Lady Penelope

Also by Lena Kennedy

Maggie
Autumn Alley
Nelly Kelly
Lizzie
Susan
Lily, My Lovely
Down Our Street
The Dandelion Seed
Eve's Apples
The Inn on the Marsh
Owen Oliver
Kate of Clyve Shore
Ivy of the Angel
Queenie's Castle

About the author

Lena Kennedy lived all her life in the East End of London and wrote with great energy about the people and times she knew there. She was 67 before her first novel, *Maggie*, was accepted for publication. Since then her bestselling novels have shown her to be among the finest and best loved of contemporary novelists.

Lady Penelope was Lena Kennedy's first historical novel. She said: 'I love history. You can learn such a lot from it. All those lords and ladies were just people like us. And I want all the ordinary people who like my Cockney characters to get the same pleasure out of history as I do.'

Lena Kennedy died in 1986.

LENA KENNEDY

Lady Penelope

HODDER

TO MY HUSBAND FRED AND MY SON KEITH FOR
THEIR LOYAL SERVICE IN TROUBLED TIMES

First published in Great Britain in 1983 by Macdonald & Co

This edition published in 2013 by Hodder & Stoughton
An Hachette UK company

1

A CIP catalogue record for this title is available from the British Library

Paperback ISBN 978 1 444 76729 2
Ebook ISBN 978 1 444 76730 8

Printed and bound by Clays Ltd, St Ives plc

Hodder & Stoughton policy is to use papers that are natural, renewable
and recyclable products and made from wood grown in sustainable forests.
The logging and manufacturing processes are expected to conform to
the environmental regulations of the country of origin.

Hodder & Stoughton Ltd
338 Euston Road
London NW1 3BH

www.hodder.co.uk

I

Chartley

The sky was blue that day, a deep sapphire lightened by circling wisps of cloud. Although it was September and autumn was already approaching, the sun was hot. Cows huddled together under the shade of the tree, their long tails flicking lazily to ward off the flies, their jaws moving leisurely as they chewed the cud. Under the hazel bushes a squirrel hopped about half-heartedly looking for nuts, as though it were too good a day to be collecting its winter store. And swallows, preparing for their great migration, chattered noisily to each other as they swooped and skimmed across the sky.

To the south lay a quiet pool over which a great willow grew. The tree's heavy lower branches trailed in the clear water and cast back a leafy reflection as if a sister tree grew in the deep green depths of the pool. There, crouched in the upper branches like a bird, was a young girl, her blue embroidered skirt drawn tightly about her knees. Her hair was the colour of autumn, like the leaves of the horse chestnut tree beyond. It was neither red nor gold and, freed from its usual plaits, it now cascaded down over her face as she leaned forward to gaze with coal-black eyes into the crystal water below and dreamily watch the little minnows that darted in and out of the leafy willow pattern on the sunlit surface.

This was Penelope's favourite seat, high up in the heavens. It was here she came when the desire to be alone possessed her, when she had to escape from her nagging old nurse, or the acid comments of her beautiful, flirtatious mother, or simply to sit quietly and think. She was generally a high-spirited and impulsive child, so moments for reflection were rare and welcome. But today sad news had come that had made her want to retreat to this spot. News that her father, the Earl of Essex, lay dying in Ireland.

With nothing except the twittering birds to disturb her thoughts, she recalled happy memories of the soft-spoken man who had always had time to listen to her. Sadness filled her young heart and her black eyes, so like those of the deer that roamed the immense parklands of Chartley Manor, misted with tears. Poor Papa, he was dying in Dublin, in a savage country far away from his family. She would never see him again . . .

'My lady!' A soft call came from behind the cherry trees that scattered scarlet and orange leaves across the grass. A small figure waved her arms frantically in Penelope's direction but then ducked down out of sight.

'Whatever's the matter with Hawise?' Penelope asked herself, screwing up her eyes to peer through the leafy foliage. Below her, not far away, she spotted two other figures. Holding her breath and hugging her knees tighter, she tried not to betray her presence as her mother, accompanied by a tall nobleman, came slowly down the path.

Stones crunched under the couple's feet as they strolled together hand in hand. Penelope had no cause to worry; they saw only each other. Deep passion glowed in her mother's dark eyes as she leaned back against the trunk of the old oak tree and said farewell to her lover.

'Good-bye, Robin,' she whispered. 'Be careful, my love,' she warned.

Familiarly, the man caressed her, his white teeth flashing in a charming grin. 'The devil takes care of his own,' he assured her.

After a long kiss, the couple parted, and Robert Dudley, Earl of Leicester, strode past the willow tree where Penelope was hidden, and on across the park to the gate where his men and mount awaited him.

From her position in the tree, Penelope could see the glint of jewels in the cap her mother wore over her luxuriant auburn hair. Her mother was looking particularly beautiful in a red velvet gown with its tiny waist and voluminous sleeves. It suited her complexion perfectly. How lovely she was, but how could she be so cruel? That very day news had come that her husband lay dying and she had been entertaining her lover without a qualm.

Suddenly her mother's shrill voice echoed up into the tree. She had discovered Hawise. 'What are you doing, girl, skulking about like that in the bushes? Come out at once!' The maid-servant slowly emerged, from behind the bush and dropped a contrite curtsy. 'Get about your business!'

The woman glowered at the terrified Hawise who

quickly scuttled off towards the timbered manor house. With a smile on her red lips as though thinking again of her lover, the Countess of Essex picked up her skirts with jewelled fingers and swept majestically past the fountains and up the lawn.

When her mother was out of sight, Penelope dropped lightly to the ground and ran home, taking a devious route through a copse, past the stables and up the back stairs to her bedchamber where Hawise stood wide-eyed and still trembling with fright. 'Oh, my lady!' she exclaimed. 'I really thought she was going to catch you this time.'

Penelope's eyes flashed with defiance. 'My father is dying and my mother receives my Lord Leicester,' she said slowly. 'Who is she to criticize me for doing what I want? I shall seek solitude in the willow tree whenever I want – and I shall do what I want.' She sniffed and pulled her head away as Hawise tried to coil the auburn hair into neat braids. 'How dare she betray my poor father like that!' she muttered through tight lips as she stared out through the window at the great gardens below. 'How dare she!'

Late that evening, a cool mist swept across the parklands drifting between the high chimneys, and obscuring the golden weather-vane. The heat had gone; outside the air was chilled. But within the west tower, it was cosy and warm. In one room, a stout middle-aged woman dozed beside a large wood fire and, in an adjoining chamber, Hawise, the maidservant, brushed her mistress's long silky tresses, as she prepared her for bed. Like all the family rooms in the house, the chamber was finely decorated. Carved oak panels and exotic tapestries covered the old stone walls; scarlet silk drapes hung down around the four-poster bed and heavy velvet curtains shut out the approaching nightfall.

Hawise brushed Penelope's hair in firm sweeping strokes until it shone like burnished gold. Her young mistress was deep in thought. 'There's a strange stillness in the air,' Penelope said at last. She shook her head. 'Poor Papa. I wonder if his spirit will come back here?'

Hawise paused in her work, brush suspended in air. 'Oh, my lady,' she cried in hushed tones, 'don't say such dreadful things. That's blasphemy!'

Penelope smiled. 'They say we never really die, so why can't we see those we love when we have passed on?'

Looking furtively from side to side, the servant made the sign of the cross. 'Hush, my lady,' she begged. 'Someone might hear you. Your papa is at peace. Let him rest.' Hawise quickly changed the subject. 'I hear that your Grandfather Knollys will be here tomorrow.' Hawise was constantly foraging throughout the house for scraps of gossip she could relay to her mistress. 'They say he will decide on what's to happen to your brother Robert.'

Penelope nodded and sighed. 'Poor Robert – the new Earl of Essex and only eleven years old. Now Papa is gone, I suppose all our lives will be very different.' She reached back and gripped Hawise's hand. The servant squeezed Penelope's hand in response.

A noise from the next room warned them that the woman was waking up. Hawise put a finger to her lips. 'Mother's waking,' she whispered. The girls fell silent. Both knew it was wrong for them to be so familiar with each other. After all, Hawise was just a servant and must keep her place.

Anne Dallon, the woman in the next room, had suckled both girls at the same time, one on each breast. She had become pregnant during her mistress's progress as lady-in-waiting to the queen. When the young lords had drunk their fill at any great celebration or feast in the noble houses of England, mistress and maid stood the same risk in those long dark corridors, fabulous gardens and isolated chambers. The young Lady Lettice Knollys was also with child after that first visit to Lord Leicester's estate, and although her husband, Walter Devereux, had no doubts about the parentage of his first child, a few tongues did wag. No high-born lady suckled her young, so it fell upon the full-breasted Anne Dallon to care for the baby girl alongside her own. And as Lady Lettice continued to live a wild and high-spirited life, it was left to the servant to bring the girls up together.

Despite the differences in their rank, time had only drawn the girls closer. Lady Penelope Devereux shared everything with her serving maid, Hawise, and could not imagine life without her by her side.

'We look almost like sisters,' said Hawise, casually tilting her head to one side. 'But your hair is fair, almost red, and mine is brown.'

'True,' agreed Penelope, 'in the shadow our faces

are much alike.' Hawise brought a hand-mirror to her mistress and, standing behind, she rested her chin on Penelope's shoulder so that the mirror reflected both their youthful faces. Indeed, they had the same long aristocratic nose, the wide brow, the narrow chin, the elongated eyes – Penelope's were black and Hawise's were hazel. Fascinated, they stared at their faces for several minutes.

'Perhaps it was the milk,' suggested Hawise.

'Nonsense,' said Penelope wisely, 'that would not have made any difference.'

Hawise shrugged her shoulders and frowned in puzzlement as she remembered something. 'The soldiers at the gate made strange talk today,' she said slowly. 'They were laughing and one said that the cuckoo had been here twice and was likely to come again this spring.'

Penelope pursed her lips. 'What twaddle!' she snapped. 'You should learn not to eavesdrop. Hand me my robe,' she added, reaching out her hand.

The next morning Penelope's grandfather, Sir Francis Knollys, arrived at Chartley Hall with his advisers. He was old and stern, and dressed in sombre colours. His white hair was sparse and thin on top, revealing a broad and noble brow. But his forehead was wrinkled with worry lines from a lifetime of loyal service to his queen. He had come today to do his best for his newly widowed daughter and her children. He had little sympathy for Lettice; her licentious ways had hardly been a secret at court. But there were the children . . .

Lettice sat before her father now, a black veil

covering her face as she wept for her dead husband. 'Crocodile tears,' grunted Sir Francis. 'We all know you are not sorry to be rid of the poor fellow. You cuckolded him often enough.'

He was saying these words when Penelope entered the room. Immediately his tone changed. 'Ah, Lady Penelope, quite grown-up, I see.' He bowed his head as she dropped a polite curtsy. 'Sad eyes,' he remarked as he scrutinised her. 'Soon be looking for a suitor.'

A nurse then brought in Penelope's younger brother. Immediately all attention was focused on the new Earl of Essex. Almost ten, Robert Devereux was tall for his age, and handsome, with a mop of chestnut curls. He hugged and kissed his grandfather with a genuine display of charm and affection, and then stood boldly upright beside the table while the advisers shuffled their papers and discussed his future with his grandfather.

From her place beside her mother, Penelope watched the scene and was slowly possessed by a strange feeling. Something told her she would soon be leaving this lovely home. The thought filled her with melancholy. Glancing sideways, she surveyed her mother's beautiful face under the veil. It looked sullen rather than sad. The Countess was already dressed in her travelling cloak, waiting to be taken on the long journey to Wales to receive the body of her late husband now on its long way home across the stormy Irish Sea. He was to be buried in Camarthen, the place of his birth.

The air was tense among the gentlemen; there was much discussion. Eventually they rose and Grandfather

Knollys gave instructions for Robert to ride back with him to London.

After everyone had gone their separate ways, Penelope and Hawise met in the gallery. 'I've never seen Mother so disturbed,' Penelope confided. 'Robert is to be a ward of Lord Cecil, the Chancellor. Mother cannot abide Mildred, Lady Cecil.'

'Does that mean he will not come home to Chartley any more?' enquired Hawise, wide-eyed with concern for young Robert.

'When he comes of age he can return; then he will turn Mother out.'

This seemed to please Hawise. A small grin appeared on her pink lips and dimples in her cheeks. 'Sometimes, I'm very glad that I am low-born. I may not be free; I'll always be a servant. But at least I'll be able to choose my own husband. That's more than you will.'

Penelope's face flushed with annoyance. 'What are you saying, Hawise?' she demanded. 'You know I shall choose my own man! I've always said I would.'

Hawise shook her head, sad to shatter Penelope's childhood dream. 'They are already looking for a husband for you,' she said. 'He must be wealthy because your father left nothing but debts. They say your brother Robert is the poorest earl in England.'

Penelope stamped her foot as two red spots of temper appeared on her cheeks. Her black eyes flashed. 'How dare you, Hawise! I'll do as I please. Get on with your work!' she ordered.

Penelope spent the rest of the afternoon in her willow tree, thinking about all the changes in her life happening now because of her father's sudden death. She thought of poor Robert in the care of the dreadful, pious Lady Cecil, and she wondered if she would be sent away too. Perhaps she would have to go north to live with Catherine Hastings, Lord Leicester's sister, who had been in charge of her younger siblings, Dorothy and Walter, since last year.

The swaying leaves of the green willow and the gentle ripples on the silver pool soon calmed her, and later she heard that she was to stay at Chartley for the time being at least. Penelope was overjoyed not to have to leave her beloved home in Staffordshire, and hoped that she would never have to.

Penelope spent much of the autumn while her mother was away riding her pony around the grounds, appreciating more than ever the natural beauty around her. When Hawise could escape from her duties, she would join her mistress, walking beside the pony as they ambled about.

'My mother says that the queen hates her Ladyship, your mother,' declared Hawise one morning as they wandered through the woods. The pony's hoofs thudded rhythmically on the carpet of leaves that covered the ground.

'Don't be so silly, Hawise,' scoffed Penelope. 'My mother is the queen's cousin. My mother's grandmother was Mary Boleyn, sister of Anne Boleyn, the queen's mother.'

'It's because she stole Lord Leicester from her,' Hawise insisted.

'Your mother is an old scandalmonger,' retorted Penelope.

'The queen might cut off your mother's head,' returned Hawise.

'Don't be so absurd!' Penelope was quite cross, but nonetheless stared apprehensively towards the house. It was a familiar view that she loved dearly; the large manor looked so small from such a distance, the river a strip of silver ribbon, the lake a small silk handkerchief. She noticed then a large procession coming along the tree-lined drive. 'It's Mother!' she exclaimed. 'Mother's come home!' She pushed the pony into a trot. 'Come on, Hawise, I must greet her in the house.'

The two girls hurried quickly down the hill – Lady Penelope sitting elegantly sidesaddle on her pony, and the pretty maid-servant tripping along beside her. Penelope was surprised to feel so happy that her mother was returning from Wales at last, but then she did love her, despite their frequent clashes.

As they drew nearer, they noticed another group of riders approaching the house from the west gate. 'Who can they be?' said Hawise, stopping to stare at them.

'Hurry!' Penelope urged. 'If Mother catches you, she'll have you whipped.'

Behind the house they parted. Hawise went in through the back door, but Penelope slipped in through a window, crouching low as she passed her mother's room, but pausing momentarily to peek in.

The Countess, already stripped of her travelling gown, stood poised, her hand freeing the lovely red-gold hair that rippled down to her waist. For a second

Penelope admired that white silk robe that contrasted with those black passionate eyes, so like her own. Unaware of her daughter's presence, Lettice was looking towards the far door as if expecting someone to enter.

And then, indeed, the door flew open as Lord Leicester burst in, dusty from riding and still wearing his long muddy leather boots. Without a sound their bodies met as they clasped each other tightly. Leicester picked her up and bore her down onto the bed, holding her in a hot embrace, and ripping the beautiful silk robe in his haste. Penelope watched in horror and, as a dry sob escaped from her throat, she turned and fled down to her chamber where she threw herself on the floor, weeping hysterically. She cried so hard that neither Hawise nor Anne Dallon could quieten her for many hours.

Later that day orders came for Penelope to join her mother in the great hall for supper. Hawise helped her into a yellow satin bodice and skirt, with a tight waist and embroidered sleeves. Her hair was coiled around her head and covered with a jewelled caul and a court bonnet. 'You look beautiful,' declared Hawise. 'Just like a queen.'

'I don't feel it,' complained Penelope. 'I shall not be civil to him.'

'To Lord Leicester? Why ever not? He is handsome and brave and, besides your mother is in love with him,' scolded the maid.

'I shall *not*!' Penelope repeated stubbornly.

The meal was unbearable for the young girl. Her

mother was very merry and chattered like a monkey;
Lord Leicester and his men were all noisy and drunk.
A young man was seated next to Penelope. He had
gentle manners and thoughtful brown eyes. Valiantly,
he tried to engage her in conversation, but she simply
put out her tongue and looked away. Lord Leicester
watched her for a while with keen grey eyes. Despite
the drink, he was very alert. Reaching across the table,
he put his hand under her chin and he stared directly
into her black eyes. He did not like what he saw –
hatred, rebellion and rage – and he let her go without
a word.

After the meal the ladies retired, leaving the men to
continue their celebrating. Penelope sat with her
mother before the crackling fire. The Countess worked
at her embroidery frame with nimble fingers, occasionally looking up at her sulky daughter. 'I did not like
your behaviour at the table, Penelope,' she said sharply.
'My Lord Leicester brought his guest especially as
company for you.'

Penelope sniffed and looked away. 'He need not
have bothered,' she retorted aggressively.

Her mother paled and her lips tightened. But she
was too angry to say more.

'Have I your permission to retire, Mother? I've got
a headache.' Penelope excused herself.

'Yes, you had better retire,' replied the Countess in
acid tones. 'And in future you will eat in your chamber
until you learn to behave.'

Penelope thrust out her chin defiantly and narrowed
her dark eyes as she caught her mother's stare. 'It is

you who should learn to behave, Mother,' she said icily. 'My father scarce cold in his grave and already you are bedded with another.'

A slim hand shot out and dealt her a stinging blow on the face. 'Get out of my sight, you vixen! How dare you speak to me like that?' The Countess rose from her seat and took a threatening step towards Penelope, who quickly ran from the room, blinded by frustrating tears, tasting the blood that trickled from the cut caused by the rings on her mother's hand. From the shadows in the corridor, Hawise appeared to comfort her, and back in her room, Anne Dallon gently bathed the wound. 'You should not provoke your mother,' the servant said. 'You know she has a quick temper.'

'I hate her!' cried Penelope, wincing from the pain of her cut mouth. 'I hope she gets punished.'

Anne muttered a furtive prayer. She knew her mistress played with fire and had done so for many years. 'Now, my lady, calm yourself,' she coaxed. 'The ways of the great ones are not for children to question.'

Penelope turned, her head held high, her fine figure upright. 'You may be correct,' she said in a low trembling voice. 'But I am no longer a child; my mother has seen to that.'

In the south wing, Lettice lay in the arms of her lover, her slim white body pressed close to his. She was feeling contrite. 'I struck Penelope,' she wept. 'I could not stand that look, the condemnation in her eyes.'

'You must send her away, madam.' Lord Leicester stroked her loose golden hair and nuzzled her ear as he spoke. 'She is wilful and headstrong,' he advised. 'She will need a tight rein.'

Lettice shook her head fiercely 'I cannot bear to part with her. I don't mind being parted from Dorothy and Walter,' she said, 'but that child, in spite of her attitude, I am afraid to lose sight of.' She paused. 'Penelope was our love child,' she added in a whisper.

Leicester laughed. 'It is often the case,' he joked.

The Countess raised herself on one elbow and looked at him quizzically. 'Surely, my lord, you don't commit yourself after all this time?' she asked with a smile.

He did not answer. Lettice's eyes flickered as she moved her soft body closer and stared with amusement quite unashamedly down at her lover. Leicester's strong arms surrounded her and pulled her to him as their lips met.

In the morning, from her perch on the window-seat, Penelope watched Lord Leicester leave. She felt nothing but hate as she watched him mount his impatient black stallion and ride away, clattering down the drive followed by his men. Beside him rode the slim youth, the guest whom Penelope had treated so ill. She did not know who he was and did not care, although she did reluctantly agree with Hawise that he sat well in the saddle.

Lettice had at last made her decision – or rather Lord Leicester had made it for her. All his life he had ruled her. She had never been able to resist him. When she was sixteen Robert Dudley had stolen her virginity, but he had had a wife then, so there had been no talk of marriage. To avoid the disgrace Lettice had been married to Walter Devereux, then Lord Hereford, later the Earl of Essex. That had been fifteen years ago but still Robert possessed her. Each day she risked royal anger and she knew the Queen hated her. But now she was a widow and Leicester's wife had died long ago. Lettice looked in the mirror and smiled at herself, pleased by her youthful features. 'Well, merry London, here I come once more,' she murmured. For a moment a line of worry creased her smooth high brow. 'I must get Penelope settled. I cannot risk taking her with me.'

For several days Penelope was confined to her rooms. Her meals were served by Anne, and Hawise was kept constantly busy and not allowed to talk to her. Penelope was used to these bouts of punishment, so she was not unduly worried, but she was aware of a feverish amount of activity going on in the house. That morning boxes and bales were being loaded into wagons, and a party of armed men waited at the gatehouse. Finally, Anne came in and told Penelope to prepare to travel to town with her mother.

'I don't want to go,' the girl grumbled.

'Now, my lady,' warned the flustered Anne, 'this time you must obey.'

'What's going on?' demanded Penelope.

'Your mother is going to live in London to attend Her Majesty. You must travel with her,' Anne informed her.

'Taking me to Court? I don't believe it.' She challenged the harassed servant.

Anne did not reply but went on silently packing her clothes.

Well, thought Penelope, it would be nice to see the capital, and to gaze on the splendour of the Royal Court. Perhaps she would not mind going with her mother at all. She quickly dressed and skipped down to join the company in the hall. The Countess was bustling about and giving orders to the servants. She avoided her daughter's anxious gaze.

When all the arrangements had been made and everything was ready to go, Penelope knew something was wrong. 'Where's Hawise?' she demanded.

No one answered, and it was too late to back out now. The huge wagon was stuck in the mud outside the gate and all hands had gone to retrieve it. Then they were all ready – the men on their restless mounts; the Countess, dressed magnificently in deep purple, on her frisky white mare; and the army of servants in the wagon. Unceremoniously Penelope was tucked up beside a groom. 'It's too dangerous for you to ride alone,' declared her mother. But Penelope did not care. Her eyes were red with weeping, and her body exhausted from sobbing because Hawise was not to ride with them. 'I'm sorry, Penelope,' her mother had said firmly, 'but she must stay here with her own mother. It's time you grew up.'

With a last sad look at her lovely willow tree, and beloved Chartley, Penelope rode out into the world of strangers, feeling completely alone.

2

Bisham Abbey

The long ride to London was very tiring. It took several days and they spent the nights in coaching inns on the way.

When they finally did arrive, Penelope found that she remembered the town house – even though she had not been there for years. She could remember the tall facade and the smart liveried servants coming down the marble steps to assist them. As her mother organised the house, Penelope wandered down the long gallery, gazing intently at the grim-faced portraits of her ancestors.

Later, she went on to the balcony to look out across the great river. How she hated the dirt and noise of London! She had been shocked by the crowded streets and the noisy babbling voices and particularly by the putrefying human heads stuck on poles on Tower Bridge. At least it was pleasanter out here. Brightly coloured boats and other river craft jostled each other as they made their way along the water. In the distance she could see the towers of Westminster Hall and, across the river, great expanses of green fields and pastures. Deep in thought; Penelope watched the sun go down. It was a deep orange and seemed to blend with the blue of the evening sky and the smoky pall of the city.

Her reverie was suddenly interrupted by her new maid, a homely girl called Tabitha, whose wide face was flushed and mottled from running. 'My lady,' she panted, out of breath, 'her ladyship, your mother, requests your presence. I've been all over looking for you.'

'Stop fussing,' snapped Penelope in disgust. She was missing Hawise, and so resented this other servant who had taken her friend's place. 'I don't know why you've been running; nothing can be that important,' she added scornfully. But then she went off to meet her mother.

The Countess was pacing impatiently up and down the marble hall, her plain black silk gown sweeping behind her. She wore an open lace ruff at the neck and a lace cap on her fair hair. Penelope was struck by her beauty.

Lettice smiled. 'There you are, child. I have to travel on tomorrow,' she told her. 'I don't want to leave you in town, so I am sending you to stay with my cousin Elizabeth.'

'But where?' cried Penelope in astonishment.

'At Bisham,' replied Lettice sheepishly. She paused, nervously anticipating her daughter's response.

'To Elizabeth Hoby Russell!' Penelope's voice rose with shock and danger. 'Why, Mother, you said you hated her!'

With an agitated flutter, Lettice continued to walk up and down. 'Now, child,' she said, almost pleading, 'don't be difficult.'

Penelope did not say a word. She stared at her mother, her mouth in a sullen line.

'I'm a widow left without substance,' continued Lettice. 'Your father left me nothing but debts. Elizabeth is a grand lady, with a daughter your age, and you will receive an excellent education.'

'Well, I refuse to go,' Penelope shouted, stamping her foot in rage.

'You must be instructed to fulfil your station in life,' her mother insisted. 'I have been so neglectful of you, child, allowing you to run around with the servants. It's entirely for your own good, believe me, Penelope.'

Her daughter still said nothing, but scowled, refusing to respond.

From the far corner a tall figure emerged. 'You will do as you are bid, Lady Penelope,' ordered Lord Leicester sternly and the girl shivered as if a grey goose had walked on her grave. 'I beg your permission to retire, Mother,' she gasped and fled to the privacy of her own chamber.

There was nothing Penelope could do. Arrangements had been made for her to travel to Bisham in Lord Leicester's barge. It was safer to travel by water, they were less likely to be attacked by robbers or catch the terrible smallpox. The Countess was terrified by the thought of her own lovely face being blemished, and was equally concerned about her daughter's pretty features, too. She presented Penelope with a blue taffeta cloak, lined and trimmed with ermine. As they parted, she placed a kiss on her frowning brow. 'It's better that you go, child. It did me no good to spend my youth at a licentious court.'

For a moment Penelope stared hopelessly into her mother's eyes. How much she wanted to put her arms about her neck and beg her to let her go home to Chartley, to loving Hawise, and her beloved pony! But pride held her in check. She stepped back and allowed herself to be escorted down the slippery stone steps to the highly coloured barge, and into a comfortable cabin beneath a blue-and-gold canopy. Below the deck, the strong arms of unseen oarsmen piloted them down the Thames.

Inside the cabin sat Madame Lucy, the chaperone who was to travel with Penelope to Bisham. She was a severely dressed old woman without a trace of a smile on her wrinkled face. Horrified at being in London, she held a small bunch of herbs that she frequently sniffed to ward off evil town germs. Ignoring Penelope, she ordered the terror-stricken Tabitha to keep out on deck, and then began to mutter to herself as if in prayer.

The smell of the herbs and the overpowering stuffiness of the cabin were too much for the country-bred Penelope. As the barge moved up-river she pushed aside the elaborate drapes and stepped out onto the small deck. There she saw, leaning against the side, another passenger – a noble youth of about sixteen, dressed in long white pantaloons and a short doublet in black and gold. A short, fancy cape hung rakishly from one shoulder. There was something vaguely familiar about him, but, deep in her own misery she did not think much about it. He bowed low. 'Greetings, my Lady Devereux,' he said.

Glumly, she stared at him, then looked down the river towards her disappearing home. The brown eyes that looked at her, had a humorous twinkle in them. 'Why so sad?' he asked in a gentle voice. 'It is not Traitors' Gate we are heading for, but down the sweet river to scenes of real beauty – you to Bisham and I to Oxford.'

'Have we met before?' she enquired, now noticing his handsome figure and courtly manner.

'At your own home, not long ago,' he replied.

At last she remembered and blushed at the memory. 'Pardon my rudeness on that last occasion,' she apologised. He was the youth she had ignored at her mother's table.

The young man smiled gently, watching as a red-gold curl escaped from her hood and blew about in the wind. He reached out and raised her hand to his lips. 'You will be a lovely, fascinating woman soon,' he said quietly. 'Don't fight. Allow them to cultivate you. Even the loveliest rose will deteriorate if allowed to grow wild.'

And something in his tone made her heart miss a beat.

'Come in here at once, Lady Penelope!' the old chaperone called from the cabin. Without a word, but glancing back at the young man, she dutifully returned to the stuffy cabin, a peaceful glow warmed her. That soft kiss on her wrist had been rather nice. She could hear the splash of the paddles as the barge cruised on, and through gaps in the drapes she could see that the river had begun to lose its muddy look; there was clear water, soft ripples and luscious green banks each side.

At eventide they came to a small Norman church that stood almost at the water's edge. Tired from her journey, Penelope thought that the ivy-mantled tower seemed to imbibe from the river a spirit of peace and beauty. The unseen oarsmen deftly manoeuvred the barge up against the bank to allow Lady Penelope to step out onto the wooden landing followed by her breathless red-faced maid, Tabitha. Trying to look cheerful as she greeted her gloomy awaiting aunt, her eye just caught sight of the youth watching her from the deck as the barge made its way on towards Oxford. She had a pleasant sensation in her chest but she did not return his smile.

Bisham Abbey had originally been the home of the Knights Templar. It breathed out an air of ancient sorrows. In the Reformation it had come into the possession of the Hoby family who had swum so well in the troubled Tudor waters. Philip Hoby had married one of the famous Cooke sisters and came by the abbey upon the death of his brother. Then misfortune began to dog his steps; he died in France while on an embassy, leaving a highly strung wife with three children, one yet unborn. Elizabeth Hoby was a lady of great learning but she made no effort to recover from her husband's death. She clung to her grief and was known at Court as 'Our Lady of Splendid Sorrows'. She wrote pages of morbid poetry and built large memorials in honour of her dead husband. She remarried soon after her widowhood a timid member of the Russell family, but he did not live long.

It was this air of gloom and sadness that greeted Penelope as she entered the great abbey with its unadorned walls and cold stone corridors. After the warmth and cosiness of Chartley, Bisham was bleak and comfortless. Even when she met her pale-faced cousins – the girls sitting stiffly upright as they worked at their embroidery, and, the nervous little boy, their step-brother, twisting and turning in his seat as if unable to keep still – Penelope's heart felt heavy.

The loneliness she felt that first day was to continue throughout her stay. The Hoby sisters were quite devoted to each other and had no time for her. They whispered loudly together in corners and smugly concentrated through the long sessions of learning which they (and now Penelope) were forced to undergo each day. There was music, Latin, French, reading, writing and every subject that would cultivate them to become fine ladies. Always a rebel, Penelope resisted much of this education, hiding to escape the lessons and daily playing pranks on the tutors, reducing them to nervous exhaustion, until her severe aunt intervened.

'Well now, Lady Penelope,' declared Elizabeth Hoby Russell one morning, 'I shall myself teach you Latin and, I can assure you, you will learn.'

Penelope felt a shiver run down her back as she saw Lady Elizabeth's thin lips pressed tightly together and the frigid eyes surveying her in anger.

The only ray of sunshine in the dungeon in which

Penelope found herself was small Patrick Russell. He was only seven years old, and small for his age, but an interesting and nervous boy, who, like Penelope, was often hiding away in corners. Sometimes, as Penelope strolled disconsolately about the gloomy abbey, he would suddenly appear, apparently from nowhere, to inform her that he was hiding. From whom she was never quite sure. Sometimes they played together, running through the austere cloisters. Patrick would wave his thin arms and hoot and shout to hear his voice reverberate around the walls, returning as a ghostly echo. Then Penelope would do the same and laugh gaily at the effect. They did have fun together and Penelope's heart went out to this thin under-nourished boy whose fear of his mother surpassed all other feelings.

It was Patrick's inability to learn that so frustrated his learned mother. One son had grown up and gone out to be a success in that ambitious society outside. He had learned to read and write long before he was as old as Patrick, and Elizabeth Russell reminded her youngest son of this repeatedly, as hour after hour she rammed Latin verbs at him, standing over him while he tried so hard to write. Patrick's little hands trembled nervously, as the ink once again blotted heavily over his copy book. Each time this happened his mother would lose her temper and viciously lash him with a thin cane until finally, weeping and grovelling, the boy would fall to the floor, begging her to stop. These frequent and violent scenes distressed the sensitive Penelope, who, when his mother had gone, would cuddle the boy and steal sweetmeats from the kitchen to comfort him.

Lady Elizabeth also meted out strict punishment to her sickly daughters, but seemed curiously afraid of Penelope's dark, scornful eyes and she never touched her. On the frequent visits of her sisters, Anne Bacon and Mildred Cecil, Elizabeth Russell would complain. 'Lettice's daughter has the makings of a wanton. I shall be extremely glad when she leaves my house; I do not wish to be thought responsible.'

'Of course, my dear, you have our sympathy,' replied her sister Anne with a sly look in her eyes. 'But what is bred in the bone must come out in the flesh.' She smiled knowingly.

'Someone must inform Lettice that you wish to be rid of her,' said the practical Mildred one day.

'Well, it's hardly possible at the moment, is it?' whispered Anne leaning forward conspiratorially.

Her elder sister smiled and nodded her head slowly. A small cap decorated with emeralds sat on her snow-white hair. 'Yes, I did hear a rumour that she has secretly married Lord Leicester.'

The three sisters raised their eyebrows elegantly, and dropped their mouths in feigned surprise. Was it not the choicest piece of gossip of the year?

Anne smiled and sat back in her chair. 'I should not like to be Lettice when the Queen learns of what she had done,' she said.

'But who is to inform Her Majesty?' Mildred showed some concern.

Elizabeth shook her head as she looked at her sisters.

'What a lot of trouble it will cause,' she said. 'The Queen will not take the news lightly.'

Together the ladies discussed the delicious gossip about how the mother of the wayward child who had been foisted on them had had the audacity to steal the queen's favourite.

'One wonders where it will all end,' declared Anne.

'It's nothing to do with me,' said Elizabeth. 'I always tried to discourage our cousin from behaving so badly.'

'At their age it's disgusting,' said Mildred. 'And with Walter Devereux so newly in his grave. As yet Her Majesty does not know, but perhaps I'll drop a hint . . .' She paused before continuing. 'Yes,' she added emphatically, 'it has to be faced. Otherwise dear Elizabeth will have that child on her hands permanently.'

While the sisters were holding this family conference, Penelope was clinging on to young Patrick by his thin legs as he hung over the river bank fishing for minnows. Earlier, they had been in the old church, where Patrick had shown Penelope the magnificent tomb that his mother had erected in the memory of her first husband and his brother – complete effigies of two knights in full regalia laid on top of the tomb below a huge plaque carved with poems in Latin which she valued so highly.

'He was not my father. My father is buried in his own family tomb with the Russells,' Patrick had stated proudly.

After they had left the quiet church, they lay on their backs in the green meadow, staring up at the summer sky, which was so blue and soft, and at the white clouds which looked like flocks of sheep drifting by.

'Would you like to be an angel, Penelope?' asked Patrick. 'With lovely white wings?'

'I don't think so,' Penelope replied dreamily. 'You have to be dead to be an angel and I've got a lot of living to do first.'

'I would! I'd like to fly,' cried Patrick. 'Like the birds in the sky!' He got up and pirouetted about, flapping his arms like wings.

'Oh, you are a funny little boy!' laughed Penelope. 'When I get married you can come and live with me.'

Patrick whirled around again and dashed back towards her, throwing himself breathlessly down on the moist grass. 'Really Penelope?' His thin face was alive with happiness. 'I'd be so happy with you.'

Penelope cuddled him close. 'I know, darling. You are unhappy here, always being beaten. Don't be so afraid of everyone. You must learn to stand up for yourself.' She kissed the top of his head and held him tight as she felt a rush of love for the poor nervous child. She was so much stronger than he. Would he ever survive in that cut-throat world outside?

From the river they went to the library where huge, leather-bound volumes were held in position by chains. In spite of his inability to read and write, Patrick possessed an excellent memory and loved to browse in these lavishly illustrated books and pore over the pictures of angels and saints drawn by the previous inhabitants of the abbey, the monks. Penelope would hold the heavy volumes for Patrick to look at and guide his little hands over the golden pictures. This was a forbidden pastime, for they were not even allowed in the library. Today as they marvelled together at the pictures, a deep sepulchral voice startled them both.

'My Lady Penelope! How dare you enter the library!'

Penelope's laughter died in her throat as she turned to see the black, forbidding shape of Madame Lucy, the chaperone who had brought her from Chartley to Bisham. Penelope had never learned what her duties were but Madame Lucy was often seen wandering around the abbey muttering to herself. Penelope had often wondered if she were praying to God or the devil.

Patrick shrank away in fear as though anticipating more punishment from his mother for his disobedience, but Penelope grabbed his hand and pulled him to her. She was not intimidated.

Perhaps Madame Lucy could see the fight in the young girl, braced ready to defend herself and Patrick, and chose not to go further. She raised her head and clasped her hands in front of her black habit. 'My Lady Elizabeth wishes to see you immediately,' she said and then she disappeared.

And later that afternoon, Penelope was told by Lady Elizabeth that her mother had married again and she now had a stepfather.

For a while there was a period of peace while Elizabeth Hoby Russell went to London to arrange her eldest daughter's marriage. She returned to the abbey some weeks later, in a fever of excitement over the latest scandal at court. Standing in a cold corridor, Penelope overheard her discussing the gossip one evening with an unseen companion. 'It really was to be expected, of course,' Lady Elizabeth was saying with relish. 'What did Lettice expect? How could it be otherwise? Yes of course, I assure you, she is finished. People have to protect their own interests and it became necessary for someone – of course, I'm not sure who – to inform Her Majesty. They tell me that the Queen raged all day before driving Lettice from court. And she actually dealt my cousin a physical blow – you know how quick and violent she is.'

Outside the door, Penelope stood very still. Her heart was beating hard against her breast. So her butterfly mother had been driven out of court because she had married Lord Leicester. Penelope did not care about her mother's marriage, for Robert Dudley had long been her lover. But to fall from the Queen's grace was a family disaster. An overwhelming desire to return to Chartley seized her.

Patrick squeezed her hand sympathetically when he saw tears flooding her eyes. As panic gripped her, Penelope could not shake off a vision of her lovely mother, without a head.

'I'm glad I'm not as handsome as my mother,' she whispered weepily.

'But Penelope,' insisted Patrick with a sudden adult tone, 'you are so much more beautiful.'

'I don't want to go to court just to find a husband,' Penelope sobbed. 'I want to look for someone who really loves me.'

'I'll marry you, Penelope,' said Patrick gallantly. 'When I grow up I'll marry you.'

Through her tears, Penelope smiled. 'You're a good boy, Patrick,' she said. 'I shall always love you.' And she suddenly felt better, a little confident that this latest news might not prove so disastrous after all.

Later that year, Penelope lost her young friend. Lady Elizabeth was becoming increasingly impatient with Patrick's slowness and now always stood over him as he wrote his letters. This had the effect of making him tremble even more than usual. Fearfully his tiny hand would try to manipulate the long quill pen and he would whimper as large blots appeared all over the page. Repeatedly he was made to go over his lessons until the pages were clean and neat. During these tortuous mornings, Penelope would watch Patrick's agonies, glaring helplessly at Lady Elizabeth's hard, pale face above the high stiffened ruff, and the small mean eyes that glittered so cruelly as she stood, hands folded, watching the boy fumbling desperately with his task. These occasions invariably ended in a blow as his mother would finally lose all patience. And each day the poor child would end up weeping on Penelope's shoulder.

'Don't be afraid,' she would beg of him. 'Don't let her bully you. Stand up to her when you get so many blots.'

One morning even before his mother had arrived, Patrick's book was full of blots. As he heard Lady Elizabeth's quick footsteps in the corridor outside, he trembled visibly. 'What am I to do?' he wailed, looking helplessly at Penelope.

She had to act quickly. Climbing on the windowsill, she pushed the books deep into a crevice in the wall. 'When your mother asks you for your books,' she said to Patrick, 'tell her that you have lost them.'

Patrick's eyes were round with terror. 'But that would not be honest, Penelope. It would be a sin,' he whispered.

'No matter,' declared Penelope. 'We'll pray for forgiveness later. Your mother is not going to box your ears this morning and never will while I am around.' Her full lips set in an obstinate line, and her dark eyes gleamed as she awaited the arrival of Elizabeth Hoby Russell.

Lady Elizabeth was in a particularly fractious mood. Her brow was lined with a deep scowl. 'Good morning, Penelope,' she said icily. 'Now, Patrick, read out your lesson. And I'll hear you next,' she said, looking at Penelope.

'I didn't do it,' Penelope stated sullenly, without looking up.

Lady Elizabeth drew herself up in anger and astonishment at Penelope's answer. 'We are all aware that you are lazy and ungrateful, Lady Penelope,' she said coldly. 'Thank God I shall soon be rid of you.'

Penelope gave her an insolent smirk. Immediately, Lady Elizabeth's face grew red with rage. Twitching nervously, she directed her attention to her small son, who cowered in front of her. 'Read out your lesson, Patrick!' she commanded.

The boy winced and, like a tiny goldfish, his mouth opened and shut. No words came out.

'He can't find his copy books,' Penelope cried triumphantly.

'Can't find his books? What a dreadful falsehood,' cried Lady Elizabeth. 'Go, get them at once!' She pointed an accusing finger at the quivering Patrick, who did not move. He was rigid with fear as his mother's gaze rooted him to the spot. 'Now, sir,' she declared. 'It seems that you have become an accomplished liar as well as an idle fool. Tell me at once, what have you done with those books?'

Still Patrick did not answer. As a swift hand came out to deal him a blow to the side of the head, his thin wobbly legs buckled. His small body seemed to spin; then he fell and his head struck the corner of the table with a sickening thud. Blood gushed from the wound as he hit the floor.

His mother towered over him, her hand raised as if to deliver another blow, but Penelope had already rushed to her playmate and gathered him in her arms. Patrick's eyes were up-turned in his head; blood from his head poured all over her. A strong hand pushed her away. Madame Lucy who had witnessed the scene from the back of the room, came forward and silently carried the boy from the room in her thin arms.

Wringing her hands anxiously, Lady Elizabeth followed Madame Lucy out of the room – her face dead-white with shock at what she had done.

As their footsteps died away, Penelope was left alone in the silent room. Kneeling on the bloodied floor she put her hands to her face and wept openly for little Patrick, her young friend. By the window, in a chink in the wall, were those fatal copy books. Getting up, she reached out a hand to retrieve them, but her heart sank as a sob rose in her throat. It was all her fault. It was she who had forced the little boy to defy his mother. *She* was responsible. Stunned by the terrible thought, she threw herself back on her knees. 'Dear God,' she prayed, 'please don't let Patrick be dead.' With her young heart almost bursting with grief, she prayed for a long time, hoping, praying and hoping that Patrick was all right, that nothing serious had happened to him after all. Thus in the gloomy portals of Bisham the character of the woman Penelope was to be began to take shape.

And that night all sleep in the house was disturbed as the grey-clad figure of Elizabeth Hoby Russell roamed the cloisters, wringing her hands and weeping hysterically as she tried to wash the blood of her child from her hands, crying out pathetically to her Maker to forgive her.

3

Wanstead

Patrick Russell was buried quietly in the church that he was so fond of. Elizabeth and her remaining daughter Isobel now lived in a remote part of the house. Apart from a daily visit from Tabitha, Penelope was left entirely alone. More homesick than ever, she roamed the deserted rooms. Snow covered the fields and hedgerows and the days seemed endless. Tabitha wept incessantly that the house was haunted and she wanted to go home. Her mistress, cold, silent and remote, grew taller and thinner and lost her merry smile. Then at last, in February, she left Bisham, travelling in a comfortable coach. She sat inside with Anne Bacon, while Tabitha sat up with the coachman. The abbey had brought its final misfortunes on Lady Elizabeth Hoby Russell and her family. The sickly Isobel was dying and Lady Elizabeth herself had lost her wits. Raging madly, she was now restrained and guarded by the forbidding Madame Lucy.

In spite of her cold, pious manner, Anne Bacon was kind.

'Am I going home at last?' Penelope asked.

'No, child, you will join your mother at Lord Leicester's estate, God willing.' After this she seemed rather uncommunicative, and only wept tears for her poor afflicted sister. Penelope sat immersed in her dreams until at last, they reached the streets of London.

Penelope and her maid were deposited at the gates of Lord Leicester's house in the Strand. Her mother was in the hall to meet her. Penelope could not deny that she looked more lovely than ever. Although she was slightly stouter, her hard eyes seemed softer, and she held up her beautiful head with her usual grace. She looked happy, as indeed she was, now married to the man she loved.

Lettice received her daughter in a warm embrace. Penelope's heart fluttered in her breast as she hugged the stiff whalebone waist, and tears of relief crept into her eyes. How good it was to belong again!

'Poor little darling!' cried Lettice in an exuberant manner. 'What a dreadful time you must have had. We are going to stay here in London for a day or two while we replenish your wardrobe, and we'll be off to our nice new home in the country, Wanstead.'

Penelope frowned and drew away from her mother. Her mouth dropped sullenly. 'I want to go home,' she stated flatly. 'I want to go to Chartley, where I belong.'

Lettice shook her head. How the child could annoy her! 'That's not possible,' she said. 'Now that I am married to Lord Leicester we will share his home.'

Penelope scowled and bit her upper lip, as she automatically thought of ways to hurt her mother. 'I heard you were dismissed from court,' she said airily, thrusting her chin in the air.

Lettice flushed angrily. 'Little pigs have big ears, I presume.'

'It makes no difference to me,' returned her daughter with a shrug. 'I never wish to be seen at court myself.'

Lettice could not hold back her anger. 'Oh, yes, you will! By God, I'll see that you do. I swear by all that's holy that no flesh and blood of mine shall be slighted.'

Penelope smiled mockingly, satisfied at having irritated her mother.

'Lord Leicester's sister will present you at court next year, or I'll know the reason why,' snapped Lettice. Impulsively, she swept from the room while her daughter stood, a mocking smile still on her lips, confident that her mother had been defeated. Then, as she gazed about the immense hall, thinking about the exchange with her mother, a slight figure emerged from a shadowy corner to drop a demure curtsy before her.

'Your servant, my lady.' It was Hawise.

Penelope dashed at her and, regardless of decorum and not caring who saw them, she flung her arms around the maid's neck. 'How I've missed you so!' she cried, hugging her tight as salty tears fell down her cheeks.

A gentle hand removed her cloak and wiped the tears away from her face. 'Come, my lady,' murmured a cajoling voice. 'I'll take you to your room.'

Penelope felt like a little girl once more, as her beloved and devoted maid led her to the privacy of the bedchamber. There, together again at last, they giggled and crunched sweets and told each other of their lives since they had last seen each other. Cold, gloomy Bisham Abbey was almost forgotten. They laughed freely and hugged each other.

Hawise had grown plump and very attractive. She had developed firm breasts and a trim waist; her dark brown hair was glossy and well cared for and her merry hazel eyes shone brightly with affection. Hawise was still as lively and as full of gossip as ever; Penelope listened hungrily to her amusing account of her journey in the Queen's Progress to the northern manors, being one of a bevy of serving maids. To their delight, the girls found that they were as close as always.

'I was so lonely without you, Hawise,' Penelope confided as she was prepared for bed.

'It won't happen again, my lady,' Hawise soothed her. 'We are going to live in a grand house, called Wanstead. I've been staying there for some time,' she whispered excitedly. 'And,' she added with a flush in her cheeks, 'I've got a lover.'

'Oh, no! Hawise.' Penelope's mouth dropped open as she turned to look at her maid. Her expression of shocked disappointment was unmistakable.

'I'm quite old enough,' declared Hawise very sharply and somewhat defensively. 'So are you. A suitor will ask you for your hand shortly, if I am not mistaken,' she added mysteriously.

Penelope sighed. 'Oh, do be quiet, Hawise,' she said impatiently. 'I'm so weary. I just don't want to do anything that will take me away from you again.'

'Don't fret, my lady,' murmured Hawise, as she tucked her mistress up in bed. 'I will never, never leave you.'

When the coach first turned up the magnificent elm-lined avenue to Lord Leicester's great manor at

Wanstead, Penelope felt a sudden thrill. Despite her hatred for her stepfather she was touched by a sense that she was coming home. Wanstead was not Chartley, and never could be, but the huge house with its hundred mullioned windows, overlooking a glittering lake and acres of well-kept gardens, was like a shining jewel in a deep, dark forest. It could never be her home while it belonged to Lord Leicester but at least coming here was better than returning to Bisham Abbey, and Wanstead was a place of great beauty, she consoled herself.

Penelope had learned more details about her mother's marriage from Hawise's gossip. Officiated in the chapel at Wanstead, the union had been kept a well-kept secret from the jealous queen and now, at forty years old, Lettice was bearing Leicester's first legitimate child. When the Queen finally learned of her Sweet Robin's treacherous behaviour, a royal storm had broken and he was now confined to house arrest in Greenwich Park, while his new wife made full use of the grand house that had originally been made so beautiful in order to entertain the queen. Penelope was not impressed.

'It was time he married her anyway,' she announced spitefully. 'He was her lover for long enough.'

'I know, my lady,' Hawise replied gently, 'but this child will be born on the right side of the blanket, and my Lord Leicester is the greatest man in all the land.'

'Not in my estimation,' sneered Penelope.

'They say he's got lots of by-blows,' giggled Hawise. 'In fact,' she added, lowering her voice, 'it's been suggested that even I might be one.'

Penelope sniffed. 'Stop this nonsense immediately, Hawise! I don't want to hear such talk.'

But now as they drove past the great elms up to Wanstead, Penelope's eyes gleamed bright with pleasure. Increasingly, she was feeling that she belonged amid these grand old trees and golden towers.

During the next few days she dreamily explored the grounds, taking in the maze, and the fabulous glass grotto. Within the house itself, she admired the high, pointed ceilings, the carved panelled walls, the hall with its warm tapestries and sumptuous displays of silver armour and jewelled weapons. But throughout, everything was subdued by enormous portraits of Queen Elizabeth herself. Penelope often looked up to survey the white mask-like face, the bright red hair and the shrewd glittering eyes that seemed to watch the massive hall with scorn. Robert Dudley, her favourite courtier, had spent an untold fortune on this place to impress the fiery, inscrutable monarch. And now her cousin and arch-enemy, Lettice Knollys, was its proud possessor and filled the house with guests with carefree abandon.

Each day there were gay boating parties on the lake; every evening lanterns lit up the gardens and lovers sauntered through the maze. Large, merry hunting parties rode out at daybreak, and each night a huge feast was laid out in the main hall and dancing and gambling went on until dawn.

Penelope was allowed to roam free amongst the guests or gallop alone through the forest on a frisky bay horse. The fresh air and the freedom healed the wounds of the past few years. And in the warm, idle atmosphere of Wanstead, so different from the austere cold gloom of Bisham, Penelope slowly lost her bitter look, her hollow cheeks and her pallid skin. Slowly her beauty blossomed. And Lettice, heavily pregnant but still active as ever, was proud of her young daughter whose red-gold hair and unusually dark eyes fascinated the good-looking courtiers who idled their time away at Wanstead.

It was not before long before Leicester was restored to the Queen's favour, and he returned home bringing with him his young stepson, Penelope's brother. Robert, Earl of Essex, was now almost thirteen, at university and already quite a young man of the world. His rich chestnut hair hung in curls. His graceful carriage, charm and pleasant appearance won him much admiration. Lord Leicester had great hopes for his stepson, who was already in the queen's favour. And now, for a short while, the family settled down amid the rural beauties of Essex.

In the privacy of her bedchamber, Hawise shared her secrets with her mistress. She told Penelope of the passionate desires of her lover, a youth called Peter Bodkin, who came from the strange land of Flanders and rode with Lord Leicester's men. She told of secret meetings in a derelict hut in the woods, how he loved her and was going to take her to his home across the sea. Penelope was sceptical.

'He will betray you, get you with child. Then Mother will turn you out.'

Her maid's merry eyes danced in amusement and she

shook her head impishly. 'It's not so easy to get pregnant,' she explained. 'It's just a matter of self-control.'

Penelope was not interested. 'Nevertheless, I worry about you. You must stop this affair at once.'

'Don't be so silly,' cajoled Hawise. 'I can take care of myself. Come, tell me of your latest admirer.'

Penelope smiled. 'His name is Philip Sidney – he's Lord Leicester's nephew. He is a little older than I and he knew and served under my father in Ireland. It was my father's dying wish that I marry him.'

Hawise wriggled with excitement. 'So you may yet marry the man you love,' she said encouragingly.

Penelope shrugged. 'I am not sure that I like him,' she replied without enthusiasm. 'He is very solemn and austere. And he writes poetry I don't understand.'

Hawise fussed over her, giving a final polish to her shining fair hair. 'I hope you find lots of happiness, my lady. I never want to leave you, but if Peter asks me, I shall run off with him.'

Penelope turned quickly, her face white with concern and panic. 'Don't you dare think of such a thing, Hawise!' she cried. 'Promise me you will never do that.'

Hawise looked away to avoid Penelope's glare. 'I'm not sure that I can,' she murmured apologetically. 'I love him too much, my lady.'

That night, as Hawise crept out to meet her lover under the starry sky, Penelope tossed restlessly in her bed. Her thoughts were in turmoil. She had to prevent Hawise from destroying her life, she knew that. Come what may, she vowed as she finally fell asleep, she would not allow Hawise to make a fool of herself.

Meanwhile, life continued to be lazy and wonderful at Wanstead, as Lettice began to squander the fortune that her husband had accumulated in his years of loyal service to the queen. Penelope, becoming conscious of her growing beauty, used the almond eyes of her heritage with increasing effect. The admiration she aroused warmed her. Only Philip Sidney, to whom she was promised as his bride, averted his sad brown eyes from her flirtations.

'He is so sombre,' Penelope complained to Hawise. 'His friends are much more fun.'

'It's so nice to belong to someone,' sighed Hawise dreamily as she undid the hooks of Penelope's bodice one evening. Her thoughts were of her Peter, so fresh and clean and cheerful. His English was limited, but his words needed no interpreting – theirs was the universal language of love.

As Penelope watched Hawise's calm happy face, her lips tightened. She still did not approve of her maid's love affair and felt compelled to prevent her from becoming too deeply involved. At that moment, she knew what she had to do.

Hawise always kept her nightly rendezvous with her lover under the highest oak next to the old keeper's hut. Tonight Penelope was going to stop it once and for all.

Darkness was descending. The birds lay hushed and silent in their nests and the moon rose high in the sky. Hawise stood at the window patiently waiting for her mistress to retire.

'Hawise, fetch me a clean shift. This one is soiled,' Penelope called sharply.

Annoyed about being delayed but ever-obedient, Hawise went into the ante-chamber to get a clean night-shift for her mistress. Immediately, the heavy door slammed shut. Spinning around in dismay, she watched the key being turned in the lock. Faintly through the thick door she could hear Penelope's voice.

'There will be no more love walks for you, tonight or ever. And if you call out, I'll tell Mother of your lover.'

'Oh, my lady, I beg you, release me,' pleaded Hawise, hammering her fists on the door.

Catching up her abundant hair in a caul and placing Hawise's dark cloak about her shoulders, Penelope ran through the house and crept out towards the stables. Jumping on her mount, she then rode furiously through the dusk down the leafy forest path to meet Hawise's lover herself, to tell him that he could see her servant no more . . .

At that precise moment, a party of armed men were also riding two abreast through the forest. Lord Leicester was returning from London after a particularly irritating session with his queen. She may well have forgiven her dear Robin, but she was certainly making him pay for his past mistakes. Robert Dudley felt tired and disillusioned; life was catching up with him. He could barely keep up with the hectic scramble for success and the incessant demands of Lettice. And now the Queen insanely jealous, was draining him of his last vestige of pride. He just hoped that Lettice would give birth to a boy. A recognised son of his own, a legitimate heir, might make it all worthwhile. His handsome face was drawn and his sensuous mouth set in a grim line, as he cantered through his estate thinking about these matters.

From the other direction he suddenly saw a rider go past, cloak sailing out in the wind.

'Who rides so swiftly through the forest at nightfall?' he asked of his servant.

The sergeant-at-arms smiled into his beard. 'It looks suspiciously like my Lady Penelope,' he said.

Leicester frowned. 'Damn that little vixen!' he growled. 'What the devil is she up to now?' He signalled a halt. 'Bring two men. We will go after her,' he ordered.

Penelope was feeling very afraid of the dark forest and, oblivious of the company behind her, urged on her mount. In the distance she could just see the keeper's hut. That was the place. Now to tell the low-born lout to stay away from her lovely Hawise.

Jumping down, she hitched her horse to a tree, pulling the cloak tight about her. The night was still, but the forest seemed to be full of strange shapes and noises that made her shiver nervously.

She had been waiting for five minutes when at last a figure appeared beneath the ancient oak under which she stood. Two arms like whip-cord went around her. 'Hawise,' a voice whispered. Penelope felt hot lips pressed down on hers so hard she shut her eyes. He held her in such a tight embrace that she felt weak and limp. No man had ever held her so close before. She wanted to pull away and put him in his place, but she could not. All the strength had gone from her limbs.

With a crash the bushes near them parted as Lord Leicester's horse dashed through. A sharp, commanding voice rang out: 'What the devil are you about, my Lady Penelope?'

Startled and bewildered, in the same glance, Penelope saw her stepfather's angry face and Peter Bodkin's terrified look. Bodkin was a mere serving man caught now in a compromising position with the daughter of a noble house. His blue eyes were round and scared as he cried out fearfully in his own tongue. Lord Leicester's men took hold of him by the scruff of the neck and pushed him roughly to the ground. Penelope did not see what happened to him next because she was then quickly bundled onto her mount and escorted back to the house. She did not see, but the cries of Hawise's lover echoed in her ears all the way home.

Back in her chamber, Penelope found that Hawise had gone to sleep in her prison. White and distraught, she confessed her actions. 'I only went to warn him off for your own safety,' she insisted. 'But he mistook me for you. There was no time to explain before Lord Leicester was upon us.'

Hawise held out her arm. 'Give me my cloak, my lady,' she said very calmly.

'I'll protect you. I'll take the blame,' babbled Penelope who had now lost all self-control.

Hawise's face was expressionless as she flung the cloak around her shoulders. 'That's not important,' she said in a hard, bitter tone. 'My concern is for Peter. I must find out what has happened.'

After she had left, Penelope lay wide awake, anxiously awaiting the return of Hawise and praying that the news would be good. It was not until the birds were twittering and moving restlessly in the eaves, ready to rise and greet the dawn that her maid returned. Hawise slipped quietly into the chamber and lay down on a small trestle-bed crying as though her heart would break.

Penelope dashed from her bed and knelt before her. 'Why do you weep so, Hawise? Please tell me,' she begged.

'My Peter is dead,' Hawise cried. 'Run through the heart by Lord Leicester's men as he tried to escape.' She turned her face to the wall and cried uncontrollably.

Numb with horror, Penelope stared at her knees as she knelt on the cold stone floor. Reminded of another time when she had felt such remorse, visions of young Patrick Russell came vividly back to her. Once more her impulsiveness had caused a death. 'Oh, dear God,' she cried. 'I must be cursed. How else could I be so unlucky?'

Her mind did not dwell on the weeping girl who had lost her first lover but rather on the unkindness of fate that caused her to bring disaster on those she loved. Frightened, she crept back to her bed where she sat for a while, hands clasped in a tragic manner. Fiercely she battled with the devils that threatened to destroy her, and, at length, emerged, cool and calculating, as she was to do many times in her stormy life.

Next morning, the great house echoed with the sound of battle as the Earl of Leicester and his wife argued about Penelope's behaviour. They frequently quarrelled so the angry sounds were not unfamiliar in the house but anyone with any sense stayed well away until the storm had passed.

'That child must be a born strumpet to indulge in an affair with one so low born.' Lord Leicester's eyes flashed angrily as he paced the wooden floor.

Lettice held a restraining arm out towards him. In spite of her extended stomach, she looked tall and majestic – certainly an imposing sight. 'Not so hasty, my lord,' she said. 'You do not know the truth of the matter as yet.'

'I have my eyes,' he snapped. 'They told me all I need to know. Send that young drab to France. They still have convents out there that know how to deal with these awkward wenches.'

The insult was too much for Lettice. 'How dare you demean my child!' She began to screech like an angry hen. 'How dare you say such a thing!'

It was Leicester's turn to restrain her. 'Control yourself, my lady,' he pleaded. 'Think of the child within.'

'This child?' she cried dramatically, banging her fat belly. 'Have you forgotten that you have probably fathered others?'

'Let us discuss this matter calmly, Lettice,' he urged, concerned for the safety of his heir. 'Be reasonable. This girl has always been wayward.'

'I shall discuss nothing of the matter,' Lettice

declared obstinately, 'until I have got to the bottom of this whole sordid business. Penelope is wild, but no fool. She is very aware of her noble blood and would in no circumstances forget or compromise it.'

Leicester sighed. 'All right, my lady, have your own way,' he said coldly; 'I shall return to London. Send me news of the birth of your child.'

'As you wish, sir.' Tears were not far from her lovely eyes, but Lettice was too proud to surrender.

Leicester made for the door, where he half turned. 'One more word, my lady, and then I'll leave. Philip Sidney's father was always opposed to the match between his son and your daughter. I shall make doubly sure that Penelope does not wed my nephew.'

After her husband's departure Lettice wept a little, but not for long; she knew that he would return soon. It did not bother her that Penelope had lost an ardent suitor. Philip Sidney was poor and a bit of an ass. Her child would look higher up the social scale if she had her way. No one was going to make her children suffer for her own mistakes and loose morals.

Later that morning, mother and daughter faced each other, both obstinate, proud and wilful.

'Now, Penelope, I'll have the truth of this matter, or by God I'll beat it out of you.' In a furious temper she tackled her errant daughter.

Penelope's pale face assumed a cold, sarcastic smile. 'So my Lord Leicester has informed you of my misdeeds.' She shrugged insolently. 'So that is all there is to know.'

Lettice raised a hand as if to strike her. The cold

sarcasm was more than she could endure. Then a small figure came forward, eyes red with weeping. 'I will tell you the true story, my lady,' Hawise whispered.

Piece by piece the full account of the night's events was dragged out. Instead of fury, it was met with a sigh of relief from Lettice. 'Oh, dear, what else could one expect from a child of Anne Dallon? It's entirely my fault. I should have kept a more observant eye on you, Hawise. I shall have to send you to Grandfather Knollys' house, so that if you are with child, there will be someone there to take care of you for the sake of your dear mother, God rest her soul.' Then sharply she turned to her daughter. 'You stay confined to your chamber. I have other plans for you, my child,' she stated almost jubilantly. But she did not explain the plans then.

Once her mother had left, Penelope comforted Hawise. 'Don't fret,' she said. 'As soon as I am wed I'll insist you come back to live with me.'

'Oh, I loved him, Penelope,' wailed Hawise through her tears. 'I do not care for anything any more.'

Penelope hugged her tight. 'Try to be brave,' she whispered gently. 'We have to learn to face up to adversity. It's the only way to survive. Only the strong can win!' Defiantly she added: 'In future, no one is going to stand in my way. I shall live my life as I please.'

4

Arranged Marriage

After Hawise's departure there was an emptiness in Penelope's heart. She moped about the great house, her full lips in a sullen droop as she contemplated a plan of escape from the never-ending round of music lessons, dancing lessons and courtesy visits to the surrounding gentry. Heavily laced up in whalebone, her lovely hair curled and frizzed and pushed into a high lace cap, with a stiffened ruff that always seemed in danger of throttling her, she accompanied her mother on long, tedious visits to her wealthy and highborn neighbours. Lettice, whose body was wide and distended – not many weeks from her time though this did little to deter her – as magnificently clothed as always, conducted her uncooperative eldest daughter on a tour of the noble family mansions, determined to make a good match for her now that the betrothal to Philip Sidney was at an end.

Soon, however, the atmosphere at Wanstead was enlivened by the arrival of Penelope's younger sister, Dorothy, who had been living in the north with Lord Leicester's sister for several years. Dorothy was fair and petite. She could point her toe gracefully, sing and play in tune. All these accomplishments were much harder for her elder sister to acquire, for Penelope was tall, stiff and awkward and in music, tone-deaf. Fervently, Penelope wanted to unbind her stiffened coiffure, to swing onto her mount and gallop swiftly through the forest, far away from the whispering, highly scented gossips in the house and, most of all, from the dark, sardonic humour of her mother who laughed insensitively at her slow progress.

Then in August the young Earl of Essex, Penelope's brother, arrived down from university. He had grown tall and very attractive, and was unusually precocious. With him came his inseparable friends – a blond, courteous boy named Christopher Blount; and a dark, sombre Welshman named Merrick, whom Penelope did not think much of.

'How can you stand that streak of misery about you?' she asked Robert one day. 'Doesn't his gloom rub off on you?' She had enjoyed getting to know her brother again. To their mutual delight, they found that they had much in common.

'Your tongue will be the undoing of you, Penelope,' replied her worldly young brother. He lolled gracefully against a tree, his white silk hose immaculate under a highly embroidered slashed doublet. He was unusually sleek and self-assured for one his age.

It was at the end of this long hot summer that Lord Leicester's wish was granted. Lettice retired to the lying-in chamber to give birth to a son just as the elms in the drive assumed their golden-amber attire. He was a puny child, but a son and heir all the same.

Around this time, after the young men had departed, Penelope and Dorothy were sent to stay with Lord

Leicester's sister, Catherine Hastings, with whom they were to begin their initial training before being presented at court. First, however, they were to be maids-of-honour at their cousin Mary Sidney's wedding. Nervous, spotty Mary was to marry a duke, an old man who had been married twice before. She was only fourteen – the match having been arranged by her uncle, the efficient marriage broker, Lord Hastings. Most important, the marriage was blessed with what every great family wanted: royal approval.

The day of the wedding ceremony, poor Mary, pale and wobbly-kneed, clung weeping to her aunt Catherine as Penelope and Dorothy decked her out with the family jewels. Her satin wedding gown was peppered with pearls – but the splendour of the garment made Mary look mousier than ever.

The ceremony took place without a hitch, but afterwards, on returning from the chapel, it was time to welcome Her Royal Majesty to the fabulous manor of Wilton.

Now dressed in a wide, stiffened ball gown with a heavy coronet of diamonds weighing down on her thin neck, poor little Mary was eventually guided down the wide staircase to take her place beside her elderly husband. From high up in the minstrel's gallery, the Devereux sisters watched the glittering company of ladies in their high jewelled wigs and shining gowns, and the simpering courtiers in their colourful slashed doublets, French hose and jewelled capes hanging with carefree abandon from one shoulder. Huge candelabra lit up the black-and-white marble floor and the excited faces of the guests as they waited for their monarch to appear.

At last she arrived, Great Gloriana, sweeping across the floor like a great galleon. Flickering shadows played on the red wig and her wrinkled, mask-like face. She was wearing a lavishly jewelled blue satin bodice with immense hanging sleeves, and a flounced French farthingale skirt. A fan-shaped ruff around her neck and a wired head rail trimmed with sapphires behind her head made a frame for her sad face and added to her height and regality. Holding a fan in one hand and silk gloves in the other, her small, beady eyes swept the room and seemed to miss no detail of the adoring throng surrounding her.

'She is terribly grand,' whispered Dorothy in awe.

'Oh, I don't think so,' retorted Penelope brashly. 'Why, she's only half that size and that's a wig she's wearing. Some say that she is completely bald.'

'Hush, Penelope.' Dorothy put a warning finger to her lips; there was always someone listening, ready to carry tales to Her Majesty.

'I wouldn't be in Mary's shoes for anything,' cried Penelope watching her cousin cringing under the royal stare.

'No,' agreed Dorothy, sweetly, 'I do feel sorry for her, marrying a man that old.'

Penelope grimaced at the sight of the old duke bowing to the queen. Such a fate would never befall her, she vowed.

Once Her Majesty had retired, the party moved out into the gardens. Lanterns hung in the trees. Fireworks lit up the sky and Dorothy skipped gaily amongst the guests. But Penelope hung back, pensive and rather sullen in the shadow of the rose arbour, taking in the drowsy perfume of rose and honeysuckle that pervaded the night air. It was not long before the black silk-clad figure of Philip approached. Penelope was surprised to feel an excited flutter in her breast as he took her hand. It had been quite a while since they had last met.

'Shall we dance, or discover the hidden beauties of the rose garden?' he asked.

Penelope looked at him with her black eyes and smiled. 'I don't wish to dance,' she murmured. They strolled the avenue of sweet-smelling flowers to a rustic seat.

'I want to say goodbye, Penelope.' Philip spoke with a sadness in his voice and his brown eyes seemed so melancholy as he knelt and kissed her hand. She wanted to caress the brown curls that grew at the nape of his neck as his head was bent before her, but she resisted the impulse.

'I'm going to France tomorrow, Penelope, on a Royal mission,' he informed her. 'I shall not forget you. You will always be my love, but we can never marry now. You do understand?'

Penelope was irritated by the presumption in his words.

'I am sorry at your departure, sir,' she answered primly.

'But I intend to choose my own husband. I shall marry whom I like.' She paused and glanced at him sideways. 'Does that surprise you, sir?' she asked.

Philip rose to his feet, a smile hovering about his sensitive mouth. 'It not only surprises me, madam. It astounds me. I certainly wish you the best of luck.' Silently he took her arm and escorted her back to an ever watchful chaperon.

When Penelope related this incident later to Dorothy, her sister did not seem a bit surprised. 'I believe that Philip Sidney is in love with you,' she said cautiously.

'Nonsense!' returned her unsentimental sister. 'Philip loves himself and his silly poems.'

Philip departed for France the next day to begin a diplomatic career. Now that Lettice had borne a son, he was no longer Lord Leicester's heir. Like the Devereux, the Sidneys were an impoverished family. Noble heritage had given much land, but very little capital. And since Philip would not now inherit his uncle's wealth he would have to marry for money.

For the remainder of that year Penelope and Dorothy moved on, visiting various noble houses, in the train of Lady Hastings who, childless herself, was determined to make good matches for her brother's stepchildren. At the Twelfth Night Presentation Ball at Hampton Court, the Devereux sisters officially 'came out'.

Penelope always remembered that tense moment of presentation – the low curtsy, and the graceful retreat without turning her back on the great queen. There had been beads of perspiration on her smooth, alabaster brow; and the uncomfortable stiff collar forced her to hold her head up high. At first malignant glances darted from the Queen's deep-set eyes, but then she eventually smiled, showing her rotten, black and yellow teeth. At the time, Penelope was terrified but afterwards she agreed with Dorothy that it was not as bad as she had expected, considering the queen's opinion of their mother.

It was at the same Twelfth Night Ball that Penelope was introduced to her future husband, Lord Rich. He had just come of age and inherited a huge fortune which his father had acquired in dubious property deals during the Reformation. Robert Rich was a second son – his elder brother had died before his father – and wealth was new to him. Brash and vulgar, he swaggered about the court, accompanied by a string of male toadies.

Penelope first saw him from behind the huge pillars in the throne room. She did not know who he was but she was tempted to laugh out loud at the squat, pompous youth, for she was head and shoulders taller than he. When introduced, Lord Rich bowed low over her hand, proclaiming his delight in a thin and squeaky voice. There was also something about his face which disturbed her, and then she realised that he had odd-coloured eyes. One was blue, the other green. They made his face look absurd. His thin lips looked cruel and were set in a hard line, while his gaze, despite the eyes, was cold and speculative.

At the time Penelope was unaware that he had chosen her to be his future wife. So it was with amusement that she had observed his ugly body clad in the thick, padded doublet above spindly white-hosed legs.

'Lord Rich is much like a spider,' she commented to Catherine Hastings afterwards. 'He has a fat body and thin legs and he squeaks just like an animal as though there is something missing in his throat.' She laughed and wrinkled her nose in disgust.

The demure Lady Hastings was shocked by Penelope's words. 'Lord Rich is very wealthy and stands in good stead for a knighthood. He would be an excellent match for you, Penelope,' she insisted.

Penelope laughed. 'Don't bother,' she replied rudely. 'I'll never marry as odd a looking fellow as he.'

Had she been aware of the matrimonial plans being made, she might not have been so casual.

Lady Hastings sighed, but pressed on with the plans, for she had promised her brother that she would get this wayward child off his hands as soon as possible. Of Lettice's brood, this girl was the most troublesome. Dorothy was happy and pliable; Walter, quiet and studious; and Robert a favourite with all – particularly the ageing queen. But Penelope seemed to cause ceaseless trouble wherever she was.

In early spring, the court circular announced the engagement of Lady Penelope Devereux to Lord Robert Rich of Leighs in Essex. When Penelope discovered what had been planned behind her back, she was horrified. Several times she tried to run away; and she cried and screamed and sulked. But her tantrums had no effect except to make Catherine Hastings send the girl back to her mother at Wanstead. There too, her pleas fell on deaf ears. Her mother simply confined her to her chambers with a bevy of sewing maids to complete her trousseau.

Lettice was worrying about her sickly baby son and had no time for any nonsense from Penelope. Lord

Leicester, who had known much honour and many misfortunes, derived great happiness from the son that Lettice had given him and she could not bear the thought of them losing him. All her other children had been hale and hearty, but this lovely golden-haired boy was constantly ill, suffered bouts of strange, nervous convulsions and needed extensive care and attention. In response to Penelope's early insistence that she 'would not marry that little toad at any price', the harassed Lettice had slapped her sharply and dismissed her. Finally, when the tantrums and tears continued, Lettice hit on the idea of bringing Hawise back as maid to her rebellious daughter.

This was a clever move. On the day before Penelope's wedding, Hawise came home to Wanstead. She looked paler and much thinner, but also much more mature. Sadly, she had been delivered of a still-born child while staying at Grandfather Knollys' country house, by a loyal old nurse who had brought up many Knollys children. Penelope and Hawise embraced as sisters, unable to speak, so great was their emotion. And Hawise's presence made all the difference; henceforth Penelope seemed to calm down and finally accept that she had to go through with this hated marriage.

'I've heard that Lord Rich is really quite nice,' the gentle Hawise said encouragingly.

Penelope sniffed. 'He is so much smaller than I,' she complained.

'But, my lady, he is very wealthy and has a large estate,' said Hawise wisely. 'And think how nice it will be to be your own mistress and have me for your personal attendant.'

'But Hawise,' protested Penelope, 'he is so peculiar to look at. Every time I see him I want to laugh.'

'Well, that's better than crying,' replied the practical-minded maid. 'I've shed so many tears for love, I never want to do so again.'

Penelope felt a lump in her throat as she reached out and squeezed Hawise's arm. 'I'll never forgive myself for what happened,' she said. 'I know I was to blame. How can I ever recompense you?' Her own problems suddenly seemed so minor compared to what Hawise had suffered.

Hawise smiled. 'You will, my lady, by your marriage. I'll then be able to live in your household and never need anyone again. Just to care for you will be enough and your children will be mine.'

Penelope turned towards the maid, her black eyes shining with emotion. 'You are so good, Hawise,' she said softly. 'And you're right about what I should do; I will make no more fuss and merry Lord Rich tomorrow.'

The next day, with the reassuring help of Hawise, Penelope was eventually arrayed in her wedding gown, a grand creation of white and gold, behind which trailed an ancestral train, embroidered with precious gems and the emblem of the noble barons from whom she was descended. Followed by a crowd of small cousins from other branches of her illustrious family, Penelope walked slowly down the aisle on the arm of Grandfather Knollys, who was upright and quiet on this solemn occasion.

As the church music rang in her ears, she suddenly faltered at the grotesque sight of Lord Rich watching her hungrily as he waited at the altar. Her grandfather grasped her arm firmly and pressed on. Penelope swallowed hard and, reminding herself of Hawise's words the day before, lifted up her veiled head and allowed herself to be escorted to the end.

Those guests who saw Penelope's hesitation exchanged meaningful glances, but if they had expected to witness a choice scene, they were disappointed; the knot was securely tied with the blessing of the church in the gracious chapel of Wanstead.

Afterwards, amid the excitement of the wedding feast, the bride sat quiet and aloof. Her runtish husband, beside her, had eaten and drunk his fill, and now slobbered expectantly at her side. Penelope gritted her teeth at the thought of being bedded with this oaf that night. What would it be like? She hardly dared imagine it for fear of panic overwhelming her. She had to try not to be so afraid. Hawise had told her a little of what to expect, but she had said it was a good experience, that it made one feel happy. That certainly would not be true for her; Penelope felt sure that nothing would ever make her happy again.

During the long carriage ride to Leighs, black despair swept through her. Even Hawise failed to console her. They had gone on ahead of Robert Rich, who had stayed on after the family guests had left, feasting and drinking with his friends, planning to follow his bride and join her later.

When the carriage transporting Penelope and Hawise arrived at Leighs, the sight of the gloomy towers did nothing to abate Penelope's rising fear. Nor did Hawise's calm comforting words as she prepared her mistress for her marriage bed.

Wishing for all the world that she would fall asleep, Penelope lay alone in a musty four-poster bed surrounded by grimy drapes. But sleep would not come, and she was wide awake with her heart beating madly with fear when her drunken husband finally came staggering up to bed. Outside, his companions made lewd noises, as the candles were snuffed out by a discreet servant.

Lord Rich clumsily tore off his clothes and jumped hungrily into bed, grabbing Penelope's body with his rough hands. She shrank away from him but he pulled her tighter, grunting loudly and fumbling beneath the bedclothes. Penelope could do nothing as he pressed his hot sweaty body down on top of her, ripping her shift in his haste. Twisting round in terror, she tried to push him off with all her might, but she was not strong enough; he grabbed her arms and pinned them against her sides. Her nostrils curled at the smell of his foul breath as he ran his hands over her exposed body. With a cry of defiance, she lifted her head and sank her teeth deep in his shoulder. Rich howled with pain and rage, gripping her arms so tight that his nails hurt her flesh.

'Right,' he snarled. 'You're my wife.' He grabbed hold of her long fair hair and jerked back her head. With his whole weight on top of her, he pushed his male member into her body. Penelope gasped; it was so much larger than she had expected. Although she struggled and fought like a tigress, she was helpless, and escape from the horror only came when she finally lost consciousness. Thus ended her wedding night – so unlike how she used to imagine such an occasion would be.

Hawise was beside her bed in the cold light of dawn. Cool administering hands soothed Penelope's fevered brow, bathed her aching body and changed the blood-stained bedding. Her lovely mistress lay silent and defeated but inside, her heart was consumed with a burning, bitter hatred. She could not tolerate more.

'Hawise,' she pleaded later. 'Go and find my grand-father, he will rescue me.'

But Hawise only shook her head. 'It will do no good, my lady. You were married by the church and you must stay married now.' Calmly, Hawise tried to make her mistress see reason.

'I'll kill myself!' threatened Penelope. She thrust out her bruised arms. 'Look at what the brute did to me!'

But Hawise hardly seemed to notice. 'It will not be so bad next time,' she said calmly. 'You must try to be a little more cooperative.'

'Never!' sobbed Penelope. 'I hate the filthy beast.'

'Hush, my lady,' said Hawise. 'It's not so bad. It's a fate most women must endure.'

'Not I! I'll die first!' screamed Penelope.

All that day and for the rest of the week, Penelope refused to leave her chamber, seeing none but Hawise behind the locked door. Each time she thought about her wedding night she burst into a fit of uncontrollable weeping.

One day, when Lord Rich rode out on a hunting party with his friends, Hawise tried to reason with her. 'Now come, madam,' she urged her in soft tones. 'Your husband has left the house. Let us look over your new home. It's very fine, but badly neglected. Rise now, my lady, and supervise your own supper table for when my Lord Rich returns with his guests.' Diplomatically she endeavoured to get Penelope to accept her fate.

'I am not leaving this room until someone fetches Grandfather Knollys,' Penelope declared obstinately.

But Hawise would not listen. Instead, she busied herself cleaning up the gloomy chamber where cobwebs hid in corners, and talked brightly about the house and grounds in an effort to interest her mistress in the size and wealth of the huge estate.

At last Penelope did rise from the bed but she just stared disconsolately out of the window. 'My God, how desolate it is,' she moaned. 'There is nothing but wild marsh out there.'

In the evening there were sounds from the hall below. Lord Rich and his rowdy friends had returned, but his bride still stood in the window. The setting sun cast red shadows on her golden hair. In the dining hall, long tables were laid. All the family silver and gold was tastefully arrayed. The guests hung about the fire awaiting their hostess. Harassed servants ran up and down the stairs. And a stern-faced Hawise came to chide the lady of the house. 'You are behaving very badly, madam,' she said.

'I don't care. I shall be leaving this horrible house tomorrow,' announced Penelope. 'You'll see, I'm not staying here.'

She heard slow, deliberate footsteps coming along the stone corridor and stop outside the door. 'Have I the pleasure of your company, madam?' Lord Rich's shrill voice echoed through the locked door.

Penelope froze and did not answer.

'No matter,' she heard him sneer. 'I'll return to town. I shall not bother you for a while.' With that he walked back down the echoing corridor.

Lord Rich kept his promise. After supper he rode out very merrily with his drunken companions. Loud and vibrant with the chink of harness and the rattle of hooves, they galloped out of the courtyard while Penelope kept her lonely vigil at the window. The fact that he had gone off without a fight acutely disappointed her.

'Thank God that oaf has left,' she said. 'Now I must contact my grandfather. He must get my marriage annulled immediately.' It all seemed so simple to her, but the series of pathetic letters she wrote never reached Sir Francis Knollys. Neither were mount or coach ever made available to her to ride out of her gloomy home. After several weeks she became despondent as she realised that she was more or less a prisoner. As Hawise had pointed out, these were Lord Rich's servants and they had received their orders. There was no way of escape; Penelope was tied to this cold, untidy house on a wind-swept marsh for as long as her husband wished.

Accepting that she could not escape for a while, she began to explore her surroundings. Leighs had at one time been a priory. There were many lovely stained-glass windows and an ancient, peaceful chapel – now seldom used. The house was filled with Spanish fittings and furnishings collected by the sticky fingers of her husband's ancestors. The kitchens were old-fashioned, and underground in a rat-ridden basement; the servants were dirty and very lazy. One day she descended the kitchens like a firebrand and, asserting herself with Lord Rich's servants, demanded that they clean the place up. Then, still unaware that her letters were going nowhere, she sat down to await the result of her plea to Grandfather Knollys to get her marriage annulled.

Hawise was extremely happy in her new home, and more effectively than Penelope, started to restore law and order in the great house. The rotting rushes were swept from the floors and replaced; she moved her mistress to a smaller, cosier bedchamber and was thoroughly enjoying herself. Before now, she had been a mere servant, taking orders. But now, as her mistress's loyal companion, she could issue them. In her new-found glory she began to turn Leighs into a suitable home for her beloved mistress.

The cold days of early spring began to pass and a fresh, invigorating salt breeze blew over the marshland. Penelope would sit with Hawise sewing in a small parlour, and the gentlefolk of the district paid her courtesy visits. She had become acquainted with the bailiff and the rector from the village. Slowly she began to feel freedom and importance as mistress of a large estate, and began to enjoy it.

One day her mother paid a flying visit. Lettice, as

always, was quite unsympathetic to Penelope's feelings. 'Thank God you have settled down at last,
Penelope,' she cried. 'From the tales I've heard I am
more than shocked at your lack of cooperation.'

Her daughter's dark eyes flickered with anger. 'I am
not sure what beastly rumours have reached your ears,
madam,' she said in a controlled voice, 'but I give no
thanks to you. I was completely unprepared for the
onslaught of that animal and all my letters of appeal,
even the ones to you and my stepfather, have been
ignored.'

'Don't be so foolish, Penelope,' her mother scolded.
'Everyone has to get used to being married.' She spoke
sharply, but nonetheless looked anxiously at her
daughter who, with hard, tight-lipped mouth muttered,
'I swear by all that's holy that if that beast comes near
me again I'll run a dagger through him.'

'Nonsense!' exclaimed Lettice. 'Why must you be
so dramatic?'

Although her voice did not betray her thoughts,
Lettice's already harassed face looked shocked at the
venom in her daughter's tone. Stiffly she rose with a
rustle of silks. Sniffing the perfumed nosegay she
carried, she said, 'All I can say is that Lord Rich did
not marry you for your beauty or your atrocious
manners, but to beget an heir of noble blood. You
should think yourself most fortunate.'

Penelope also arose, tall and very fiery. Narrowing
her eyes she hissed at her mother. 'You must be correct,
madam. I know I possess neither your beauty nor your
avid appetite for men.'

The cold sarcasm in her daughter's voice made Lettice flinch but immediately she had regained her composure. 'Well,' she shrugged, in a matter-of-fact way, 'providing you are pregnant, he will probably leave you alone for a while. I don't blame him,' she added. 'You have a vile temper.'

'I'll pay that little toad out in full measure,' threatened Penelope. 'And I'll certainly not bear a child by him.'

Lettice peered into her face and smiled. 'I don't think you have a choice. It looks to me as if you are already with child.' Throwing her fur-trimmed cloak about her shoulders, she turned to go. 'Of course, it's all in the hand of fate,' she murmured.

Penelope gasped as though cold water had been thrown into her face. It had not ever occurred to her that she might be with child.

'Well, goodbye, dear,' said Lettice breezily. 'I'll spread the news in town.' She paused and then added more kindly, 'He might not bother you for a while.' With a flurry of fur and feathers, she had gone.

From the main entrance Penelope watched her mother depart. She rode away in a black-and-gold coach drawn by six prancing milk-white steeds with two fabulously clad footmen behind and a coach load of attendants following.

It was in this extravagant, ostentatious manner, that the Countess of Essex travelled to London to seek her lord. In the streets of London, plain folk stopped to stare at this elaborate cortège, and under the impression that it was their queen, waved and cheered loudly.

Lettice revelled in the homage she received and smiled and waved back.

It did not take long for news of Lettice's behaviour to reach the ears of the monarch. Queen Elizabeth was furious to hear that her brazen hussy of a cousin was parading about town in an outfit only right for a queen, and she summoned her immediately.

When she received the summons to court, Lettice was delighted, for she was convinced that she was at last to be acknowledged as Lord Leicester's true wife. She arrived in a magnificent gown, handsomely bejewelled for this special occasion. Radiant and happy she stepped forward to pay her respects to her great and glorious queen.

At the sight of her, Her Majesty's small eyes narrowed and her lips clamped down hard. 'Only one sun is allowed to shine here,' she said simply. Reaching forward she boxed her cousin's ears in the presence of the whole court, including Lettice's own husband and son.

Mortified, Lettice fled back to Wanstead, determined never to return again. She was accompanied by Sir Christopher Blount, her son's friend, because neither the young Earl of Essex nor Lord Leicester was granted permission to leave the side of his imperious Sovereign. It was a terrible disgrace which few people would forget.

When Hawise brought this choice piece of gossip to her mistress from the servants' hall, Penelope was angry and hurt for her foolish mother. She began to hate the Queen and all she stood for more than ever.

Now ten weeks pregnant and with a sick feeling at the pit of her stomach, she awaited with apprehension the impending return of her lord and master.

'When he comes back, you must make an effort,' insisted Hawise. 'He is the father of your child.'

Penelope sat glowering as if trying to think up some vicious plan to outwit him.

'The servants say that he is not an ogre,' pleaded Hawise. 'Just a silly young man whom lecherous acquaintances make use of.'

Penelope sniffed airily. 'Don't be so afraid, my little maid. I shall handle him, I can assure you.'

Tall and majestic, a white hard-faced mistress descended to the lower regions of the house once again. Pots must be re-scoured, the larder re-stocked. Her eyes were like two black opals and her mouth was set in a sullen line. With strict discipline, she stirred the servants from their lethargy to become the established mistress and ruler of her own home at last.

Hawise was worried by the sudden change. Motherhood and the dreaded return of her husband seemed to have wrought some transformation in Penelope's personality. And the steely strength that seemed to shine from her made poor Hawise convinced that Penelope really did mean to murder Lord Rich.

Lord Rich arrived home to the delicious aroma of roast sucking pig and the feverish activity of the staff. There was no sign of his wife, but a message was brought to him informing him that she would join him at dinner with their guests. Upstairs, with expert care, Hawise was helping Penelope dress in a bodice of black-and-gold brocade, with balloon sleeves lined in scarlet. Her sleek hair, pulled back and piled high, was shining with jewels and made a perfect halo for her pale face. Grandmother Knollys' famous black pearls hung about her neck and, set in gold, dangled from her ears. 'Pearls are for tears,' she had said moodily as Hawise placed them about her neck.

'Fie, fie! How morbid you can be!' scolded Hawise. 'These are worth a king's ransom.' Valiantly the little maid tried hard to hide her tears of concern for the heartbreak of her mistress.

Lord Rich was waiting for her at the foot of the staircase. Her red-gold hair gleamed in the flickering candlelight. His piggy eyes were slightly mocking, but he was clean and polite, and together the tall Lady Rich and her small husband welcomed their guests – several ladies and their husbands including a sea captain whose white teeth flashed merrily above a dark beard as he told tales of a recent voyage to the New World, where he and his men had come across a new race of savages called Red Skins.

Proudly erect and smiling, Penelope entertained her guests; her noble blood did not let her down. But all the time she was aware of Lord Rich's strange eyes surveying her with sneering amusement from the other side of the table. And little spasms of fear ran through her each time she heard his high squeaky voice. Immediately the meal was over she begged permission to retire. With a low bow and a loose grin Robert Rich escorted her to the door.

Once inside her own chamber, Penelope tore the

rings off her fingers. 'Get me out of this tomfoolery, Hawise!' she cried. 'I did my duty and that is all I ever intend to do.'

After several days out hunting and late nights carousing with his drinking companions, Lord Rich eventually departed once more to London. Before he left, he paid his wife a brief farewell visit. Penelope was in her parlour working industriously at an embroidery frame. The afternoon sun slanted through the stained-glass window, painting her a myriad of colours. Her husband approached somewhat nervously. Looking up, she calmly laid down her work and gazed very seriously at this irritating little man whose child was within her. Surely there would be some mutual feeling? But all she saw was empty frustration.

'I came to bid you farewell, madam. I am about to go back to town,' he announced in his thin tone.

Graciously she inclined her head and waited.

He fidgeted with his hands, finally placing them behind his back. 'I will see that you have all that is necessary for your confinement. I have already engaged an excellent physician who will arrive a few weeks previously.' He paused. Penelope said nothing. 'God willing, we will have a son,' Lord Rich muttered piously, breaking the silence. Again, Penelope did not respond as he paused. He hesitated for a moment but then seemed to change his mind. Bowing low, he swiftly departed.

Expressionlessly, Penelope watched him ride away with his men. But the moment he had gone from sight, she began to laugh and skip about the room, twirling the flustered Hawise around and around by the arms. 'He has gone!' she cried. 'At last I am free of him.'

'Calm down, madam,' insisted Hawise drawing away.

'It's all very sad. After all, he is your husband.'

Penelope stopped in her tracks; a frown wrinkled her brow. 'By God, don't you dare pity him! I was bought and sold like a slave. What right has he to the use of my body because some bungling priest said a few holy words over us?'

'Hush, my lady,' whispered Hawise, who looked really worried.

A slow smile had crept over the face of her mistress. 'I discovered today,' Penelope said with satisfaction, 'that he is afraid of me. That power is a weapon I shall wield with great pleasure.'

Hawise was speechless and just stared at her formidable mistress in trepidation.

The hot, dry summer came and dried up the mud in the Essex countryside. There were dangerous deep holes and ruts in the highways and byways, but most places around Leighs could be reached. Penelope had at last obtained the use of a heavy lumbering coach that had previously belonged to the late Baron Rich, and, accompanied by Hawise, she would pay courtesy visits to her surrounding neighbours, including the Lucas and Howard families with whom she discussed the latest gossip from court and the rumours of approaching war. Nowadays she spared no expense; she made use of the massive fortune that the parsimonious old rascal, the late Baron Rich, had accumulated.

Penelope was her mother's daughter and did not care if she was living beyond her husband's means. She was determined to enjoy his wealth.

It was late summer when they travelled to Wanstead to visit her mother. Lettice was very distressed, having been recently bereaved of her little son, the sickly child who had brought her and her much loved lord so close to one another. Now he was dead, a terrible gap had been left in their lives.

Penelope found her mother sitting in the garden superbly gowned in deep mourning. At first sight, Lettice seemed as proud and regal as ever, but violet shadows beneath her eyes betrayed her heartbreak. She looked tired and, Penelope thought, a little older. Lettice welcomed her daughter graciously, but it did not take long for them to clash.

'Pregnancy does not suit you,' Lettice remarked unkindly. 'It makes you look enormous.'

Ever conscious of her size, Penelope flushed, but she refrained from answering back and, without saying a word, she seated herself beside her mother. Today, for some reason, she felt perfectly capable of coping with her mother's caustic comments which usually subdued her.

'I am truly sorry for your loss, Mother,' she murmured softly.

For a second, tears flashed into Lettice's passionate eyes. 'It was not unexpected,' she replied politely. At that moment, a handsome blond youth came across the lawn to stand solicitously by her side. 'Get someone to bring out some cool drinks, will you Christopher?'

Obediently the young man left for the house.

Appraisingly, Penelope watched him. So that was why her mother was taking it all so bravely. Lord Leicester had returned to the bosom of his queen, leaving the handsome Christopher Blount to care for his stricken wife and huge estate.

'There is bad news from the low countries,' Lettice informed her. 'Robert thinks it possible that England will send an expeditionary force out there to aid the Dutch against the Duke of Parma.'

Penelope was not interested in politics or military campaigns and did not reply.

'So you may be fortunate enough to rid yourself of your own illustrious husband,' continued Lettice. She spoke in a humorous tone, but the undercurrent of sarcasm was still there. 'Young Robert is already playing tin soldiers, ruining his legacy, fitting out a troop of soldiers in tangerine velvet. Squandering the little left of his father's estate.'

Penelope disliked the spitefulness of her mother's tone and did not respond. Instead, she peered absent-mindedly towards the lake beside which she could see a lone figure.

Her mother's glance followed hers. 'It's Philip,' she said. 'Why don't you join him?'

'If he wishes to converse with me, Mother, he will come over,' Penelope replied impatiently. There was a dangerous glint in her eyes. Sorrow had made her mother insufferable, and Penelope could not now resist the urge to retaliate. Christopher Blount was returning, his blond hair shining in the bright sunlight as he crossed the green lawn.

'If my brother rides to war he will take his close companion with him, no doubt,' said Penelope as she sullenly eyed the handsome youth.

But Lettice was not to be goaded by this malicious thrust. She rose gracefully and smoothed down her gown with her slim, white hand. Casually she put her hand on Sir Christopher's arm. 'Forgive me if I retire. I will see you at supper, no doubt.' Lettice had noticed that Philip was coming in their direction and was making a discreet exit.

As Philip reached Penelope, he held out his hand in greeting. Without a word she took hold of it and the couple wandered hand-in-hand through the rose arbour. Penelope was quiet, still conscious of the way her heart had leaped as her old suitor had approached. Philip was looking very handsome and courtly. His rich brown curls had been neatly trimmed and his face was much thinner. She had heard that he had been ill in France and had returned home to recuperate. She could not deny that she was happy to see him and she struggled with her confusion as she tried not to lose the calm that she had acquired. But she was acutely aware of his body beside hers and of the heat gener-ated by their clasped hands.

Once they were clear of the house, Philip stopped and turned to her. 'Are you happy, Penelope?' he asked gently.

She held onto his soft, warm hands, and shame-faced, averted her head. 'Don't rub salt into a gaping wound, sir. You know my answer,' she said sourly.

Philip nodded in assent and placed a comforting

arm about her waist. They walked towards a wooden bench and then in silence, fed upon the sweet nostalgia of the past, he handsome and erect, outlined by a screen of honeysuckle.

'I am truly sorry we parted,' he told her. 'If I had had half the brains or ability of my forebears, I would have fought to keep you, and stopped you marrying that lout Robert Rich,' he added bitterly.

Tears welled up in her eyes. Her dear Philip was so brave and noble. What a fool she had been not to realise it. 'Yes, it's a bad business. I am tied to the uncouth Lord Rich and you, I hear, are contracted to marry another.'

'She is too young as yet, and I am indebted to her father.' He made excuses for his betrothal to Frances Walsingham.

'So now it is too late, my lord,' whispered Penelope. Leaning forward she stroked at last the soft curls that grew on the nape of his neck.

At her touch Philip fell to his knees and wept, pressing his face to her swollen stomach. 'Oh, I am lost without you, my lovely wild goose,' he sobbed. 'This child should have been mine.'

'Don't grieve, sir,' she comforted him, as Philip, weak, sensitive and poetic, covered her hands with kisses. She hugged him close, quivering with the strange tremors within her. This noble man would have given her true love and she had only been a victim of rape. 'Everything has a remedy, sir,' she said coolly. 'When I have given Lord Rich his heir, I can still belong to you again. I promise only death will part us.' She offered herself to him.

Philip closed his eyes and shuddered. Then he rose to his feet. 'I am a knight, a man of honour. Do not tempt me, my love.'

Penelope sniffed and pushed him away contemptuously. 'Will you never learn, Philip, that life is for living? Must we be pawns in this political game?'

Philip smiled sadly and looked at her with love in his eyes. 'How I admire your courage, my lady, and your refusal to be bound by conventions. Perhaps those qualities are what I admire most about you, my little rebel.'

Penelope looked up at him with her eyes glowing like black coals. She knew she loved him, but how weak he was! She wondered if she could have really shared a life with him, when she was so much stronger than he.

The evening festivities at Wanstead were enlivened by a fleeting visit from Robert Devereux, Earl of Essex. Very full of himself, he boasted of his conquest of the old queen. Lettice seemed quite cheered up as she fawned on both her son and his friend Christopher Blount. There was no sign of Philip. He must have left as secretly as he had come.

Throughout the evening Penelope had felt that she did not belong anymore, either in the house or with her family, so she was not sorry the next day to return to Leighs. And she was quite happy to stay there until the child was born. She hoped that it would be a boy, an heir to this manor and many others throughout the land. For if it were a boy, there would be no occasion for her to bear another child. She would request permission to enter a convent. Her red lips trembled as these morbid thoughts passed through her mind.

'Are you feeling poorly, my lady?' enquired Hawise noticing the unusual paleness of her skin. 'Was the journey too much for you?'

Penelope shook her head. 'No, I was thinking of the future. How I hate this house and how I would like to live in town!' As she said this, she realised that she did not really know what she wanted; first life in a convent, now in town.

Hawise pursed her lips in disapproval. 'There are too many hazards in town,' she said, 'what with the plague and smallpox so rife.'

But Penelope did not hear her words; her pains had started.

Penelope gave birth with comparative ease to a son, whose jet-black curls stuck tightly to his wrinkled forehead. As his large mouth let out a dreadfull squall, Penelope stared down in horror at this monstrosity that had been within her.

Hawise was quite unable to conceal her delight. 'Oh, it's a boy, a beautiful boy. Congratulations, my lady,' she laughed.

But Penelope was not moved. Not one ounce of maternal love did she feel.

From the courtyard below came the sound of galloping hooves as the messenger left to take the news to Lord Rich that he now had an heir, uniting the royal blood of the Devereux and the Boleyns with his own merchant family.

The tiny child, wrapped tightly in swaddling clothes, was handed to his mother. One eye slowly opened and stared up at her. Penelope felt wrenched in half. She wanted to love him, but how could she love any child conceived in such circumstances? Shutting her eyes, she pushed the love of her first-born from her heart. 'Take him away, Hawise,' she ordered. 'I don't want to see him again. Get him a wet nurse.'

One week later she stood downstairs in the Barons' Hall surrounded by the suits of armour and banners of past battles. Her beautiful face was cold and hard as she waited to meet her husband. At last Lord Rich arrived. He walked nervously towards her, slightly tipsy, dirty and gravel-stained after travelling hard to reach home after hearing the good news.

'Congratulations, my lady,' he said, almost breathlessly.

Lifting one arm she bade him keep his distance. Robert Rich was clearly excited; beads of perspiration formed on his brow and he shifted his hands from back to front in an anxious manner.

There was a wicked gleam in Penelope's eyes as she watched his obvious discomfort. He only came level with her shoulder and she deliberately held herself very upright in order to create an even greater distance between them.

'Have you some requests, madam?' he blurted out. 'You have given me a fine son. Is there no way I can recompense you?'

Penelope's face was expressionless as she replied. 'I need nothing from you, sir, except to return to town. I hate this mausoleum.'

5

The Rebel

Much to the amazement of his wife, Robert Rich set about granting her request. Penelope was surprised because she had been quite prepared to battle with him. Lord Rich renovated and refurnished a little-used property at Stratford-le-Bow, a fairly large village on the outskirts of London, where Bow Bridge crossed the River Leigh as it emptied itself into the Thames.

The house was a tall, three-storey dwelling, one that his illustrious grandfather had acquired when milking the Papists so thoroughly during the Reformation. It had been a nunnery and was completely obscured from the road by a high wall and a line of immensely tall, rather lovely, sycamore trees. It possessed a long-established garden with vines and even, in a sheltered place, an orange grove, though the trees did not bear fruit. There were many little niches where statues had stood, empty now and hung about with bindweed. A square courtyard, a lily-padded pond and a splendid view into London from an upstairs balcony added to its charms.

Penelope was entranced. For though old and neglected, the place had a kind of sweet stillness about it that captivated her, and she felt as if the spirits of the past still dwelt there. She visualised white-clad novices sitting in the sun; happy children playing about the pond; high voices raised in songs of praise. Always sensitive to atmosphere, Penelope felt that here she could be happy. The front of the house faced the main road to town and gave a complete change of view. A toll gate at the end of the rickety bridge crossed the River Leigh. It was the main highway into the city and it amused her to watch the motley procession that went back and forth across the bridge – carts alive with chickens or green with vegetables; drivers shouting or swearing; folks arguing at the toll gate. All around, the air was alive with living.

'Oh, isn't it fun?' she laughed to Hawise after they had been there a few weeks.

'I don't think so,' replied the maid. 'It would have been a lot more sensible to stay in the country.'

'Oh no! It's going to be so exciting. Why, I was buried alive at Leighs,' declared her mistress.

'The plague may come. Smallpox is very rife,' said Hawise gloomily.

Radiant in a new gown of apple-green velvet, Penelope refused to have her spirits dampened. She had dispensed with the stiff, cumbersome ruff and now wore a high-backed lace collar, her white bosom almost bared.

'You are looking very lovely today,' said Hawise, hugging her fondly.

Penelope laughed gaily. 'You know, my little maid, for some reason I feel happy once again and I am not even sure why.'

Hawise pursed her lips primly and said nothing.

'Oh fie!' declared Penelope. 'Don't tell me, Hawise, that those hell-fire preachers at Leighs have been getting at you.'

'We are all in God's hands,' replied Hawise frankly.

'Fiddle-faddle!' snapped Penelope. 'I can well do without all that hell-fire stuffed down my throat every hour of the day.' She was referring to the strong Puritan tendencies of the Rich family and all the refugee parsons who seemed to reside with them.

'Now, now, madam,' warned Hawise. 'Don't mock, or folk will get the impression that you are a heretic.'

'Nothing like that,' Penelope laughed dismissively. 'Just a rebel.' She grinned charmingly at Hawise, and remembered then that it had been Philip who had first called her a rebel. Thinking of him now, she wondered how he fared. She had had no news of him since the summer. The house at Stratford had improved Penelope's relationship with her husband and he bothered her very little. They ate an occasional meal together but otherwise he divided his time between the nursery and travelling to town, where he was closely concerned in a profit-making venture involving privateering voyages to the New World.

Penelope began to make shopping expeditions, buying beautiful materials from the market in St Paul's churchyard. Seamstresses could be employed for very little in this poor area. She had hundreds of gowns made and many drapes to beautify the house. The servants at Stratford were noisy but extremely lively and capable, and much easier to handle than the staff at Leighs. She was very content and fearful only that she would not be able to keep her husband at arm's length for ever.

In March they went to Hampton Court as guests of the queen. It was the first time they had appeared together in public and they attracted much attention. Gracious in a gown of white-and-silver brocade, her hand on the arm of her small, but very proud husband, Penelope walked the long length of blue carpet to be presented to Her Majesty. As before, the Queen's shrewd deep-set eyes badly disconcerted her, as did her twisted smile of amusement. Queen Elizabeth graciously received Lord and Lady Rich but she scrutinised them with a critical eye.

'She's laughing at us,' Penelope whispered indignantly. 'How dare she!'

Of course they did look ridiculous: Penelope's tall, slender figure and Robert's short, square shape. No matter how well dressed they looked foolish as a couple. She could not fight back the fury and humiliation in her breast. 'Oh God,' she muttered. 'Forgive me, but I hate her.' Other eyes in the court surveyed her with much admiration; and the melancholy brown eyes of Philip Sidney, flamboyant in his knightly regalia, followed her.

Philip caught up with her later in a private corner. 'You look magnificent,' he whispered. 'A star shining above all others.'

Penelope lowered her eyes and the corners of her mouth twitched. 'How nice to meet again, dear cousin,' she murmured.

Philip put her hand to his lips, which felt hot and dry. His long eyelashes flicked back as he saw a merry twinkle in the large dark eyes he knew so well.

'I am residing at the old house in Stratford-le-Bow. Am I in danger of a visit from you, Philip?' she asked with a coy smile, glancing at him sideways.

As someone approached their corner, Philip tactfully withdrew with a courteous bow. Although he had not said a word, she knew that he had accepted her indirect invitation, and that she would make him very welcome.

Too much excitement at court and an excess of wine made Robert Rich very maudlin on the way home. In the carriage he had wept pathetically, but then he tried to fondle Penelope, who resisted his advances stiffly. On arrival home she abruptly called the servants and ordered them to escort their drunken lord to his own bed.

The next morning at breakfast, he rose unshaven and disreputable-looking, and came to the table in the crumpled clothes he had slept the night in. His fresh, clean wife looked at him disdainfully. 'You might at least have done me the courtesy of completing your toilet,' she remarked acidly.

Robert Rich snarled like an enraged animal. His head was throbbing and left him in no mood for sharp comments from his wife. 'Bitch!' he yelled, throwing his wine cup across the room. Within minutes he was on his horse and galloping away to town.

'Oh dear,' joked Penelope, delighted by the effect of her remark. 'What a nasty temper.'

Hawise looked so solemn. 'I think you are extremely unkind, madam,' she said.

'When I need your opinion, I'll ask for it,' Penelope replied tartly.

At midday she went upstairs to the front balcony and looked through the narrow slit windows towards the bridge. The view from there was a source of entertainment for her: robust country women bustled along balancing huge baskets of produce on their heads as they headed for the market where they would sell their wares; men shouted at their donkeys or horses, urging them to pull the carts and waggons faster; armed men in their shining armour rode through the crowd, whips cracking, voices rising as they jostled the pedestrians to one side.

Today, she noticed a baker being led to the stocks by a crowd of angry people, his underweight loaf tied about his neck. The angry crowd cursed and jeered at him. Later on Penelope watched a thin ragged child deftly picking pockets as a loose woman was being beaten up by the mob. Suddenly, she was almost overwhelmed by an urge to escape, to leave her rich dwelling, to run down the bridge and dive right in among the squalid mob. She had had this feeling before but it was particularly strong this morning.

Turning heavy, languorous eyes away from the bridge, she followed a winding path that went down past the Norman church to a small wicket gate that no one ever seemed to enter. High beech trees in full foliage made a striking frame for the church's tower. A pair of white doves nested in the belfry, and sparrows and finches hopped about squabbling on the flower-bordered path. The sudden change of scene curiously affected her; here the steaming heat of the main street with its noisy, highly-coloured population, there the cold, dark shape of the church. She shivered, and at the same time felt a rush of despair, a desperate longing to be loved.

As though a prayer had been answered, she watched in astonishment as a rider in a russet-brown cape jumped his horse easily over the wicket gate and cantered gently down the path.

'Why, it's Philip!'

Pulling her gown around her, she ran quickly downstairs and out of the small arched side door to greet him. She was wearing only her scarlet gown and slippers, and her long hair was unbound and hanging in heavy tresses down her back. Holding out her arms to him, she cried impulsively, 'I knew you would come, Philip, my love.'

Ardently he knelt to kiss the white hand he had so longed to possess. And, as Penelope stroked his bowed head, he rose and pulled her to him, pressing her tall, lithe body to his own.

At twilight Hawise was sitting in the garden valiantly pretending to sew. Jabbing at the material, she stabbed her finger with the sharp needle, causing blood to mix with the tears which spilt on to her immaculate work. She had just seen Philip discreetly leaving by the wicket gate. As dusk descended, Hawise had watched two shadowy shapes entwined in a goodbye embrace.

Now her beloved mistress stood alone and very still but soon she came and stood beside her maid, putting out her arms as if to embrace the world.

'How wonderful the garden smells at night,' she exclaimed. With her eyes half-closed, she drew in deep breaths through her nose.

Hawise regarded her in silence, shocked by her lack of shame.

Noticing her stony look, Penelope smiled. 'Grudge me not, my little maid. Tonight I have really been loved,' she declared as again she breathed in the sweet summer air, wrapping her arms about her.

'It is strange behaviour for a noble lady whose son is yet six months old,' muttered Hawise without a smile.

'Come now, my pious Hawise,' mocked Penelope, still glowing with the fire of love. 'Did that old parson at Leighs capture you as well as my gloomy husband?' She shivered in wicked delight at the memory of the pleasures she had enjoyed that afternoon. Now at last, she knew about love.

'I am very shocked, madam, and cannot hide my feelings,' replied Hawise.

Hawise's disapproval annoyed her. Scornfully Penelope stared at her. But then she sighed and said, 'Cease this foolish moralising and help me with my bath.'

Hawise obeyed readily enough, but silently and sullenly. The bond between them was strained.

'It is a deadly sin, madam,' Hawise finally said as she poured perfumed water down Penelope's smooth white back.

Penelope was ready with her retort. 'Have you forgotten your own lover?'

'Certainly not,' Hawise replied stiffly, 'but what I did with my body was unimportant; you are a noble lady and it will hurt many . . . All I can do is pray for you, madam.'

'Well, you'd better do it thoroughly,' Penelope said with a wide smile, 'because I fancy that in the near future I am going to need your prayers.'

All through that sultry month of August tumultuous fires raged in Penelope. Cherishing her precious memories, she waited and yearned. But her lover came no more. Hawise watched with increasing anxiety as her mistress allowed all domestic routine to slide and roamed the house in a purposeless manner without even a glance for her baby son. Every day she stood by the narrow window staring in the direction of the path that led up from the church, aching to catch another glimpse of Philip's chestnut curls. The crowd still milled about down by the bridge in sunshine and shadow, but she barely noticed it while there was still no sign of her lover. And every evening, dressed in a flowing house-gown and with her hair unattended, she paced the courtyard, her shoulders hunched, her eyes half-closed, and her mouth in a sullen droop.

'Be calm, madam. Sit for a while,' Hawise would beseech her. She knew that there was no way to placate her mistress once she was in this rebellious mood, so she waited patiently for the flames to die down, each day dreading the return of Lord Rich.

One hot evening Penelope dashed up the stairs with

a determined expression on her face. Half an hour later, she came down wearing a large slouched hat with long plumes and a heavy, dark cloak, underneath which her skirt was hitched up high, revealing long, thigh-length riding boots.

'Good heavens!' declared Hawise, 'whatever are you doing, my lady?'

There was a devilish glint in her mistress's eyes as she twirled around to show herself off. 'Well, Hawise, do I look like a man?' she asked.

'What are you up to? Where are you going?' spluttered the confused Hawise.

'That's not your business,' Penelope snapped, pushing her aside. 'If anyone asks for me, you don't know where I have gone.'

Within minutes, the sound of galloping hooves echoed from the courtyard as she sped out into the darkening highway towards the Bishop's Gate, where Philip's house was in the Minories. Penelope was quite confident that she would find her lover.

As she approached Bishop's Gate, thieves and prostitutes hovered in the dark alleys; the only lights were those of the link-light boys escorting their masters to houses of ill-fame. Fearlessly she rode on until the black-and-white timbers of the house she sought showed through the gloom. With her dainty gloved hand she pounded the heavy lion-headed knocker and, as the grey-haired servant opened the door, she pushed her way in.

'I've an appointment with your master,' she growled in a gruff voice and ran past him up the wide staircase, her cloak billowing out behind her.

A soft sigh of relief escaped her lips as she opened his study door. He was there, as she had hoped, head bent over manuscripts, his handsome profile outlined in the candlelight.

Impulsively, she ran towards him. 'Oh, why did you not come to me, my lord? I have been consumed by the fires of hell just waiting each day for you,' she cried.

Dropping his quill, Philip jumped to his feet in astonishment. 'Penelope! Oh, Penelope, my wild goose. You should not have come here. Someone might recognise you.' But he spoke without conviction for he was gazing hungrily at her tall figure as she stripped off her long cloak and stood in a loose, clinging gown that scarcely covered her full white breasts.

'Relieve me of these damned riding boots!' she cried impatiently, flopping down on a cushioned bench. 'How they pinch my feet!' She lifted her leg towards him as he obediently knelt to pull off the boots.

As her slim, stockinged legs slipped out of the confining boots, Penelope's arms crept about his neck. Immediately, Philip responded by gathering her up in his arms and pressing his lips on hers. She could feel his quickening breath on her cheek as she offered herself to him. The world outside was forgotten; nothing mattered but their passion and love for each other. And Penelope felt loved as never before.

Afterwards they lay close together with limbs carelessly entwined. 'Oh, my love,' sighed Philip. 'What am I going to do about you?' He twisted her fair hair in his long, slender fingers.

'You can run off with me to Flanders,' she laughed. 'I'll get the money, and I've many jewels. This time we shall get away before that oaf returns.'

Although she was laughing, Philip knew she was serious. Suddenly he drew back, his eyes clouded with fear. 'Don't talk so foolishly, Penelope,' he said. 'Neither you nor I can afford to do such a thing. We both have our families to consider.'

Penelope threw her arms about his neck. 'Please, darling,' she begged. 'How can I live my life without you now?'

But Philip had disentangled himself from her. Getting up, he put on his clothes. 'It has to stop, Penelope,' he said firmly, but without looking at her. 'It's too dangerous, we will both be destroyed.'

Penelope sat up and threw out her arms with abandon. 'Philip, Philip my love, what do we care of propriety?' she cried.

He stared down at her with pain in his eyes. 'I am a knight of the realm.' His voice was choked with emotion. 'On no account will I dishonour my family and bring the wrath of the queen down on them.' Then his voice became cold as he said, 'I must ask you to leave, madam.'

There was silence. Penelope stared at him in astonishment. He was dismissing her like a paid whore.

Philip was buckling on his sword-belt. He turned to her, his melancholy eyes deliberately hard. 'I love you, Penelope,' he said simply. 'And I'll never love another woman more. But my honour comes before everything.'

Without a word she watched him go out of the room and gently close the door. In a blinding rage and muttering curses under her breath, she slammed the atrocious hat back on her head, struggled into her uncomfortable boots, threw on her cloak and dashed downstairs and out to the courtyard where her mount was tethered. Urging on her horse, she galloped back to Stratford-le-Bow, with tears raining down her face as she gave vent to her feelings of humiliation.

When she arrived home, the house was lit up. Lord Rich was waiting in the hall to greet her. 'Since when does a lady ride unaccompanied at night?' he demanded, looking down suspiciously at her large boots and strange hat.

'I had business that needed attending to,' she answered sharply, sweeping past him to her own chamber.

Upstairs, Hawise helped her undress and gently wiped away her tears. She did not pry, but informed her mistress that Lord Rich had been waiting several hours for her and had been drinking steadily.

'To hell with him! I'm going to bed,' replied Penelope sulkily. But her husband was already at the door. With narrowed eyes he crossed the room and sat on the edge of the bed, leering drunkenly at his angry wife. Uncouthly he dismissed Hawise.

'Leave me, sir!' Penelope ordered. 'I will talk in the morning.'

Lord Rich ignored her. Pushing Hawise out, he closed the door, and approached the bed. 'It's about time I took my rightful place in my marriage bed,' he declared savagely.

Penelope suddenly felt nervous and tried another approach. 'We will discuss it tomorrow,' she pleaded, holding her arm to her brow as though in pain. 'I've a severe headache.'

Her husband grabbed her wrist in his strong, wiry hand. 'It's time we produced another child,' he sneered, pulling her towards him.

She automatically pulled away. 'I want no more children of yours!' she screeched venomously. 'Let go of me, sir!'

'The choice is mine, not yours,' he snarled, moving in closer.

'Am I a slave that you think you just use my body and soul?' Her voice rose in fury.

Grabbing her bare breast tight, his fingers plunged into her soft flesh.

'I hate you!' she screamed. 'I can never love you. Don't you understand that?'

He was drooling in his excitement; saliva ran down his chin. 'You're my wife and you will do as I please. I shall take my pleasure when I choose and I don't want to hear any more arrogance from you.' His grip tightened.

Desperately, she tried to pull away, in a sudden fear that the horror of her wedding night was about to be repeated. With a swift movement he pushed her on her back and climbed towards her. Penelope fought like a trapped animal, biting, scratching and struggling, but it was no use. He had the brute force of bestial desire.

She knew she could not hold out. Suddenly she stopped struggling and went limp. 'Take your damned pound of flesh,' she sobbed. 'Take it, damn you, and be done with it.'

Taken aback by her capitulation, Lord Rich hesitated. 'Love me, Penelope,' he mumbled pathetically. But he rolled her over as his lust grew.

Sickened, she turned her face away while he satisfied his sexual urge, grunting like an animal throughout.

When he got up from the bed, his energy spent, she could not resist a last bitter taunt. 'If you think your foolish fumblings and meanderings make any impression on me, you are very much mistaken,' she said coldly. 'You disgust me, sir.'

Robert Rich's face flushed with wounded passion. 'Why, you bitch!' he cried, dealing her a severe blow across the mouth. 'Your behaviour disgusts me!'

After he had gone, Penelope cried out for her maid. 'Hawise! Hawise!' she wailed. 'Come to me. Oh, how I wish I could die!' And Hawise sat up through the night comforting her dear mistress in her arms.

The open and often public battles between Lord and Lady Rich became one of the main topics of court gossip. Penelope did not care; in fact, she even announced to one and all that she hated the little toad. Many jokes were made about them and people asked each other how Robert Rich had managed to get such a shrew pregnant twice in as many years.

Now that his wife was expecting a child again, Lord Rich avoided her as he had before, spending much time at the gaming tables, and at meetings with various young men of commerce who were intent on making a fortune quickly. When he did occasionally descend on Penelope, he was received with open hostility. In retaliation, he began to poke and pry into the household accounts, and finally accused her of wanton extravagance and engaged astute agents to tie up her marriage dowry. At this point, Grandfather Knollys stepped in to the battle. The grand old man would never interfere in domestic problems, but where family finance was concerned he would have no trickery. Penelope's money was her own, left by his late wife to her eldest granddaughter. Lord Rich was forced to retire from that battle, defeated.

Meanwhile, Penelope's second child grew lusty in her womb. At loggerheads with her husband, deserted by her lover and heavily pregnant, Penelope felt trapped and very depressed. A fleeting visit from her mother in the spring did little to improve her mood.

She had been unprepared for the jovial exuberance of the perfumed, extravagantly dressed Countess, when she arrived with her entourage and Sir Christopher Blount in tow. Bad-tempered and irritable, she had to listen to long drawn-out accounts of how well her young brother Robert was doing at court where everyone thought him so gallant and successful. Poor Lord Leicester, she was informed, was suffering badly from indigestion, which did not improve his temper. 'And, my dear,' babbled Lettice, without noticing her daughter's pale face and dark shadows under her eyes, 'to top it all, your sister Dorothy has run off with that terrible Tom Perriot.'

'I don't blame her,' Penelope replied flatly. 'She's been in love with him for a long time.'

Lettice frowned and waved a dismissive hand in the air. 'My dear, he is a penniless rake. She will rue the day, I can assure you,' she insisted.

With her hands resting on her high stomach Penelope sat listening to her mother's voice. It tinkled and babbled like a swift-flowing brook as it poured from Lettice's carmined lips. Penelope was feeling exhausted and hoped fervently that her mother's visit would end soon.

But Lettice was saving her choice titbit until the last minute. 'I went to a wedding last week,' she said with a sly smile on her lips. 'Your ex-suitor, Philip Sidney, married that pale-faced little ninny, Frances Walsingham.' She raised her eyebrows. 'And only just in time, too, by the size of her,' she added gleefully.

Penelope showed no response. So that was the real reason for her mother's social call. Well, she was not going to let her see that the news disturbed her. 'I did hear of it,' she murmured softly. 'Just a marriage of convenience, I believe. She is so young and her father was a good friend of Philip's.'

'It did not prevent him getting her pregnant,' Lettice replied tartly and Penelope shuddered and looked away, unable to speak.

When her mother finally departed, Penelope flung herself on her bed and wept until she was drained of tears. She had accepted Philip's betrothal to Frances Walsingham. He had said that he was marrying her because he was indebted to her father. Why, then, this news? It shocked her deeply. Had Philip been lying to her about his feelings for Frances? Had she now lost him forever? Until now she had always assumed that they would be together again one day. But now everything looked very different. When the tears ceased to flow, it was only sleep which then temporarily took away her pain.

In April she gave birth to another son; this time a bonny blue-eyed baby as fair as his brother had been dark. Again, Lord Rich came visiting, excited and anxious to make peace with her, highly delighted with the new addition to his family.

'We may be incompatible, madam,' he said, 'but we can certainly produce fine sons.'

'That is very clever of you, sir,' she sneered, refusing to accept the olive branch he had held out to her.

Knowing better than to attempt further reconciliation, Lord Rich retired again to his separate life away from her.

To Hawise's amazement, Penelope loved and fussed this new child. She announced that she would dispense with the wet-nurse and feed him herself. Obstinate and wilful, she would not be persuaded that it was beneath her station to nurse her new-born babe. 'He's mine. I'll take care of him,' she said brusquely. And there was nothing Hawise could do about it.

Strangely enough, her new maternal feelings were also extended to her previously neglected elder son. Delighted to be accepted at last by his mama, the dark, curly-haired toddler came into his own.

Although she was delighted and relieved, Hawise

was sure that this burst of maternal affection could not last. But it did, and was to mature over the years as Penelope's love for her children blossomed.

At high summer they returned to Leighs when smallpox had reached an epidemic level at Stratford. And it was here in the family house that the nursery became a happy, warm place as Penelope turned her devoted attention to her children. Lord Rich, fortunately, remained in London, having by some insidious means, obtained for himself a small post at St James's. There he never allowed anyone to forget for a moment that he was related by marriage to the Queen's favourite, Lord Leicester, Master of the Horse. But even though he was not at Leighs, Penelope still had little peace from him. With a monarch like Elizabeth, small gains could easily be lost, so he sent persistent requests for his wife to attend court functions with him. Elizabeth was known to smile on well-arranged marriages.

Penelope refused to go to London for a long time but, finally, she relented and allowed Hawise to get her ready for the fabulous New Year Ball, an annual affair held at Hampton Court. Her hair was twisted and curled until it stood in a frizzy halo about her head; the jewelled head-dress rested on top of it; the Rich family diamonds were about her neck and in her ears; her fingers were loaded with rings; her gown of dark purple silk had silver-lined sleeves and a tight silver-laced waist. From there billowed a voluminous skirt.

'My lady,' cried Hawise as she did the finishing touches, 'you look really beautiful.'

Penelope shrugged nonchalantly. 'I've no desire to appear in public. The whole procedure bores me.'

'Come on. Think what your mother would give to be back in that throne room.'

'I am sure she would give her life,' Penelope replied wearily. 'But I hate it. All that spite and treachery. Everyone betrays everyone else just to stay at the Queen's side.'

'But, my lady,' protested Hawise, 'it is tradition and has always been so.'

'Tradition!' Penelope sniffed dismissively. 'Each one has his own axe to grind – a son for a knighthood, a daughter for the marriage market. How I detest those cantankerous, overpowering females and those slimy, soft-tongued courtiers!'

'Those are strong words, my lady,' said Hawise. 'But please smile because you will be the grandest lady there.' She stepped back to admire her handiwork.

Queen Elizabeth had called Penelope's mother a brazen hussy and chased her from the court, but she smiled benignly on her lovely daughter, Lady Rich, ablaze with the family jewels, and mother of two sons of her own kin, the Boleyn heritage. Yes, the royal hand of favour was indeed extended to Penelope, who remained very cool and rather aloof while her small husband danced about like an excited frog.

The large, black, brooding eyes grew hard as Sir Philip Sidney then presented his bride, the tiny Frances Walsingham who was neatly dressed in black-and-gold with a high neck-line and immaculate white ruff. Philip looked pale and stern, but was as richly dressed as ever.

'Little vixen,' Penelope muttered under her breath. 'Pasty-faced and skinny, and only sixteen. What can he see in her?' Then jealousy twisted in her like a knife when she noticed the small but tell-tale bulge of the girl's stomach. With a sour taste in her mouth, she looked away.

Once the queen had retired and the gentlemen moved on to the gaming tables, Penelope returned to her lodgings alone. The long corridors were still and silent. Only the rustling of her skirts disturbed the air. From a shadowy corner a figure stepped out in front of her. She pulled up quickly, very startled, and met a pair of sad brown eyes. Philip stood in her path, his arms held out towards her, entreating her.

'I've nothing to say to you, sir,' Penelope said, thrusting out her chin. 'Let me pass.'

His hand was on her arm. 'Pity me, Penelope,' he begged. 'I am haunted by our love. Please let me hear you say that you have forgiven me.'

Haughtily, she drew herself up to her full height. 'Forgive, Sir Philip? What is there to forgive? Nay, I should congratulate you.'

He caught her hand and pressed it to his lips. 'I am a penniless knight with more debts than I care to mention. What else could I do but marry money?' he pleaded.

'That is no affair of mine,' she replied, looking away and trying to control her fluttering heart.

'I pledged my honour to care for her,' continued Philip. 'Her father is in extremely bad health.' He poured forth excuses.

'I confess you did that extremely well,' she scoffed. But she did not pull her hand away; she allowed it to rest in his.

'Oh, Penelope,' he cried. 'I am but a weak fool, but I'll never love anyone as I do you.'

'Much good that will do me now, sir,' she sighed, but she moved closer and put her hand to his cheek. She could not prevent a smile spreading across her lips. Opening the door of her chamber, she gestured for him to enter.

'Don't dally outside, sir,' she whispered urgently. 'We may be seen.'

They stepped into the darkened room and immediately fell into each other's arms in a passionate embrace.

'Oh, my darling,' she cried, as he showered her with kisses, 'one touch from you and I am lost.'

'My love,' returned Philip. 'There is no answer for our love.' As he picked her up in his arms and carried her to the bed, his eyes were wet with tears.

The next day, Lady Rich returned home to Leighs with shining eyes and a buoyant step.

'How was the ball?' Hawise enquired, anxious to hear all the details. 'Did you enjoy yourself?'

Penelope hugged her tight. 'Oh, I had a wonderful time,' she gasped, her cheeks glowing with excitement.

'I'm so happy for you, my lady,' replied Hawise, not a little puzzled by her mistress's change of attitude towards society life.

It did not occur to Hawise then that Penelope was once more involved with her lover. But it became obvious that spring when Philip came riding up the drive one sunny day and Penelope fell into his arms in greeting. Hawise was saddened to know that her mistress was indulging in a clandestine affair once more but she was helpless to do anything to stop it, either then or at any time during that sultry summer while it continued.

Lord Rich was not around at all, being off on one of his electioneering campaigns, when he toured the countryside bullying his tenants to vote as he wished.

Philip cared little for politics, immersed as he was in his poetry and his love of the black-eyed Penelope. He frequently came to Leighs, undeterred by the fact that his neglected wife was due any day to bear his child. When the old beech trees turned a golden brown and a cool autumn mist descended on the Essex marshland, still the lovers met. Floating idly down the river in a small boat with a coloured canopy, Philip would strum on his lute and sing the passionate sonnets he had composed to her, while Penelope would lie back on silken cushions dreamily listening to his musical voice. They would moor the boat to get out and make love passionately in a lonely spot screened by tall, dark reeds with only the golden marsh marigolds to share their secrets. Life was wonderful. Penelope had never known such happiness; regardless of all danger, she drank her cup of joy to the dregs.

There were times when Philip was very despondent or when an item of gossip would send him into despair. He was still desperately afraid for his family honour and feared that this love affair might destroy it.

Bravely and loyally, Penelope encouraged him. 'Do not torture yourself, my love. Is it our fault that we are not man and wife? That we are male and female is quite sufficient for me. Is not this God that worries you a God of love?'

'But we are committing a deadly sin. We will be punished in the hereafter,' he would say, fearfully, from time to time.

'God in Heaven, have I a lover or a gibbering parson?' Penelope would reply mockingly.

'But I cannot give you up,' he would say. 'You are my star, my guiding star. I pray that I too may gain your fearless attitude to life.'

'You must not keep worrying,' Penelope said one day. 'I care for none but you. I'll leave Lord Rich this day if you will take me to Virginia. We can start a new life.' She knew that Philip was planning to make a trip to the New World next spring.

'It's not settled yet, Penelope. I still have to get Her Majesty's permission.'

'How strange,' she sneered, 'that every act of ours needs royal permission. How I hate that red-wigged old baggage.'

The noble Philip was truly shocked. 'You must not talk like that, Penelope. You are such a rebel. Sometimes it's hard to understand you. We are of noble blood; we owe allegiance to our monarch.'

Penelope sighed. 'I'm sorry,' she said, 'but I have reason to be bitter. My father ruined his estate and lost his life in the service of the Queen for little reward. And if he had lived, you and I would have been properly wed. It was his death-bed wish that it be so.'

Philip shook his head sadly. 'We cannot fight our fate, Penelope. Life is mapped out for us,' he said seriously.

Lord Rich returned from his campaign tour in September and Philip came no more. Having been refused royal permission to sail to Virginia he was recalled to court, given a knighthood and dispatched to Flanders on an embassy. Penelope was very sad but could do nothing about it.

The coming of the New Year brought much excitement to Leighs, for not so far away at Tilbury, Lord Leicester was recruiting an army to protect the Lowlands from the Spaniards. The house at Leighs was frequently invaded by Penelope's brother Robert and his numerous friends. The young earl had formed his own company of Horse Guards and fitted out his men in tangerine velvet. They were now encamped nearby, while their Colonel-in-Chief made merry at his rich sister's house.

Debonair in his military attire, sun-tanned from a recent sea voyage, Essex was brimming over with good spirits and health. That he was so popular with the ageing queen was no wonder. His sunny smile, his deep-blue eyes, fringed with heavy lashes, his chestnut curls, his youth and charm could compete with any favourite. Robert had always been Penelope's favourite brother, and that same dry humour which she found so particularly aggravating in her mother, she enjoyed in Robert who used it more skilfully.

Since the birth of her second child Penelope had filled out; her bust and hips were now much more pronounced. This seemed to add to her height.

'Ye Gods!' jested her brother, as she moved across the hall to attend to her guests, 'she is like a galleon in full sail.' Turning to Penelope's little husband, he exclaimed loudly, 'I give it to you, sir, not many could have tamed that amazon.'

Robert Rich stuck out his chest as if someone should pin a ribbon on him. Instantly, two warning spots of temper appeared on Penelope's face – angry, glowing marks that always betrayed her feelings. Wisely, she withdrew to the gallery and watched the throng down in the hall from a distance. Constantly on the look-out for Philip, she felt detached from the excitement below. But Philip did not come. He had already left for his appointment in Flanders.

Penelope rose at dawn to watch the young men ride out to war, all of them excited by the belief that battle would bring them glory. How well her brother Essex sat his mount, with Sir Christopher Blount riding close beside him. Her younger brother, Walter, was also there. He must have arrived from the north during the night, having left his studies to ride with his magnificent elder brother. Her husband followed, his short shape seemed ridiculously wide and weighed down by an inordinate amount of equipment. The brave company, riding so merrily to death or glory, filled her with pride.

Several weeks later alone at Leighs without husband or lover, Penelope awoke to the realisation that she was once more pregnant. Casually, she dismissed it from her mind. She would cross her bridges when she came to them. So she spent her time going out visiting with Hawise or amusing her children. There was no hurt inside; in fact, she had seldom felt so completely calm. That her husband would deny that this was his child she was quite sure but secure in her love for Philip, she did not care.

There was little news from the war front. Occasionally word of a few skirmishes would filter back to the lonely marshland at Leighs but Penelope had little idea of what was happening in the Low Countries where her stepfather and brothers travelled and fought so flamboyantly.

A long letter arrived from her mother one day informing her that she was intending to join her husband in Flanders because he was likely to be made governor there. Lettice described in great detail the huge retinue and wardrobe that she was planning to take with her and she did not fail to add that Frances Walsingham was already out there with her Philip.

Even this last piece of information did little to ruffle the peace which had descended upon Penelope. And she was not unduly surprised when she later heard that Queen Elizabeth had absolutely forbidden her mother to sail for Flanders. 'Poor Mother, why is she so foolish?' she asked Hawise. She had sympathy for her irresponsible mother even though they seemed impelled to hurt one another every time they met.

Autumn came once more and the apples and berries hung richly ripe, asking to be harvested. Out in the fields at Leighs the corn was reaped and the fields were alive with workers. As mistress of this vast estate, Penelope was kept continually busy, conversing with the bailiff, organising farm suppers, filling the larders with potted preserves. The world outside did not seem to exist for her any more. She was extremely popular and very fair in her dealings with worker or tenant farmer.

'I never thought I'd get used to this gloomy old place,' she told Hawise as they sat contentedly sewing in the peaceful, well-tended garden. They sat near the sundial, surrounded by rows and rows of late summer blooms banked by the highest of hollyhocks. The air was fragrant and sweet; Penelope thought she could almost taste it in her mouth.

'Life is how you make it,' replied Hawise philosophically.

Her mistress had paused in her sewing to munch at a rosy apple. Her small white teeth crunched into the red skin with obvious enjoyment. 'It's strange how fond I am of apples since I carried this little one.' She chewed pleasurably. 'I believe I'm learning to enjoy being pregnant. It makes me feel quite restful.'

Hawise looked concerned as she was reminded of her mistress's secret. 'How will you approach my Lord Rich when he returns?' she asked anxiously.

Penelope grinned happily and patted her fat stomach. 'We will make him doubly welcome, now that there are two of us,' she jested.

Hawise frowned disapprovingly. There were times when her mistress really annoyed her.

Several weeks later one misty night in November, Robert Rich returned from the battle front. Wearily he dismounted and his servant helped him inside.

'Run downstairs, Hawise!' commanded her mistress, having spotted him from her window. 'Find out why he has returned so soon.'

Penelope slowly and carefully dressed in a wide farthingale to hide her pregnancy, then came down the wide stone stairs with a cool demeanour. A log fire blazed in the vast fireplace. Lord Rich, grotesque in padded hose, dirty and rather grey of countenance, fussed and fidgeted in front of the fire, snapping and shouting at his man servant who was plying him with hot drinks.

'Welcome home, my lord,' Penelope said with heavy sarcasm.

'You can keep your damned insulting remarks to yourself,' he snarled. 'I am very sick, and have returned home to restore my health.'

'I am genuinely sorry, sir. Can I assist you?' A mocking smile still played about her lips and there was a look of sardonic amusement in her black eyes.

'Take yourself out of my sight, you bitch!' he yelled. A strange, rumbling sound came from within him as he dashed from the room to relieve himself, leaving behind a vile odour.

'My goodness.' Penelope wrinkled her nose in disdain. 'Whatever is that smell?'

Apologetically, Lord Rich's servant explained. 'My lord has an infection of the bowels, my lady. It's very prevalent in foreign parts.'

Penelope drew herself up. 'You can inform your master on his return that I wish him to stay in his own quarters,' she said. 'I do not want any strange diseases transmitted either to myself or to my children.' Gracefully, she retired. Hawise had heard this order and was almost in tears. 'That was most unkind of you, madam,' she protested.

'Don't criticise me, Hawise' retorted Penelope. 'After all,' she added lightly, 'I'm only what life has made me.'

Lord Rich kept to his bed for a week or two, and then left discreetly to journey to a spa for the benefit of the waters. Once he had gone his wife heaved a deep sigh of relief. 'Get me out of this whale-boned corset, Hawise. It was so tight I could hardly breathe. At least I was able to conceal my size for a little longer. There was no sense in meeting trouble halfway.'

The next week brought a visit from Penelope's aunt, Catherine Hastings, looking decidedly harassed. Although this kind-hearted woman had brought up many of her husband's wards, she had always been particularly fond of the Devereux children; Walter and Dorothy had been her special pets. Now she called on their elder sister to relate her latest tales of woe. Dorothy had run off with that no-good Tom Perriot, and Walter had given up his studies to follow his illustrious brother to war, leaving his newly wed wife, Beth Deakin, to weep her heart out.

'Oh dear,' wept Lady Hastings. 'It's all so distressing.'

Penelope tried to console her, but inside a new and sudden fear was building up. Her aunt's mention of

Walter going off to fight brought concern for Philip's safety. She had not worried before but now she was afraid for him

'I see you are pregnant once again, Penelope,' sniffed her aunt. 'How fortunate you are to be so prolific! What I would have given for a child of my own!'

Penelope smiled but quickly changed the subject. 'How fares your nephew Philip?'

'He is quite well,' sighed Cathcrine, 'but he has asked for permission to return home. His father is very ill, you know and, as you may have heard, his mother, my poor, dear sister Mary, died two months ago.' She wiped her eyes with a silk handkerchief. 'Oh dear, what a depressing year this has been!'

Once Lady Hastings had left, Penelope was extremely thoughtful. 'It would have been a waste of time to ask her to keep a secret, not to mention my condition,' she told Hawise scornfully. 'I'm sure she will tittle-tattle to everyone everywhere. Mother will be told, and the entire Sidney family. And from there it will be transmitted to Lord Rich, wherever that damned oaf is lurking. Then I'll be watched and spied upon from all directions,' she sighed. 'Well, I'd better get used to the idea, I suppose,' she added philosophically.

'Well, madam, in the end you have to face the consequences of your actions,' Hawise reminded her.

There was not much that Penelope could say in reply to Hawise's practical comment. But, all the same, she still clung on to straws, hoping that fate would be

on her side. 'All is not necessarily lost,' she said opti-
mistically. 'I'm sure that Philip will come home to his
sick father, and when he does, I will discuss the matter
with him.' Her mouth was set in a determined line. 'I
cannot and will not go on forever with this life,' she
said. 'Philip will save me.'

Hawise frowned. 'But madam,' she protested, 'there
is no need. Your marriage will protect you . . .'

But Penelope was not listening. She had picked up
her skirts and, with her head held high, was already
heading back to the house.

6

The Tragedy of Hawise

Slowly a plan developed in Penelope's mind. News had reached her that the Queen had recalled Lord Leicester from the Low Countries, so she knew that Philip would return home to England with his uncle. His father, Sir Henry Sidney, had died – a fact that was confirmed in a long, gossipy letter from her mother. Penelope knew that she had to contact Philip; he had to be told of her predicament. No doubt he would go first to his own house in the Minories. She decided to send Hawise with a letter to him there.

'He will return with his uncle, my Lord Leicester. Of that I am sure,' Penelope informed her bewildered maid.

'But, madam, be sensible,' begged Hawise. 'I cannot see the point of it all. You now have a husband and a family. Surely it is time for this nonsense to cease.'

'Please, Hawise,' cajoled Penelope. 'I must warn him before the word spreads too far, for I am sure my Lord Rich will be very vengeful.'

'But surely your marriage is a protection for you,' repeated Hawise. 'Please reconsider, madam,' she begged.

Those hard, dark eyes stared straight at the maid. 'If

Philip will have me, I will go and live with him as his mistress. I care nothing for propriety and I will not forsake him. You must help me, Hawise, otherwise there will be bloodshed.'

Thoroughly confused and very frightened, Hawise eventually gave in and agreed to deliver the letter.

'I will give you that dark-green velvet dress that you have always admired,' declared the jubilant Penelope, generous now that she had got her own way.

'Madam,' protested Hawise, nervous about the nature of her mission. 'I know so little of London. I shall be lost in that big city,' she cried.

'I'll get that fine, strong lad, young Ned, from the village, to escort you. He will take you into London, and Sir Philip will make sure that you are returned safely afterwards. As soon as you arrive at the Bishop's Gate Inn, get Ned to bring Sir Philip there, and then order him to ride straight back home. And he must be told that I do not want my affairs circulated around the village.'

Hawise listened to Penelope's instructions without a word. She knew that it was very difficult indeed to restrain her mistress once she had made up her mind.

A few days later the gentle maid obediently laid her head upon the block of her mistress's impetuosity. She dressed in the fabulous green gown with a stiff, circular farthingale which held out the soft velvet folds as it nipped in tight at the waist. There was a gold-embroidered bodice and a yellow swirl of silk petticoat to match the silk lining of the large open-ended sleeves.

'You look magnificent!' exclaimed Penelope,

stepping back to admire her. She pushed Hawise's glossy brown braids into a plumed hat, put a jade necklace about her neck, and diamonds in her ears. Clasping her hands together, she was almost over-whelmed with emotion and delight. 'So it's true,' she cried. 'It *is* only the gown that makes a lady! Hawise, my dearest Hawise, you will match the finest lady in the land.'

With feminine vanity Hawise smoothed down the shining folds. 'It does suit me,' she murmured in agreement.

'But for your colouring, you could be me. It's remarkable how much alike we are!' cried Penelope. 'It will give Sir Philip quite a shock, I can assure you.' She slipped a crested ruby ring upon Hawise's finger. 'Take good care of that,' she warned. 'It bears the ancient crest of the Bourchiers, from whom my family is descended. It will convince Philip there is no trickery.

'This letter and this packet of money is for him. Keep them hidden in your bosom. Give them only to Sir Philip himself. Now here is a purse of money for yourself. Spend freely and enjoy yourself. It will be a great adventure for you, my love.' Then she kissed the terrified Hawise goodbye.

Hawise left on her journey, weeping as if she knew she would never return. She rode through the misty lanes of Essex, her escort behind her on a constant look-out for thieves and vagabonds that thronged the country-side. All the time her fear grew. The first night they rested at a wayside inn and the next day they were joined by another travelling party. There was safety in numbers on those treacherous dark highways where robbers lurked behind every bush.

Most of the travellers were in a jovial mood, singing songs and sharing jugs of ale. But Hawise rode silent and aloof, with a harassed expression on her usually pleasant features. A long russet cloak covered the fine gown but her hat felt uncomfortable. She still felt worried as they rode in to the City of London through the Bishop's Gate in the evening. The crowded streets and the musty smells confused her.

Ned left her at the inn and rode to deliver the letter to Philip's house in the Minories, as he had been told. The innkeeper discreetly conducted her up the stairs to a private chamber, but from a small dining-room on the side, eyes watched her go by. And two fashionable young noblemen looked at each other in surprise. They had dined well and were slightly tipsy.

'Do my eyes deceive me?' whispered one, blinking hard.

His companion shook his head and stared back at the stairs. 'That was definitely Lady Rich,' he murmured.

The other raised his eyebrows and smiled slyly. 'This is just the spot for a lovers' tryst,' he said. 'Is it possible that she has not heard the news yet?'

'Well, sir,' said young Tom Walsingham, clumsily pulling himself to his feet. 'I am just the man to inform her of my brother-in-law's death.' Swaying slightly he walked towards the stairs.

In the hotel bedchamber, Hawise sat staring at the

faded hangings around the bed. With her hands folded in her lap, piously she muttered a little prayer. When she heard the gentle tap on the door, she leaped to her feet, breathing a sigh of relief. Thank goodness Sir Philip had come promptly, she thought. Now she could tell him what she had to, and return home to Leighs as soon as possible. 'Enter!' she called.

The heavy wooden door opened and a strange young man stood in the doorway. He seemed a little unsteady on his feet, but he bowed low very courteously. Hawise's mouth dropped open as he spoke.

'Greetings, dearest Penelope,' he said. 'I am sorry to be the bearer of bad news, but your glorious cousin, whom you await, will not be coming here tonight. Sir Philip was killed on the battle front.' There was irony in his tone, for he was the younger brother of Philip's wife, Frances.

Hawise stepped back and let out a cry of astonishment. Instantly, the drunken youth realised his mistake. 'I beg your pardon, madam,' he said, backing away. 'I mistook you for another.'

As she heard the young man's heavy steps down the stairs, Hawise sank down on the bed and began to weep. The ruby ring seemed to burn her finger, the packet of money weighed heavy against her breast. All her life decisions had always been made for her. Faced now with such a crisis, she was completely flummoxed.

A few seconds later, she suddenly realised she was not alone in the room after all. An untidy young girl emerged from behind the curtains where she had been hiding. She was small and skinny, and her hair stuck out wispily from a lop-sided cap. She had an ugly but strangely attractive face. Her nose turned up at the end in a most ridiculous manner, her mouth was very wide and her teeth uneven. 'Don't cry, ma'am,' she whispered. 'Your husband will turn up.'

The girl's appearance and her strange London accent startled Hawise. But seeing the wide, sympathetic blue eyes, she relaxed.

'I'm Rosie,' said the girl. 'I work here.' She began to pull back the bedcovers and straighten the pillows. 'I'll help you get to bed, ma'am. Things will look brighter in the morning.'

But Hawise had begun to panic again. 'Oh dear, whatever shall I do?' she cried. 'Tell me, Rosie, is it true that Sir Philip Sidney is dead?'

Rosie's eyes widened. 'Oh, lordy, yes, ma'am. Everyone's talking about it. He's a hero, he is. Gave his water to a common soldier when he lay wounded, and died himself.'

Hawise was feeling faint. 'Whatever shall I do? I came here to bring him a message. I don't know what to do.'

'Wish I could help you, ma'am,' said Rosie. 'Don't like to see a pretty lady cry, and that's such a lovely dress.' Her eyes caressed the green and yellow folds.

Hawise wiped her eyes and looked thoughtful. 'Perhaps you can help me, Rosie. Do you know where Lord Leicester's house is?'

'Yes, ma'am. It's in the Strand,' Rosie replied brightly.

'Can you take me there tonight? I'll give you money.'

She pulled the leather purse from her breast and held some of the gold coins in her hand.

Rosie's eyes gleamed greedily. 'Can't go tonight,' she said. 'It's a long walk from here. Ladies can't walk about here at night, it's much too dangerous.'

'But I must go,' Hawise insisted. 'I've friends in Leicester House who will help me.'

Rosie gnawed her fingers and looked longingly at the green velvet gown. 'I'll tell you what, I'll ask my young man. He is a link-light boy what directs the gentlemen to the houses of pleasure.'

'Find him, Rosie,' said Hawise, giving her a coin. 'I'll rest here until you return.' Rosie helped Hawise out of the beautiful green gown and eyed the leather pouch and the other packet in the bodice. As Hawise wearily laid her head on the pillow, Rosie slipped out of the room to find her young man. She ran down the stairs with an excited glint in her blue eyes.

Harry, the link-light boy, was loitering in the alley. He was corpulent for his age; bad eating and drinking habits had destroyed his youth. Tiny bristles stuck out all over his chin as he endeavoured to ape his betters and grow a fashionable beard. 'What's up with you?' he demanded of the breathless Rosie as she hurried towards him.

'I got something for you, Harry,' she whined. 'A real lady, she's got lost. Got packets of money hidden everywhere. Lovely clothes – and a real gold ring,' she gabbled excitedly.

'Hold hard,' said Harry, 'I'm not getting mixed up with no titled lady.'

'Well, she's not a noble lady, just standing in for her mistress who's got a lover. Wants to go to Leicester House tonight, and asked me to help her.'

Harry nodded thoughtfully. 'Well now, that's different,' he said. 'Might be easy late at night.' He rubbed his porcupine chin. 'We'll see her. Come on, lead me to her ladyship.'

With his lantern on a long pole they went up the back stairs of the inn.

'Can I have her dress?' whispered Rosie. 'It's lovely – all green velvet and yellow silk.'

'We'll have to see,' growled Harry. 'You go in and get her. I'll wait for you out here.'

Rosie crept into Hawise's chamber and roused her from her sleep. 'It will be all right, ma'am,' she consoled her as she assisted her into her clothes. Again Rosie's eyes appraised the soft folds of the gown and this time they also looked greedily at the signet ring on Hawise's finger.

Trembling visibly and as pale as death, Hawise followed Rosie and Harry out into the evil night.

'Hold up your skirts, ma'am,' whispered Rosie. 'The streets is very mucky.'

In front of them, with lantern swinging, walked fat, red-coated Harry. Hawise was suddenly gripped with fear. 'Dear God,' she prayed. 'Let us soon come to Lord Leicester's house.' She knew she would be safe once she got there, for there were servants there she had known since childhood. But it was a long way, and she was so terrified . . .

Harry had slowed down. 'Something's gone wrong

with the cursed light,' he grumbled. The flame was flickering as though about to go out. Strange, dark shadows lurked in doorways. Eerie cries broke the still midnight air. A stray cat dashed across their path; an old woman in rags croaked and held out a skinny hand for alms. Sick with fear and shivering with horror, Hawise held up her skirts and timidly followed the weakening flame that Harry held before them.

Suddenly they stopped in an alley. 'Wait here,' Rosie ordered tensely. 'Harry has to see to the light.'

Now they were in complete darkness standing in a smelly recess. Before Hawise could know what was happening, a door opened behind her and a rough, grimy hand covered her mouth, stifling her screams as she was dragged inside the house. She passed out as a fist gave her a great blow on the back of the neck.

'Plenty of money here,' said Harry, with great satisfaction, ransacking Hawise's motionless body. 'And a damned fine ring too,' he added, pulling it from her finger.

'I want her dress,' whined Rosie.

'Get it off her, then, and before I finish her. You don't want blood on it, do you?'

Rosie went down on her knees and gleefully took off Hawise's gown and her white kid boots. Harry had discovered the letter. He could not read so he threw it into the fire which burned low in a rusty old grate. While Rosie was still struggling into the gown, Hawise regained consciousness. She moved a little and then moaned with pain and horror.

From a murky corner a bed creaked and an old

cracked voice called out, 'Harry, Harry, is that you Harry? Get me some water, me throat's on fire.'

'Shut up, Mother, for Christ's sake,' yelled Harry. 'And you get out of here, while I finish her, you silly cow,' he roared at Rosie who had pulled the dress on over her own old clothes and stood there grinning blissfully.

She put a restraining hand on his arm. 'Don't do no more, Harry,' she said. 'She was a nice lady. Don't hurt her no more.'

'Stop interfering,' he hollered, but she clung to his arm.

'Come on, Harry. We got enough money. Let's get out of town. Don't do her in.'

'What'll I do with her, then?'

'Shove her in bed with your old mother,' suggested Rosie.

Harry laughed. Picking Hawise up, he gave her another hefty whack on the temple and threw her on to the bed where a filthy old woman lay in a heap of rags. 'Harry, Harry,' the old woman croaked. 'What's that?'

But the door closed with a slam as Harry and Rosie danced off to celebrate their newly acquired wealth.

The old woman tossed and turned, screaming in her senile delirium. Clad only in a long white shift, Hawise tried desperately to raise her head from the filthy bed. As the light of the morning came through the broken windows, it showed her the horror of her surroundings. She tried to cry out, but no sound came from her bruised throat. Her neck seemed to have lost the power to support her head.

In the heat of midday the old woman finally stopped thrashing about and lay still – an old bag of bones peaceful in death. Gathering up her fading energy, Hawise threw herself from the bed onto the dirty floor. She was unable to move, and lay there sweating and vomiting. Through a red, misty haze she could hear children laughing and playing outside. As she passed from life to death, she was sure that she could hear her beloved mistress calling out to her across the green lawns of Chartley.

Soon after Hawise had departed, Penelope was seized by violent pains. At first she thought that she had just been eating too many apples, but she was soon proved to be wrong. She went into premature labour, but it was not until a week had passed before the child was born.

Weakened by her ordeal, but otherwise healthy, Penelope sat up in bed nursing the baby girl whose auburn hair scarcely covered her head and whose dark-blue eyes could do little else but turn as dark as her mother's. 'I'll call her Lettice,' she had told the servants. 'She reminds me of my mother.'

Now she munched sweet figs dipped in sugar while the child clung to her full breast. 'I'll feed her,' she told the shocked servants. 'I don't want any wet nurse for her.' She was sorry that Hawise had not yet returned from her mission. At least she would understand how Penelope felt, and not look at her disapprovingly as the other servants did. Again she felt a warm surge of maternal love for this new little one. Ever since Henry, her second child, had been born, Penelope had enjoyed motherhood, and continued to love her small children with great intensity. And now there was another one to cosset and cuddle.

Lord Rich returned to Leighs without any warning. He burst into the room as she lay back against the pillows, placidly feeding her baby and eating sweet-meats. Her golden hair was spread luxuriantly over the pillow and her white breasts were exposed. Good health glowed upon her cheeks and her mouth was full of sweet figs.

Robert Rich stopped in the doorway, gazing at her in astonishment. He opened his mouth to speak but no words came out. Calmly and fearlessly, Penelope stared back at him. Then his shrill, piercing voice cut through the air. 'Then it's true!' he screeched. 'By God, I can't believe it. You managed to cuckold me, you bitch! You filthy bitch! God in Heaven!' He shut his eyes and clapped a hand dramatically to his brow. 'I have been matched with a whore.'

Penelope calmly removed a stray fig pip from her lips and hugged her baby closer as her husband came forward and stood over her, waving his arms threateningly. 'I'll swear before God Almighty that I'll kill him, whoever he is,' he shouted. 'I'll never allow shame to be brought to my noble house.'

'There is no need to excite yourself, my lord.'

The coolness of her tone enraged him even more. 'Just look at you!' he screamed. 'Like some damned fishwife sitting there suckling that bastard brat.'

Her eyes flashed warningly, but her voice remained

steady. 'Calm down, sir,' she said. 'Or you will do your-self an injury. Would you have the whole household know how I have cuckolded you?'

Robert Rich wiped the sweat from his brow and muttered sanctimoniously as if seeking guidance in prayer.

Slowly a cold, sneering smile appeared on her face. 'I doubt if your puritan God can help you now, sir. But perhaps your illustrious queen can,' she said, her voice loaded with sarcasm. 'Having been called a red-headed bastard herself, she may well be very sympathetic.'

'By God!' Lord Rich snarled. 'You bitch! Must you torture me? You know that none of us can afford to offend Her Majesty.' He stood before her breathing heavily, his nostrils flared, his ugly face red with rage. But then suddenly his eyes glinted and an evil grin spread across his lips, as if he had seen the light. 'Ah,' he said slowly. 'We are forgetting the child's real father in our haste, madam.' One side of his face lifted in a sneer. 'What say you to a certain well-favoured poet who at this moment lies dead in Flanders?'

Penelope's heart missed a beat. Her jaw dropped and she sat bolt upright in shock. The child rolled from her lap on to the bed and began to scream so loudly that a maid quickly ran into the room, grabbed hold of the child and fled.

Penelope quickly recovered her composure. 'You are a liar,' she accused her husband staring into his eyes challengingly.

'So, I was correct,' he leered. 'I did not have to look so far.'

Penelope rose from the bed and, in her night shift, stood towering over him like an avenging angel. 'Tell me the truth, sir. I demand it!' she yelled.

'Demand, madam?' He laughed. 'You are not exactly in a position to make demands of me.' He snorted and turned away.

Cold fear crept through Penelope's body. Clutching her throat, she stood white-faced and pathetic, waiting for him to tell her what she so badly needed to know.

'Your lover is dead,' he said without turning around. 'That paragon of virtue and prudence who seduced my wife and left his brat for me to support is lying dead on a battle field in Flanders.' With a muffled cry, he suddenly ran from the room.

Penelope refused to believe what he had said. Surely he was just playing a sadistic trick to get his own back at her. She had to discover the truth about Philip – from someone . . .

Where was Hawise, now that she really needed her? Trying to remain calm, she decided that the best plan was to stay in bed out of her husband's way until Hawise returned and Penelope could find out what was going on. Pretending she was ill and too weak to rise, she had the servants bring all her meals to her chamber.

It did not take long for the house to be echoing with whispers as the staff gossiped among themselves about the strange situation. Hawise had disappeared and the master raged about the corridors like a caged animal, finding fault with everything, and indulging in terrible quarrels with his tenant farmers, while the mistress was confined to her room.

Still Penelope waited for Hawise to return from London but after two weeks there was still no sign of her. Unable to stand the strain any longer and knowing that she would have to find out about Philip some other way, she sent for the sour-faced parson who was frequently at her husband's side. He was a strict Calvinist – breathing fire and brimstone with every word he uttered. Recently he had begun to hold meetings in the hall at Leighs and the servants were forced by their tyrannical master to attend. The mistress went to the village church, not because she was pious, but because it was the law of the land. How she hated this hatchet-faced parson who officiated at Leighs! She shivered when she thought about him. But she knew that he might be able to help her now.

'What is it you require of me, my lady?' he asked grimly as he entered her chamber with no vestige of a smile on his long thin face.

Penelope smiled at him. 'I might ask you to read out of the good book to me, sir. It's a long day,' she said affably.

The parson saw straight through her friendly manner. 'What is it you wish to know?' he demanded, sourly.

'News from the battle front,' she gasped out pathetically. She knew he understood.

The parson nodded. 'We are victorious at Zutphen,' he said, 'but unfortunately, a good, religious knight was lost in the death of Sir Philip Sidney.'

She put her hand to her mouth to stop herself crying out, and almost retched as her stomach contracted in an agony of fear. 'Oh, leave me, sir!' she cried. 'I am unwell.'

Too shocked for tears, she staggered to her bureau to dispatch a letter to her mother. Her thoughts were less on Philip's death than Hawise's disappearance. If Philip had not been in London, then what had happened to the maid?

In the letter to her mother, she wrote of her concern for her friend and servant. Then she summoned Ned, the young village lad who had escorted Hawise to London.

'I left Miss Hawise at the Bishop's Gate Inn, as I was instructed,' Ned told her. 'Then I delivered a letter to a house in the Minories and rode straight back home, as ordered.' His ruddy face was creased in anxiety.

Dismissing Ned, Penelope spent the rest of the afternoon trying to imagine what might have happened to Hawise as she waited at the inn for Philip, already lying dead in Flanders. So preoccupied was she that she was totally unprepared when her husband appeared that evening with an offer of a truce. He looked so nervous as he stood in the doorway that she even felt a pang of pity for him.

'I came to inform you, madam,' he said, after gathering up all his courage, 'that it is my intention to remove my sons from your charge. I do not consider you to be a suitable influence for my sons at such a tender age.'

Penelope's lips curled angrily and her eyes narrowed to dark slits. 'I warn you, sir,' she said in an icy voice, 'do not interfere with my family, or you will be extremely sorry.'

Robert Rich seemed taken aback that his carefully prepared speech had not instantly frightened her into contrition. Off his guard, his courage deserted him. 'I beg you, madam,' he said, suddenly timid, 'to consider the harm it will do if this scandal gets out.'

Penelope sniffed, glad to see the fear in his eyes. 'I disagree,' she said obstinately. 'My sons were born legitimately, baptised Christian and are of noble blood. I will fight to the end for them,' she threatened.

'Penelope,' he pleaded. 'Please be sensible. Neither of us can afford this slur on our families.'

'That is your problem, sir,' she retorted haughtily, 'Personally, I don't care.'

'Sidney is now a national hero. Are we to soil his name?' he asked.

At the mention of her lover's name, Penelope felt weak and her lips trembled. The wound was still too raw. 'He was my real husband,' she sobbed. 'You and your damned wealth robbed us of our true love.'

'Of that I am well aware,' Robert said quietly.

A sob rose in Penelope's throat. Defeated, she sank down on a low stool, her head in her hands.

'The fault is not entirely mine,' continued Robert Rich. 'Your most illustrious uncle, Henry Hastings, was at the gate to bargain for your hand in marriage before my dear brother was cold.'

'Like a prize cow,' she muttered.

Tears flooded her eyes and ran down her cheeks for several minutes before her courage finally returned. She knew she could not be sorry for herself at this moment. Swallowing hard, she rose to her feet and allowed her temper to rise again. 'Have I not enough on my mind without having to deal with you? My maid, my loving Hawise, is lost in the big city. Go away!' she shouted at him. 'You are of no assistance to me.'

To her surprise, he did not go away. Instead he crossed the room and seated himself facing her. 'Tell me of Hawise,' he said in an unusually kind voice. 'I may be able to help.'

Penelope stared at him in amazement. This was a genuine offer of help. It had never occurred to her that a sympathetic person might exist beneath that unpleasant exterior. But he was revealing himself to her now. Slowly and sadly she explained how she had sent Hawise to London to warn Philip of the situation at Leighs.

Robert Rich listened to his wife without saying a word. But by the time she had finished telling her tale of woe, he was looking astounded. 'Do you mean to tell me, madam, that you gave a servant money, jewellery and an expensive gown and sent her off to London? You are absolutely mad. What else would you expect a servant to do but run away? You have probably set her up for life.'

Penelope shook her head earnestly. 'No, no,' she protested, 'not Hawise. We were as sisters. We grew up together.'

'You apparently have very little notion of the world outside your own sphere,' her husband said scornfully, 'but I will do what I can to find your maid.'

'I shall be eternally grateful to you, sir,' she murmured, still surprised by his desire to help her.

'But I warn you,' he continued, 'if a felony has been committed, your maid will be punished. My position as a Justice of the Peace will not allow me to overlook any trickery.' He rose to his feet. 'I trust that in the meantime you will pray for guidance and give up your wilful ways, madam,' he said.

She curtseyed gracefully, her eyelids lowered.

'If you wish to regain your position as my lawful wife, you had better learn to behave like a god-fearing matron,' he added.

For a moment Penelope felt a strong desire to giggle. What a pompous little fool he was! But she managed to stifle the laughter in her throat and remain silent as he finally bustled away looking rather pleased with himself.

7

The Armada

Despite the contempt she felt for her husband, Penelope was thankful for his offer of help, and she also began to accept her marriage. Grief for Philip and fear for Hawise had broken, temporarily, her rebellious spirit.

Slowly that depressing year drew to a close. The New Year made the world look ahead again. February brought with it the funeral of Penelope's lover, the great Sir Philip Sidney, a posthumous hero whose great debts had been so many that his body had lain many weeks in that house in the Minories while sufficient money was raised to give him the grand send-off his friends had planned. In the end, it was his father-in-law, Sir Francis Walsingham, who had borne the brunt of the expense, for he was determined that his son-in-law, the young poet knight and idol of the Protestant Party should be buried with full honours after a grand, ceremonial procession to his grand tomb at St Paul's.

As the procession wound its way through the streets from the Minories to St Paul's, the populace of London had their chance to show their respect for the thirty-two-year-old hero and cry their lamentations.

From the balcony of the house in the Strand, Penelope sat with other noble ladies as the cortège passed by. The total size of the spectacular procession was seven hundred noblemen, knights and gentlemen. And in the middle, Philip's horse was led by a footman and ridden by a page trailing a broken lance. Weeping, but discreetly hidden from view, the court ladies mourned their young hero.

Penelope sat with Philip's sister, Mary, on one side, and her mother on the other. The other female relatives sat nearby, including Catherine Hastings, and Penelope's sister Dorothy, whose new husband, Tom, walked alone in the procession, proudly holding aloft the Sidney emblem. Her Majesty did not attend; she was still in official mourning for her cousin, the unfortunate Queen of Scots. Nor did Sidney's young wife, Frances, who was too ill to leave her bed.

Penelope's dark eyes, which were to be immortalised by her lover's poetry, showed not one sign of a tear. They were cold and hard, for she had shed all her tears in her virtual imprisonment in the gloomy house of Leighs, weeping for her lost Hawise as well as for her darling, passionate Philip. During those long, sleepless nights while Robert Rich snored loudly beside her, having at last been allowed the use of his marriage bed (and seldom out of it) Penelope had surrendered to her circumstances and no longer fought against her fate.

Now she watched the burnished helmet carried on a velvet cushion by the golden-haired page on Philip's magnificent steed. Then the velvet-clad coffin slid by, carried by fourteen yeomen, and emblazoned with the Sidney arms. At the corners of the coffin, his dearest friends carried banners. Penelope looked away, scarcely able to look. Philip was not down there; he lived still, in her heart, locked up with the secret of their love.

After the funeral, Penelope returned to Leighs. It was too unsafe to stay in town because of the outbreaks of the plague, which had been brought back from France by ragged half-starved soldiers. Back home, her two sons and pretty auburn-haired daughter were a joy to her in her silent grief. Slowly she even began to accept her husband a little more as she realised that he was not really an ogre, just a clumsy oaf, as her brother Robert had once described him.

Since his return from the war, Robert Rich had taken a very puritanical turn of mind. He dressed soberly and frowned on merry-making. Penelope, in black gown and a white ruff, went about her duties like an obedient wife. Gone was her lovely carefree smile and cheerful countenance. Her mouth assumed a solemn droop and child-bearing had widened her figure. Stoically she faced up to her life as wife to a wealthy landowner. And within a year she had borne him another child – a fair little girl whom they named Isabella. Robert was not very interested in the new baby, for he cared only for boys as his heirs. But the children were happy and often their laughter was heard in the long, echoing stone corridors.

During this time, Lord Rich frequently disappeared on dubious privateering expeditions or long electioneering campaigns, leaving his wife in the company of her children. In spite of his wealth, he would not allow money to be spent freely, and he kept a strong check on all household accounts. A new gown or a small luxury was often hard to come by. However, he still kept to his part of the bargain and searched diligently for Hawise, so Penelope felt she was bound in honour to keep hers.

The crested ruby ring was found in the possession of a notorious thief who, under torture, admitted murdering a Jewish trader in the Minories. He was promptly hanged by Robert Rich. The wife of the Jew remembered a young woman in a green dress who had sold them the ring, but there was still no news of Hawise.

'Give up, madam,' pleaded Robert Rich. 'Your servant obviously sold the ring and immediately left the country.'

'I'll never believe that,' cried Penelope. 'Hawise would never be disloyal. If she lives, she will not betray me.' Stubbornly, she clung on to all hope that Hawise would return to her one day, healthy and well and beaming her bright smile to all around. Nothing could shake that belief from Penelope's mind and it was only such hope that kept her going through her otherwise dreary life at Leighs.

In the early spring of 1588, Penelope took her four children to visit her mother. It was a bright day and the end of winter. Sun greeted their heavy, low-built coach as it approached the elm-lined avenue at Wanstead. The children peeped excitedly through the curtain.

The great lake lay silvery still, ice still visible on its surface. The colourful plumes of the birds congregated sleepily on the island, contrasted with the black branches of the leafless trees. Tiny crocuses poked up through the green lawns and under the majestic cedars grew clumps of golden daffodils. The air was crisp and clean and the dark forest surrounding them gave the park an air of mystery.

Penelope breathed a sigh of happiness as the peace and beauty of the estate overwhelmed her. This always happened when she came to Wanstead.

Lettice welcomed her daughter and grandchildren with open arms. As usual, the house was full of guests. Lettice played tennis and danced like a young girl. Lord Leicester had aged since Penelope had seen him last. He had grown stout and walked more slowly, was redder in the face and greyer in the beard. But he seemed to have mellowed with age, and was very gracious to Penelope.

For the first few days Penelope avoided the bright company in the rest of the house, either staying in her room or walking alone with the children in the garden. Eventually her mother felt compelled to say something. Marching into Penelope's room one morning, she stood with her hands on her hips.

'For pity's sake, child, take off that rusty black robe. You look as if you belong to some order of nuns.'

'Lord Rich does not approve of bright colours,' Penelope replied primly, annoyed by her mother's intrusion.

'To hell with Robert Rich!' yelled Lettice. 'God in

Heaven, what's happened to you? Are you merely a puppet with your husband pulling the strings?'

'I have settled down to married life,' answered her daughter sullenly. 'What else would you have of me?'

'I suggest you get some sense,' declared Lettice. 'Only twenty-two and four children. There is more to life than sitting on your arse like a broody hen.'

Her mother's hard vulgarity sunk in. Tears sprang into Penelope's eyes.

Immediately Lettice was contrite. 'Come on, now, don't get upset,' she said. 'Get that old rag off and I will send something for you to wear. My maid will dress you and you can come down to supper. Come on,' she said hugging Penelope warmly, 'let's see that old self.'

Huge candelabra lit up the carved oak staircase. Brightly clad flunkeys lined the walls. The air was filled with high-spirited conversation and laughter. Her mother's blue brocade gown suited Penelope. The neckline was very low, exposing the top of her snow-white breasts. As she self-consciously came down the stairs, masculine eyes turned to look appreciatively at her. Wine flowed and the guests supped leisurely. Slowly Penelope began to relax. There was something about this house which made it function with carefree abandon and suggested everywhere the imprint of Lettice's personality.

Very soon her mother, closely attended by Christopher Blount, introduced her daughter to a very distinguished young gentleman whose dark hair was worn rather long and curled fashionably over his shoulders onto a fine lace collar. He had merry brown eyes and a small tuft of black beard on his chin. He was tall and handsome, though somewhat heavily built. As Penelope noticed these features, she thought that there was something oddly familiar about him.

'Allow me to introduce you to my elder brother, Charles, Lady Penelope,' said Christopher in his affable way.

As Charles caught Penelope's eye and held it for a few seconds, she knew they had indeed met previously. The first time was when as a raw youth he sat at her mother's supper table and the second was in the barge when she was going to Bisham Abbey and he to university. Now here was the finished product – a handsome courtier, professional soldier and, in fact, quite a man of the world. How plump he has become, she thought, as he held her fingers to his lips. She was in no mood for a flirtation, and surveyed him with little interest.

'Lady Penelope Devereux,' he whispered gallantly. 'You are even more beautiful than I remember.'

Penelope lifted her head proudly. 'My name is now Rich,' she said pertly. 'Or did news of my marriage escape you?'

Expert in the art of courtly behaviour, Sir Charles Blount was quite unperturbed. He escorted her into supper, led her out to dance and stood behind her chair as they watched a play until after midnight. Throughout the evening, he was in constant attendance.

After the party was over and the merry-making had

stopped, Penelope spent a restless night, mainly because of the wails of her youngest babe, who cried incessantly in spite of the efficient nurse's efforts to comfort her. Finally, unable to bear the sound any longer, she rose and brought the child back to bed with her. This was undoubtedly a child of Robert Rich, she thought as she held it to her breast until it quietened down. She had tried so hard to love and comfort this baby, but she had a strong will of her own, not to mention a large mouth which was always open and emitting ear-splitting screams.

As the baby settled down, Penelope began to think of the large, capable, well-cared-for hands of Charles Blount and his handsome figure. He was very charming, and by the end of the evening, had obviously been completely captivated by her. How easy it would be to drift into another affair, she mused dreamily . . .

The next morning her thoughts were completely changed. It was absurd to consider such a liaison with Charles. Having survived one adulterous scandal, she could not indulge in another. No, she would leave Wanstead today. She could never go through all that again.

When she told her mother that she was leaving, Lettice was most indignant. 'Leave today, Penelope? Why, don't be so absurd! I've had no time at all with my grandchildren.'

So Penelope relented, and lingered and walked in the lovely gardens with Charles Blount. Dimples appeared once more in the corners of her full, red mouth as, with the aid of Charles, she began to smile again. The roses returned to her cheeks and the sun brought out the gold glint in her hair.

Charles was not an intellectual as Philip had been, but he was calm, courteous and gentle and quite determined to win her.

'Have you no wife, sir?' she asked him one day.

His lips lightly brushed her hand, and his rich brown eyes wooed her as they sat in the summer house amid the glories of spring. The white swans glided across the lake, and snowdrops grew around the banks. Clumps of yellow primroses dotted the paths and daffodils grew in abundance under the trees.

'I never had the time to marry,' he answered languidly. 'Too poor in my early youth, and too busy since.'

'I hear you are a great success at court,' she teased him.

'Not with the ladies. In truth I am a bird of passage, my lady.'

'I disbelieve you, sir,' she mocked.

'Also,' he said more seriously, 'I am next in line for the title of Mountjoy and from an early age I have set myself the task of rebuilding the fortunes of my noble, but impoverished family.'

'Then I recommend a rich wife for you, sir,' Penelope jested. 'It's the quickest and the safest road to fortune.'

'No, never,' he declared. 'No loveless marriage for me. I've seen too much heartbreak around me.'

Penelope immediately dropped her eyes. Was it possible that Charles had heard about her unhappy life with Lord Rich? But inwardly she knew that she fascinated him and the glint of mischief returned to her dark almond eyes.

Together they took long rides into the heart of the forest, where, on mossy banks shy violet grew, and on a bed of ferns a young fawn took milk from its mother. They dismounted and rested under a great oak whose bare branches spread out to the sky; tiny leaf buds swelled as the sap rose in the old, grey bark.

Charles pressed her close to him, his body urgent with love. 'Be mine, Penelope,' he whispered. 'I promise I'll be constant to you.'

She pushed him away gently. 'I'll never be another man's mistress,' she said firmly, but inside her chest, her heart was beating with excitement.

Charles gazed at her with steady eyes. 'Ah yes, Sidney . . .' he murmured.

Penelope nodded slowly. 'So you knew also. It wasn't a secret then,' she said gently.

'Most folk did, my lady, but no one blamed you. Did Sidney not capture us all with the poems of love he composed to you?'

Penelope stared sadly out at the spring green forest. 'He used to read his sonnets to me, while we drifted up the river in a boat,' she said dreamily. She sighed and shrugged her slim shoulders. 'But now he is dead, and I am going to return, unspoiled, to the bosom of my illustrious husband. You are acquainted with Lord Rich, I presume?'

Charles grinned. 'I had that honour when he made

a sudden return from the Low Countries. Such a pother of pills and potions I've yet to see again.'

She began to laugh loud and heartily. Instantly, Charles took advantage of the situation to press hot, passionate lips on hers. Penelope's arms crept about his neck and soon they were lost in the endless time and space that belongs only to lovers.

'Come to me in town, my darling,' he pleaded. 'Wanstead is too public a place for the things I wish to say and do.'

'Behave, sir!' she giggled as he stroked her soft neck. But she leaned forward to whisper, 'I'll think about it.'

His hands caressed her more and the shiver of love, which she tried to control, almost overwhelmed her. Something about him inflamed her passions. Even with Philip she had never felt like this before.

In their last two days at Wanstead, when they romped on the lawn with the children and danced the night away, Penelope and Charles grew closer. When the time came for Lord Leicester and his party to ride back to town, they both knew that they had to meet again but that in the meantime the fires that burnt within each must be quenched. Their hands clung in a last farewell.

As the men prepared to ride away, Penelope caught an enigmatic glint in her mother's eye. 'Parting is such sweet sorrow,' said Lettice, blowing a farewell kiss to her menfolk.

Was it for her husband or Sir Christopher Blount? And was Sir Christopher her lover? Penelope was not quite sure.

Mother and daughter stood side by side at the top of the flight of marble steps that led to the entrance hall at Wanstead. Over their heads a banner waved bearing the crest of the Dudleys – the bear and the ragged staff. The same emblem was embroidered all over her mother's fine gown. Lettice was not as tall as her daughter, but the women were still remarkably alike – Lettice; her auburn hair stiff with dye to hide the grey streaks, and Penelope's of burnished gold which captured the sun. Her mother's face was cold, proud and patrician; Penelope's white and sad with a mouth that trembled at the corners as she said goodbye to her new lover.

Later Penelope sat with her mother in a cool arbour, where roses, yet unborn, hid within tiny buds.

'It's pleasant to enjoy a little peace after such a big company,' sighed Lettice. She fondled the little black pug dog that was always at her feet. Her daughter's thoughts seemed far away. 'I'll take care of the children if you wish to ride to London,' Lettice suggested tactfully.

Penelope shot her an angry look. 'I've no reason to go into town,' she replied brusquely. 'I shall leave for home tomorrow.'

Lettice gave a nonchalant shrug. 'I did consider that you might need some fabric to replenish your wardrobe. I must say, Penelope, you are looking frightfully shabby.'

'What do I care?' replied her daughter with a surly look.

'You are supposed to have married well,' Lettice

continued icily. 'But you seem to have little desire to live up to it.'

'Mother, I have already told you that Lord Rich does not approve of bright finery. I'll have little occasion to wear fine clothes once I get home to Leighs.'

'Oh, fie!' snapped Lettice, rising to her feet impatiently. 'For God's sake, come back to life, Penelope. Don't let that puritanical oaf destroy you. It's more than I can bear.' Charged with emotion, Lettice strode away, leaving her daughter feeling very disturbed.

That night Penelope lay awake thinking about her mother's sarcastic comments. And by the morning her mood had changed. 'Mother really pities me,' she said aloud to herself. 'How I hate the idea, but I know she is right. Am I not of noble blood, my family the most ancient of barons? Yet I am a rag bag, dressed in black like a worker in the fields.' Her rebellious spirit was suddenly unleashed and emerged as strong as ever. Yes, she would ride to town and spend liberally. What a mean old fool her husband was. How long was she supposed to do penance for past misdeeds?

Later that day, dressed in the brightest of her mother's riding attire, she rode off to London accompanied by a manservant.

Lettice beamed upon her departure. 'There will be much to amuse you there, Penelope,' she said enthusiastically. 'Throw off the sackcloth and ashes and have a good time. The children will be quite safe with me.'

There was an air of excitement in London as they rode through the dirty streets of the Barbican. People gossiped noisily in groups. Hot-pie vendors had ceased to tout their wares and stood around chatting. Mounted men galloped down the streets, bludgeoning people to get out of their way as they rode hither and thither.

'What's going on?' Penelope asked her manservant.

'They are all saying that the Spanish Armada is coming,' he answered.

'Fie, that's just another rumour to distract us,' Penelope replied without interest.

On reaching Leicester House she found the grooms in the stable yard also gossiping, the mounts left unattended. The rumour was spreading like wildfire, and hatred and fear of the Spaniard was running riot. Still unconcerned, she went out and completed her shopping, buying new ribbons and arranging for two new gowns to be made.

Having satisfactorily refurbished her wardrobe, that evening she stood out on the balcony of the great house in the Strand, looking down at the river that flowed leisurely by, her heart filled with the haunting shadows of desire. She had not long to wait. Soon a little boat came alongside the landing stage. Wrapped in a long, dark cloak she crept discreetly down the slippery steps. Oarsmen steered the boat just a short way down the river to Duran House where Charles had his lodgings.

He was waiting for her at the riverside. 'I knew you would come,' he whispered, enveloping her in his strong arms.

There was no shyness between them. They met and were united in love as if they had always been together.

Penelope felt no remorse. Afterwards, she fell asleep beside him, happy, contented and fulfilled.

At dawn, a messenger came for him. Charles rose and surveyed Penelope very seriously as he put on his cloak and buckled his sword-belt. 'I am loath to leave you, my love, but news has just come that the Spanish Armada is approaching our shores.'

'I've no desire to own you, sir.' Penelope could not help being sarcastic.

Charles bent to kiss her. 'Hush, do not spoil the love we have found.'

'Do not commit yourself, sir,' she said bitterly. 'There is my husband and several children to be considered.'

He raised a protesting hand as she got up from the bed and stood perfectly still. Her lovely hair rippled down over her white and shapely body.

'Oh God! How beautiful you are, my lady!' he exclaimed, stepping towards her, entranced.

But Penelope drew back, hands on her hips. 'It's possible that I would have made a magnificent whore,' she said mockingly.

Charles frowned. He was deeply distressed. 'For God's sake, Penelope. I don't understand you.'

Calmly, she slipped a long, silk shift over her head. 'Well, that makes two of us because frankly I don't understand myself.'

Charles was both mystified and annoyed. 'I beg your pardon if I have offended you, madam, but you came to me willingly.'

Immediately Penelope knew that she was being

unreasonable. Her warm smile returned, and she slipped her arms affectionately about his neck. 'I know, my lord. You have made me very happy and I am likely to ask you to do so again.'

Relieved, Charles kissed her passionately. 'Oh, God in Heaven,' he sighed. 'I don't think I am ever going to get over you.'

'Don't worry,' she smiled charmingly. 'I probably shan't let you.'

'Good,' he said.

And so they parted – Charles to Plymouth where he had his command, Penelope back to Leicester House.

Even before midday she had begun her return journey to Wanstead. Storm clouds were gathering and a fresh wind blew inland. 'Just the wind to blow the Spaniards inshore,' said her escort.

Like one awaking from a dream Penelope realised that the Spanish invasion, threatened for so long, had begun. She had to ride directly and rapidly to Wanstead to collect the children.

She found her children playing happily in the garden watched over by their grandmother. But Lettice, a trifle haggard, was worried about her husband and son, now that this emergency had arisen.

'I feel wildly extravagant,' Penelope informed her. 'I've ordered two new gowns.'

'That will set that parsimonious old wretch back a noble or two.' Lettice gave her daughter an indulgent smile.

'Do you think the Spaniards will come?' Penelope asked her.

Lettice smiled bravely. 'They will come all right, but what a welcome they will have, to be sure!' She was proud of her fighting men. 'It is just what young Robert has been looking forward to. He has taken all my men capable of fighting. How will I run this place with old men and little boys?' She chattered on nervously.

Penelope began to gather up her offspring, packing them into the curtained wagon with the homely maid, Tabitha, who was now attached to the nursery. 'I must go home, Mother,' she said. 'Lord Rich will be furious if the children are not in the safety of Leighs.'

With two armed men escorting them, the family set out home along the muddy Essex lanes. Penelope rode on horseback in front of the coach, occasionally riding back to give instructions to Tabitha. The roads were unusually crowded. As many people seemed to be leaving the capital as were on their way in. The threat of invasion had set the whole population on the move. Carts containing valuables were being taken to places of safety, cutting deep ruts in the road. Panicky horses fell and got stuck on the almost impassable road. The travellers were tired and dusty and the children harassed and complaining. The sky was orange from the glare of the beacons that had been lit on high ground. Clouds of smoke came up from the camps set up on the side of the road as the farm workers went into London to offer their services to the Queen carrying rusty pikes, and shouting and singing. But the most depressing sight of all was the beggars. Hordes of them walked in small groups: weary, dirty women carrying babies; crippled soldiers hobbling along on sticks; ragged children holding out their hands and crying pathetically for a coin or any kind of food.

'How sickening!' cried Penelope. 'Where on earth did all this rag-tag come from? And why are they all going back into London?'

'Most of them came out of the town last year when the plague was rife,' her escort informed her.

'But why are they all on the move now, for goodness sake?' she asked.

'The invasion, my lady. There might be pickings if the Spaniards come. They will loot. They're making sure they get in first,' he told her laconically.

'Vultures to the feast of death!' Penelope grimaced. 'It's unbelievable.' As she stared at another passing group, a thin, young woman, whose face was covered by a grimy mask, ran out and grasped her horse's bridle. 'Spare a coin, ma'am,' she whined, holding out a scraggy hand.

Penelope gazed down in horror at the mask and the vile eyes that peered through the holes. Her escort rode forward and drove her away. As the woman ran, her ragged shawl fell away and the remnants of a green velvet gown clinging to her emaciated body could be seen. The filthy skirt billowed out behind her and, despite the stains and dilapidation, Penelope instantly recognised the dress. It was the one she had given Hawise on the day she had disappeared.

'Catch her!' she gasped, bringing her mount to a swift halt so abruptly that it reared and disturbed the riders in front.

'Nay, ma'am,' drawled the slow voice of the country lad. 'Better leave her be. She's got the pox.'

Tired and dispirited, Penelope almost cried in vexation as the beggar girl disappeared into the crowd. It might have been her imagination, she tried to console herself. There might be a hundred dresses like that. But it was no use; she was sure that that was the one Hawise had worn. A deep depression came over her. If Hawise had been murdered it was as if she herself had killed her. And she remembered the death of little Patrick, the murder of Hawise's lover. Had she really ended three lives by her impetuous actions?

She was still full of morbid thoughts when she rode under the octagonal towers of the gate-house at Leighs, where the cold melancholic air of the house seemed heavier than ever. The servants came to attend to the sleeping children and Lord Rich came hurrying forward, sweating profusely. He smelt of a strange herb ointment that he rubbed on his chest to prevent colds. Involuntarily she backed away from him.

'So, you have returned, madam,' he said loudly. 'Who gave you permission to take my sons to that unhealthy town?'

'We were at Mother's,' she answered quietly.

Pompously he marched up and down before her. 'I suppose you are unaware that we are in danger of an invasion and here you are traipsing about the country with small children.'

'Do cease!' Penelope cried irritably. 'I am worn out with travelling. If you wish to complain, save it until the morning.'

After just one hour of exhausted sleep, she found herself wide awake once more. Her body ached, her mind was disturbed. Constantly Hawise's gentle face seemed to haunt her, dancing before her eyes. Unable to bear it any longer, she rose and walked out into the cold stone corridor. An old servant with a candle snuffer was methodically putting out the lights.

'Go, rouse Tabitha from the nursery,' she commanded him.

The small red-faced maid arrived dressed in a long blue flannel night-gown and cap. She rubbed her snub nose and yawned sleepily. 'What's wrong, ma'am?' she asked. 'The children are all sound asleep.'

'It's all right, Tabitha,' Penelope smiled at this funny looking little maid. 'I cannot sleep. I want you to get me something from the pantry.'

'Not tonight, ma'am. Someone might catch me,' grumbled Tabitha.

'You have my permission, but there's no need to wake the whole house. Bring me a jug of strong wine, and one of those skin bottles that belong to Lord Rich. They are hanging up in the pantry. Go quietly, now,' she warned the terrified maid.

A little wine at dinner was usually the limit of her alcoholic intake, but tonight she had to obliterate her morbid thoughts. Within minutes, the breathless maid returned, bringing a large flagon, a jug of wine and a bottle of ship's brandy.

'Fill up the cup, Tabitha,' Penelope ordered from the bed. 'Mix up some wine with the brandy.'

Greatly agitated, the little maid did as she was bid.

'Now sit beside me and fill it up again when I tell you.'

She sipped the first cup of the filthy liquid, grimacing at the sour taste. But then by the second cup, she had begun to enjoy it. Her thoughts tumbled over each other, jumping from Philip to Charles, Patrick and Hawise, then, with a convulsive shudder, to her husband. Why was she so ill-fated? Would she ever have lasting happiness?

She could not answer her own questions, and was beginning to feel very drowsy. It was a nice feeling. 'Fill up the cup, Tabitha,' she slurred.

The maid had dozed off and was sleeping with her head between her knees, so Penelope reached for the skin container, pouring from it into the cup over her shift. Then her head fell back and a drunken sleep overpowered her.

A few minutes later, soft steps padded along the corridor and the small square shape of Robert Rich appeared at the door. He peered into the dark chamber. 'Madam,' he called. 'Are you awake?' When he saw Tabitha sleeping beside the bed, he gave her a hard clout across the head. 'Get off to bed!' he yelled. 'How dare you sleep here?'

Tabitha was off like a bewildered rabbit to its burrow. Lord Rich stood by the bed looking down at his sleeping spouse. Penelope's mouth had dropped open and her abundant hair streamed out on to the floor. He fondled the long mane for a second, but then sniffed her breath. 'By God! The bitch is drunk!' he cried.

He gave her a slight push. She did not stir. A sadistic expression came over his ugly face as he pinched her arm. Still she did not move. Then, almost drooling, he pulled off the covers and leapt on top of her.

Penelope experienced what now happened as a nightmare, which was to recur for many years to come. An animal was trying to devour her which she tried desperately to push away, but was powerless. Arms and legs were paralysed. The creature bit and ate into her flesh as the crazed mind of her frustrated sadistic husband ran amok.

In the light of the morning she slowly came back to life. Something was wrong. Heavy-eyed she peered about the room, and when she raised an arm she saw that it was covered with bruises. What had happened to her? She wished she had not drunk so much and could remember. Rising from the bed she staggered over to the mirror, and gazed in horror at her bruised face and the bites on her breasts. She wanted to vomit. The beast! It had not been a dream. He had had his way with her in her unconscious state.

'Tabitha!' she screamed. The girl ran to her aid, but could not conceal her fear when she saw her mistress' bruised and disfigured body.

'Lock the door, Tabitha!' Penelope wept. For several days she lay in bed attended by her solicitous little maid. Her battered body recovered slowly but her mind seethed with angry plans for revenge against her brute of a husband. Tears of self-pity frequently fell like rain down her pale cheeks. And she refused to see her husband or even to accept a message of apology from him.

At the end of the week Robert Rich rode away once more, and she could go to the nursery again to love and fuss her children. She was comforted by them, but she did not forget how her husband had used her. By God, she vowed, I'll pay back that lecherous brute, if it takes me all my days. But she began to circulate once more – riding about the huge estate and walking with her children.

Rumours about the Spanish invasion were rife throughout the neighbourhood, brought in by travellers coming through the remote Essex countryside. Servants brought scraps of information to the house from the village, saying that the Spaniards had landed in the south and were now marching on London. Some said that the Spanish had burned and pillaged all the small towns as they marched. Around the village pump, terrible tales of atrocities were swapped.

In this atmosphere it was not surprising that Penelope developed an unfamiliar sense of fear and uncertainty. And it was with relief that she saw her husband come riding back home with a party of friends. Even so, she still refused to see him. She gave instructions for his guests to be taken care of, but refused all requests for her attendance at meals.

Eventually, Robert Rich came to the nursery looking very pale and distraught. He patted his sons on the head, but ignored the two little girls. 'I thought you might like to hear news of the battle that is progressing,' he murmured almost apologetically.

Penelope inclined her head very haughtily, feigning a lack of interest but really wanting to know.

'A victory has been won,' he said. 'The Armada has been chased from our shores and is now being defeated on the high seas.' His voice squeaked with excitement.

Penelope could not help smiling with relief and she felt a tug of happiness at the thought of her brother and Charles. 'Is that the truth?' she asked. 'According to the servants the Spaniards are likely to be at the gate any day.'

Robert Rich shook his head in a smug gesture. 'There is no fear of that,' he said. 'They were no match for our great queen's navy.' He strutted up and down with his chest puffed out like a little bantam cock as though he himself had fought off the enemy single-handed. 'Not with men like ours – Drake and Howard. Our country shall be eternally grateful to them. But the battle is not over yet. Our gracious queen is to visit Tilbury to review Lord Leicester's army of defence. I wish you to accompany me to the house of my kinsman, Thomas, to welcome Her Majesty,' he announced finally.

Penelope could not believe what she had heard. The audacity of the little brute! But this meant that the Queen would be making an overnight stay at Ardenhall. As always, the whole royal pack would accompany her – ladies-in-waiting, courtiers and servants. She eyed her husband with cold suspicion. To what end was he trying to use her now?

Robert Rich fidgeted nervously as he waited for her response. 'It will be an occasion for you to wear those extravagant gowns you acquired in London,' he added sarcastically as though her silence had given him courage.

Penelope narrowed her eyes at him. 'So, now you poke and pry into my boxes,' she snarled as she felt her temper rising. Her new gowns had recently arrived and were not yet unpacked.

'I do not begrudge you a new gown, madam,' said her husband trying to sound reasonable. 'But surely in these desperate times there are more needful things to spend our money on.'

'You pious little hypocrite!' she screamed at him. 'You jumped-up nobody!' She hurled insult after insult at him and pulled down the shoulder of her gown to show the bluish marks on her skin.

'Am I to be lectured by a husband who behaves like an animal?'

He looked shame-faced at the tell-tale bruises on her neck. 'I did try to apologise, madam,' he said. 'If that is not sufficient, there is little else I can do.'

'Well, I can!' she yelled. 'I intend to get lawyers to free me from you.'

'Be sensible,' he sneered. 'You are the mother of a large family. I doubt if even you could prove our marriage was unconsummated.'

His words silenced her and she stared at him in cold disdain. He was right, she sighed. She could not be rid of him on those grounds. She switched her thoughts to his request. Why not attend the celebrations? It would be probably the only opportunity she would ever have to wear those lovely gowns. 'I shall accompany you sir,' she said, coolly, 'but on no account or under any circumstances, will I ever allow you into my bed again.' Robert Rich stared at her with his piggy eyes and an old crooked smile crossed his face. Without a word, he bowed low and left.

Pursued by the Commander of the Queen's Fleet, Lord Howard, the Spanish Armada was being driven back on to the rocky coast of Ireland. The beaches of Devon were littered with wreckage and piled high with Spanish booty, but Penelope and her husband had not yet left for Ardenhall. Thomas, master of the house, was a poor kinsman of Robert, who was extremely jealous that the Queen had honoured him with a visit. As the Queen's progress was subject to the usual delay, Robert had gone off scouring the countryside for supplies to aid Leicester's army, bullying his tenants to enlist, commandeering their houses, and demanding quantities of food. He judged that success in this mission would be a feather in his cap and he was on the look-out for several more.

His wife had a shrewd idea of his ambitions as she sat in her chamber carefully painting her shoulders and breast with a white cosmetic to hide her bruises. But his requests for her presence at Ardenhall still puzzled her. Damned little fox, what was he up to? He hated his kinsman Thomas. Furiously she dabbed at the marks on her neck. She was beginning to hate them all: Charles, elated with conquest, had only used her; poor, pathetic Philip had been unable to break the ties that bound him. She felt scornful of them both with their lives ruled by the possessive, demanding queen. Blind hatred for Her Majesty consumed her.

And her assiduous, toadying little husband lusting for power and expecting her to aid him, she totally despised. But she was caught like an animal in a trap, and for the sake of her family she had hung on, but she was not sure how long she could.

In all her married life she had hardly shared any of her husband's activities. Either she had been pregnant or he was out of favour. Well, she thought now, if he insisted on her making an appearance in public, at least he would have to provide her with a suitable wardrobe. She smiled at the thought of wearing the lovely gown she had ordered in London.

On a sunny day in early August when they eventually arrived at the gates of Ardenhall, Robert Rich could barely hide his disappointment at the news that the Queen had arrived the previous night and was already on her way out of the house, well rested and about to continue her journey to Tilbury. Soldiers lined the road and held back the thronging mass of enthusiastic subjects, eagerly waiting to see their glorious Queen Bess.

Lord Rich was extremely irritable. His plan had gone awry, since he had to arrive in time to welcome her to his kinsman's home. But already the monarch was coming down the drive-way with her huge retinue, so there was little for Lord and Lady Rich to do but sit in the carriage and wait for the procession to pass.

Dressed elegantly in a plumed hat and a new scarlet travelling dress, Penelope watched the glorious pageant approaching down the tree-lined track. In an elaborate gold-fringed litter, Her Majesty sat bolt upright, a vision of loveliness in white-and-gold brocade, with her faithful Leicester at her side. Other peers of the realm walked beside the litter and a bevy of richly dressed ladies walked proudly behind. With a slow smile, Penelope watched the duchesses and their fair daughters – many of them companions of her youth – and knew that she would not be in their shoes for anything. As the mounted guard swept past with a scatter of hooves and a clink of armour, and the crowd let out a great cheer, Penelope was left quite unmoved. She felt nothing but pity for most of those old men who hobbled along behind their queen, weighed down by their heavy regalia. She almost giggled at the sight of Lord Burghley, the sour-faced Lord Chancellor sitting on top of a short-legged mule, with his hump-backed son, Robert Cecil, beside him. Most of these loyal courtiers were old; the young gallants were all away at the battle-front.

Penelope sat still in the carriage watching the procession go by but Robert Rich hopped in and out like a small frog, distracted that his plans had gone wrong. Penelope's lips curved in a slow, mocking smile. He was so ludicrous with his shrill voice and jerky movements. She watched, too, the motley throng that lined the road, seeking for the face of Hawise or for the beggar who had worn the green dress.

At last, Lord Rich decided that they should follow the end of the procession to watch the Queen review the troops at Tilbury, and then continue on to London to dine with the Cecils. As she listened to his proposed plan, Penelope realised at last what he was up to. Now that her brother, Lord Essex, was away at sea, her wily husband was cultivating a rising star, Robert Cecil, who seemed to be about to step so neatly into his old father's shoes. The feud that raged between the Devereux and Cecils was long-standing. The queen had always gone to great pains to preserve the balance between the rival Essex and Cecil factions at court. So that was why she had become important! Well, at least she knew and was ready for his crafty tricks.

She turned these matters over in her mind later that day as she sat in the paymaster's house at Tilbury with other noble ladies, watching from a window what went on outside. Her Majesty, now mounted on a white steed, rode through the ranks wearing steel armour. And when her stentorian tones rang out loud and clear, her subjects knew that Good Queen Bess was in deadly earnest. But as she delivered her rousing speech, which inspired even the weakest man in Leicester's army to match the proudest Spaniard, all Penelope could think of was how masculine the Queen was, and how old and tired her stepfather looked as he held the bridle of her mount. Queen Elizabeth, in her true element, urged on her nation to fight, declaring that she would lead them into battle herself if need be.

After the Queen's heroic speech, Penelope and her husband rode on to London to view their newly acquired property at the far end of the Strand. It was called St Bartholomew's Square but became Warwick House once Robert Rich had obtained the title for which he was working so assiduously. At her husband's decision to stay in London, Penelope did not protest. Everyone was in town celebrating the victory over the Spanish. Every great house in the Strand was lit up and overflowing with guests. Bonfires were blazing in the open spaces. The taverns were full of celebrating crowds, and drunken apprentices roamed the streets shouting the queen's praises.

For a while Penelope was quite eager to join in the round of lively entertainment. When Her Majesty returned, there was a great reception at court while she rewarded her victorious young men. And then there was a continuous round of balls and tilts, and visits to the noble houses all about them. Robert Rich, returning all this hospitality in a most lavish manner, seemed to take on a remarkable change of attitude, keeping his distance from his wife, but, presenting her with pieces of valuable Spanish jewellery acquired from the plunder of the wrecked Spanish galleons. Most surprisingly, he did not turn a hair at the sight of her new court dress with a silver corsage and embroidery of real pearls. Penelope was beginning to enjoy herself. Gloomy Leighs seemed very far away. But she often longed for the company of her children, and on this point he was adamant.

'My sons must remain at Leighs. There is too much illness in town. I will attend to their welfare,' he added pompously.

She felt that tug of angry rebellion but reluctantly, she gave in as she found herself becoming a famous hostess in this fashionable, glittering, Elizabethan society. One constant visitor to her home these days was

Robert Cecil, whose slim, sensitive fingers seemed to burn a hole in her hand as he pressed it to his lips. His deep-set eyes always seemed to caress her almost bare bosom, while his soft, insinuating voice told her how beautiful she was. Inwardly she shivered. She loathed him, finding his long, thin face and twisted shoulder repulsive. But her instincts told her that he admired her and found her sexually attractive. And she knew that it would be quite possible to use him, in spite of the keen astuteness of his mind. He called regularly, bringing brightly coloured blooms from his father's grand garden, and he would watch her intently with his snake-like eyes. Her husband, delighted at having acquired this patron from the inner court, welcomed him to the house with embarrassing effusiveness.

The new house was very splendid and had an imposing white frontage with many windows. It had been built only recently by one of the new rich merchant families. Modern and bright, it possessed neither the gloom of Leighs nor the decaying atmosphere of Stratford-le-Bow. Penelope felt sure she could be happy here. The fields of Marylebone were not far away, and the stables were filled with fine horses. In his new-found glory, her husband was most affable, sparing no expense in furnishing his magnificent town house. Each day fresh treasures arrived, all spoils of war acquired in his crafty business dealings. The Riches entertained extravagantly in the manner of their day.

London was bursting at the seams with noble young men who flocked to court endeavouring to make their mark. When Penelope heard that Charles Blount, now Lord Mountjoy, had returned to court to be knighted by the Queen, she was not surprised but she was hurt to see how he competed with her brother for the Queen's favour. At tournaments, she often watched him ride to the lists in the middle of a fanfare of trumpets, but Charles did not smile or even glance in her direction. He hardly seemed to notice that she was there. But he looked so handsome in his shining armour, with the bright plumes on his helmet waving in the breeze, that she would forget her aching heart, and hold up her head bravely and proudly.

Sometimes Robert Cecil would seat himself beside her, his thin mouth twisted in a knowing grin. 'Lord Leicester should be wary,' he murmured one day. 'Every day the grass grows greener.'

Penelope's stepfather was absent that day. After the long weary ride to Tilbury, he was very ill at Wanstead for a while, and now he was on his way to his house in the Midlands. But he was never to return. He died a week later and the court closed for a period of mourning. The distraught old queen shut herself away with her sorrow for her favourite, and Lettice came home to Wanstead. Penelope joined her there and tried to comfort her but Lettice, usually so proud, was inconsolable. Her grief was terrible. Night and day, she wandered helplessly through that large house in long, black robes of mourning. 'Oh, Penelope,' she wailed. 'Robin was too great a man to be struck down like that in his prime.'

'But Mother,' Penelope replied tactlessly, 'he was turned fifty.'

Furiously, Lettice turned on her, spitting like a cat. 'What age is fifty? All his life he slaved for this realm. And now, when he and I could have lived in peace together at last, he has gone,' she wept.

Ashamed by her thoughtlessness, Penelope put her arm around her mother's shoulders.

'I'm sorry, Mother. Don't cry so,' she pleaded.

'It was worry that killed him,' declared Lettice, 'and that red-haired virago, Elizabeth. There was no pleasing her.' Her wrath had turned from her daughter to the queen.

'Please, Mother, be careful,' warned Penelope. It was unsafe for anyone to criticise their glorious queen.

'She deprived us of our love,' sobbed Lettice as her rage gave way to sorrow. 'All my life she kept him at her side. How I hate my cousin for what she has done to Robin and me!' Her sobs became louder, echoing through the long corridors, and Penelope held her mother in her arms and comforted her until sleep finally came to wipe away the pain and exhaustion.

Lord Leicester was given a grand state funeral by which time Lettice had calmed down. And when Elizabeth ordered her bailiffs to strip Wanstead of its treasures to cover the debts she insisted Lord Leicester owed her, Lettice regained her fighting spirit. 'Let her take whatever she wants if it gives her satisfaction,' she said caustically. 'What else can hurt me now?' And with her courteous companion, Sir Christopher Blount, beside her to help her organise her new estate, she left the ransacked house and fled to Drayton

Bassett, a small house that her husband had left her, and remained there to the end of her days.

With her mother off her hands, Penelope prepared to return to London. All this time she had kept secret her new pregnancy which was now in the fifth month. She was feeling very tired and jaded, and her mother's emotional troubles had been an additional strain on her. On the advice of an old nurse at Wanstead she travelled in a litter. She had wanted to ride on horseback but the servant had been horrified by such an idea. 'Glory be,' she cried. 'Do you want a child with a crooked back like the Lord Chancellor's? Horse-riding, indeed! One topple puts two lives in danger.'

The serving woman's words sounded like commonsense and besides, Penelope knew that she was tired, so she set off with fur rugs over her lap in a well-cushioned litter carried by eight bearers.

Mist ringed the hills around London as they approached. It was now mid-winter. The bearers padded rapidly along and the gold fringe decorating the litter swung from side to side. Penelope had begun to feel slightly sick and wished fervently that she had ignored the old servant's advice and ridden on her horse. The journey had been long and tedious, and she was cramped and stiff. When the spires of London came into sight and she heard the church bells, she breathed a deep sigh of relief. But she dreaded the slow pace through the crowded, smelly entrance to the city, and she knew that she had to have a rest.

'Put me down at the Bishop's Gate Inn,' she

commanded the bearers. 'I'll rest there a while. Send someone to my house to bring back a carriage.'

As she waited for her carriage, she sat by the window of the dining room of the inn, which looked out on to a narrow alley. Scraps of food had been thrown out of the kitchen into the alley, and a crowd of ragged children and old folk were grabbing them and fighting among themselves like animals.

'How disgusting!' she muttered to herself and leaned forward to pull the window shut. But as she did so, she caught sight of a tattered green velvet skirt. It was faded and filthy, and worn by one of the beggars. Without a moment's hesitation, she rose and made for the entrance. She would catch the woman herself this time, she vowed. For it was the pock-marked beggar girl she had spotted on the road to Leighs.

To the amazement of the other customers at the inn, the beautiful noblewoman suddenly picked up her purple skirts and ran out into the alley. 'Come here, girl! I want you,' she called.

The crowd of beggars immediately scattered in panic, and the thin shape of the beggar girl streaked away like a whippet. With grim determination in her eyes, Penelope hitched her skirts higher and began to run after her. Tousled heads appeared from the windows of the houses of pleasure; languid young men watched from the doorways and loud guffaws of laughter came echoing down the alley as the noblewoman, with her skirts held high, to expose white stockings and kid boots, chased a beggar girl down the alley. The alley was blind, so at the end of it the fleeing girl turned, ducked swiftly under Penelope's outstretched arm and ran back the way they had come. Breathlessly, Penelope turned, still determined to catch her. But as she did so, a man stepped into her path and grabbed her arm to check her.

'In God's name, Penelope! What are you about?' cried the shocked tones of Charles, Lord Mountjoy.

Penelope could hardly think straight as she looked up into his heavily lashed, astonished brown eyes. 'I want that beggar girl!' she gabbled excitedly. 'Quick, get her! Don't let her escape!'

But Charles' servants had already apprehended the beggar girl and were now dragging her screeching like a throttled hen back down the alley.

'Come, madam,' Charles said firmly to Penelope. 'Let us go inside. We cannot discuss matters out on the street.' And he ordered his men to take the girl into the inn.

Soon Penelope and Charles were seated in a private chamber while outside the door his men still held onto the girl who was swearing and cursing very loudly. As his gentle hand covered Penelope's, a feeling of infinite well-being suffused her. 'I am sorry if I embarrassed you,' she apologised, 'but I simply had to get hold of her.'

Charles smiled warmly. 'I understand, madam,' he said. 'Now compose yourself and I will have her brought in. What has she stolen from you?'

Penelope shook her head quickly. 'Nothing, as far as I am concerned, but she's wearing part of the clothing that belonged to my maid Hawise when she disappeared.'

Charles looked concerned and a little alarmed. 'But can you be so sure? It's almost two years since that happened.'

'Oh! I am sure. Bring her in!' Penelope's composure had fully returned.

The beggar girl grovelled on the floor and wept unrestrainedly. 'I don't know nothing. Someone gave me the dress,' she cried.

'But you must tell me who gave it to you,' Penelope insisted, trying not to frighten the girl any more than she already had. 'Be sensible and I'll reward you well.'

The thought of a reward made the girl's eyes, so deeply sunk in her head, glint greedily. 'A lady gave it to me. She was staying at the inn where I worked.' She looked expectantly at Penelope as though expecting a reward already.

'That's not enough. I need details,' Penelope said firmly.

Charles gave the girl a prod with the toe of his long pointed shoe. 'Come on,' he said with a grin. 'Get on with it or I'll send you to the Fleet. They have a method of extracting information from the likes of you.'

The girl trembled at the thought of torture. 'Oh, I stole it!' She wailed. 'But I did not hurt the lady . . .'

And so, piece by piece, they drew out the squalid story of Hawise's last hours. They sent for the landlord of the inn who was able to identify the girl in spite of those disfiguring pox marks. 'Yes, that's Rosie,' he said. 'And I heard that her companion, Harry, the link boy was hung up in the north, last year.'

Now Penelope began to feel some compassion for

the wretched, quivering girl. Her man had been hung. Perhaps they did not harm Hawise. Shock might have brought loss of memory. It was possible that her maid was still in the area. She threw Rosie a coin. 'Get some food. Don't leave this place, for if I find you have lied, I'll have you arrested.'

Rosie grabbed the coin and fled. Charles was amused and began to laugh but Penelope's face was deathly white. 'I fail to see the humour of the situation,' she said coldly. 'I loved Hawise as a sister. I will not go home again until I have searched the whole neighbourhood for her.'

Charles put an arm about her and held her close. 'Calm down, madam,' he said. 'Let us dine, and then I and my men will assist you in your search.'

After some food and wine, Penelope's good humour and her charm returned. But Charles's personality seemed to have changed, she thought. He was more self-assured and rather arrogant. 'I could not believe my own eyes,' he said, 'when I saw you actually running. It's a long time since I saw a society lady do that.' He chuckled into his ale.

'I am surprised that you recognised me, sir.' Penelope's voice was edged with sarcasm.

Charles knew why, and looked away. 'I know, Penelope,' he said ashamedly. 'I should have called on you.'

'Is it possible that Her Majesty would have objected?' she parried.

Charles shuffled his feet and looked awkward. 'My position at the moment is somewhat difficult.' He made excuses.

'My dear, ambitious lord,' she continued in the same tone. 'I've no wish to impede your progress.'

Charles now ignored the irony and raised her hand to his warm lips. 'My love, don't blame me for being cautious. We both have many enemies at court.'

'You had better concern yourself with your own affairs,' she said loftily, 'for I have nothing to hide.'

Charles looked into her eyes and squeezed her hand gently. 'Well, nothing has changed my love for you,' he said gently.

Touched by a warm glow at his words, she dropped her gaze. Her anger had gone; willingly she let him pull her to him and envelop her in his arms.

Until late evening with Rosie's help, they followed the trail of the lost Hawise, and ended up in a derelict house in Duck Alley. It was an evil-smelling place with a slimy gutter full of swill. Most of the houses in the neighbourhood were empty, with broken doors and windows, and stripped by scavengers. Charles' men conducted them to the house of the nearby beadle. In his clean, comfortable house they rested while a servant went to fetch the local parson.

'The parson is the only person who might remember, sir,' the beadle said. 'I am only a poor, uneducated man. I does my duty, that's all, but he keeps records and such-like. That year there was a bad smallpox epidemic around here. We raided Duck Alley and took away women and children to the pest house.'

'God in Heaven,' broke in Penelope. 'What induces people to live in these conditions?'

'Poverty, my lady,' replied the beadle simply. 'Poverty and cold, grim hunger.'

Soon the parson arrived at the beadle's house. He seemed quite flustered at the sight of the noblewoman and young knight. 'Yes,' he said, 'I do recall a case of a young girl who lay unclothed upon the floor in a house in Duck Alley. She did not have smallpox, but had died from a broken neck. There were marks on her neck as if someone had tried to strangle her.'

Penelope went white as the blood drained from her face in shock. 'Oh, dear God!' she cried. 'My poor, dear Hawise.' There was no hope left.

'It was a filthy house,' continued the parson. 'And an old woman also lay there dead of the pox. At the time, I remember, I had intended to investigate, but there were many deaths and much work to be done, so they were all buried in a mass grave in the churchyard.'

Penelope sat silent and still until the parson had finished his tale. Then she rose. 'I want to see the grave,' she said firmly.

'It's quite a walk, my lady,' said the parson, looking in Charles' direction with a concerned expression on his thin face. This well-dressed woman was obviously pregnant and had no business walking about this low-class area.

'Leave matters as they are, my lady,' urged Charles. 'What good will it do now?'

'No,' she declared, obstinately, 'I have to see where Hawise is laid to rest.'

With Charles holding her gently by the arm, they

walked through the dirty, narrow streets. The parson led the way to an old small church, tucked close to the old city walls. In a remote corner of the churchyard was a heap of earth. This was the communal grave in which they had buried her lovely Hawise among the desolate victims of Duck Alley.

The horror was insupportable. She sank down on her knees as bitter sobs racked her frame. Charles picked her up and held her tight; then he sent his men to commandeer a carriage.

In no time at all he was gently laying her down on the couch in her own hall in front of a blazing log fire. 'Penelope, darling, cease. It breaks my heart to hear you cry.' He kissed her lips, and passed his hand gently over her swollen belly. But, before he could say more, pompous Lord Rich appeared.

'So stupid and wilful,' he grumbled. 'With no thought for my child that she carries.'

Charles stood aside, aloof and proud. But he watched the scene between his white, crushed, beloved and her arrogant lout of a husband with pain in his eyes. Finally, as if unable to stand any more, he quickly took his leave.

Penelope had never been ill before in her life. Always fit and healthy she had only ever been confined to bed in child-birth. But now she rolled about in bed sweating and shivering with a high fever and, to her husband's horror, covered with spots. Robert Rich, terrified of illness, did not come near her and the house was filled with rumours of smallpox or the plague. But it was neither of these dreaded diseases. To everyone's surprise it turned out that Penelope was only suffering from a severe attack of measles.

Once the crisis was over, her health began to improve steadily. She lay convalescing on her couch and began to receive visitors. Young ladies from the court dropped in to pass on gossip and to wail when they were out of favour with their royal mistress. At the root of most of these upheavals was, it seemed, the new favourite, her handsome, headstrong brother Robert who had, apparently, an even more roving eye than his late stepfather.

But when Penelope was alone, her thoughts returned constantly to Hawise, and to the horrors of her last hours. She remembered how thoughtlessly she had insisted that Hawise make the journey to Philip, and how lightly she had dismissed her maid's fears. Murderess, she accused herself, and not only of Hawise. Was she destined to bring death upon others she loved? The burden of guilt seemed too heavy to bear and Penelope fought to escape from under it, as she had done in childhood. Her depression lessened and then vanished as she awaited the birth of the child she was sure was Mountjoy's.

8

Family Affairs

During the weeks when Penelope had lain burning with fever, her husband had not come near, but had sent to the sick chamber all sorts of concoctions that he had mixed himself. She abhorred these homemade remedies. 'Dear God! Does he intend to finish me?' she had cried when some particularly obnoxious mixture had been offered her.

A fairly frequent visitor had been her brother, Robert, now Master of the Queen's Horse and still climbing the ladder of fame. He was becoming indispensable to the ageing queen, whom he reminded so strongly of Leicester, her former flame. This curly-haired youth, whose grace and audacity were the wonder of the age, had tried hard in his generous manner to reconcile his mother with her cousin, the queen, but in vain the Queen continued to refuse to receive Lettice or her daughter at court.

To his sister Penelope, on her convalescent couch, he brought his troubles, and Penelope was pleased to find that the years apart had not damaged their feelings of affection for each other. But the Devereux had always been a close-knit family.

'The court is full of intrigues, Penelope,' he told her,

his fair face very troubled. 'I have many enemies around me.'

'Cecils?' murmured his sister sympathetically.

'Not only the Lord Chancellor, but his weasel-faced son and his cronies, and that wily old seaman Sir Walter Raleigh. One grows very tired of these continuous squabbles,' he told her with a mournful sigh.

'Do not let them defeat your purpose, dear brother,' she encouraged him. 'Use all your opportunities and feather your nest as others have done.'

'That's easier said than done,' he replied. 'I've enough debts to drown me, and Her Majesty keeps tight hold on her purse-strings, I can assure you.'

Penelope nodded. 'Yes. Can I forget how she ruined our dear father after years of loyal service?'

'She is insanely jealous of all the young maidens and, by God, there are some little beauties there this season . . .' His black eyes, so like her own, gleamed at the prospect of bedding some or all of them.

Penelope showed her fine teeth in a slow understanding smile. 'Take care, dear brother,' she said gently, and patted his arm.

The Earl of Essex smiled back and planted a soft kiss on his sister's smooth forehead.

In April, when Penelope had regained her health and the rain had brought forth spring flowers, a small, very dark boy came into the world. His mother gazed apprehensively at this red-faced underweight child, for he had tufts of black hair and his eyes did not open but were red and inflamed and full of pus.

'What's wrong with his eyes?' she gasped.

'It is nothing serious, my lady,' said the nurse. 'He has an infection passed on from your own illness. In time it will pass.'

Nevertheless, each time she looked at this child she felt the chill pang of anxiety. Such a dark little stranger, almost Spanish-looking. Charles was certainly its father. His dark, good looks had come from his Spanish grandmother. But Lord Rich seemed not to notice. He was very proud of his new son whom he saw as another male Rich to share in the spoils he was assiduously accumulating. 'I suggest we call him Walter after your own father,' he said. Penelope smiled secretively and looked down at her babe. 'I'd like to call him Charles,' she said.

Robert Rich pondered this for a moment and then nodded approvingly. 'Well, it's a noble name,' he said. 'Let it be Charles Walter.'

The child was christened with much ceremony. His lace gown was a present from the French court; and Lord and Lady North were his sponsors. But he was a sickly babe who cried incessantly and did not thrive or feed. Penelope soon lost patience with him and handed him over to a wet nurse. She took long rides in the park hoping to meet Charles, but he had gone to Hampton Court with the retinue of the Queen

But her main preoccupation now was that of keeping her husband out of her bed. She was sick of child-bearing. She would have no more children, she decided. She wanted to be with her beloved children at Leighs, but Lord Rich absolutely refused to leave town and forbade her to do so either. Her life was further complicated by the amorous advances of Robert Cecil whom she tried to avoid when she could. He still called on her regularly, in spite of being contracted to marry Cobham's daughter.

In June, the heat was terrific. The whole town lay sweltering in a misty haze. The sour smell of the city rose up and encircled the houses, stifling her and making her long all the more for the clean, sweet air of the countryside. Each morning she would ride across the fields of Marylebone away to the heath high up outside London.

Returning early from her ride one day, she passed a funeral procession of carts loaded with plain, wooden coffins. Large red crosses were painted on their sides. She knew instantly what they meant. 'Dear God,' she muttered, 'the plague.' The further she rode into town, the more shuttered houses she saw with crosses on their doors. And the frightened looks of the few people in the streets told her that the plague had reached epidemic proportions. 'I must get out of town and take the child to safety,' she muttered to herself as she galloped home.

Her husband was away so she did not have to confront him. Losing no time, she packed up the town house, and with baby Charles and her household, she rode out of London to Leighs as the Black Death swept through the city.

As she passed under the stone arch of the gatehouse at Leighs, she was assailed by memories of Hawise and of the day she first entered it as a young bride with her maid. Dark thoughts entered her mind once more and Leighs without Hawise felt intensely lonely.

The children welcomed her boisterously, all anxious to view their new baby brother. Her two elder boys now attended day school in the village and assumed a very adult air in their trim velvet suits and large white collars. The little girls held each other by the hand and were accompanied by their governess, Miss Thorpe, a recent addition to the houschold. Robert had engaged her when travelling abroad. She was a neat, well-built woman who spoke perfect English and fluent German; she professed to be a war widow. Her mouth had a ready smile and the children seemed devoted to her, but she did not try to hide her disapproval of Lady Rich.

Feeling in need of a rest, Penelope handed her new baby over to this capable woman and spent her time in the garden or in her parlour catching up on her correspondence.

Lord Rich wrote at length telling her she had done well to leave the town and escape the plague that was now raging. He instructed her to put guards at the gate to allow no one to enter or leave and to admit no strangers into the estate. He himself was journeying to York and would not come home until the pestilence had passed.

Penelope was delighted by his last remark. She would be free of him for a while, and not live in fear of him visiting her at night.

The plague spread as the summer grew hotter. All the roads out of London were blocked with refugees trying to flee the sickness, but every day soldiers from the noble manors drove them all back into town. Knowing the danger, Penelope took every precaution to protect her own family. Outside the big house at Leighs the pestilence raged, but life went on smoothly on her husband's large estate. Day and night there were armed men at the gate. No food was brought in, no parcels or letters delivered. The family, servants and retainers all existed on their own produce which was quite bountiful. Leighs possessed a large dairy herd and a field of grain, a brewhouse, bakery and many orchards.

Despite the conditions outside, Penelope was happy to be home again. Once more she loved and fussed her children, and daily romped with them in the gardens – much to the disapproval of Miss Thorpe, who seemed to resent her interest in her own children. Meanwhile, the sick and dying lined the roadsides outside. Throughout the land entertainment ceased; even the court was closed as the Black Death took its toll.

During this time Penelope's whole life was her children. The baby Charles now thrived. Those tiny lids had eventually rolled back to reveal black pupils that unfortunately would always be short-sighted. Penelope took great pride and joy in teaching him to walk and talk, and she became very close to this afflicted little one who stumbled into the furniture and clung nervously to her skirt. But, as time went by, Penelope found the loneliness hard to bear – that and the continuous bickering with the governess over the children and with the long-nosed parson who had lived at Leighs so long. She found it very hard to live without any news from the world outside, but no news and no gossip ever reached her. No stranger passed through the gate for two years. One young stable boy, who sneaked out of the estate to visit his love, was not allowed to come back. Instead, he was driven back into the stricken city with the rest of the refugees. It had seemed cruel, but Penelope had had no choice but to give the order; she would take no risks with her family's safety.

At last the plague abated and news reached the gates of Leighs that it was now safe to travel at last. Robert Rich rode back home, very plump and slimy and as demanding as ever. In January he decided that he and Penelope should return to the town house which he had been improving, but again he insisted that the children should remain at Leighs.

London seemed desolate and empty when they arrived. Houses stood empty, grass grew in the streets. But that Robert had very much improved his town dwelling, Penelope could not deny. In an effort to compete with the other great families who lived in the Strand, he had enlarged the house by adding a new wing. A very ornately carved oak staircase led up from the newly decorated hall with its lavishly painted ceiling. Penelope could not help smiling to herself at the signs of her husband's growing self-assurance; the walls and stair rail were literally covered with the Rich coat-of-arms. And Robert continued to flatter and fawn on the great and powerful, flitting from St James's to Essex House, from York House to Durham House, in a sycophantic frenzy that Penelope found disgusting. Her mother, who soon came to visit, agreed that Robert Rich would eventually wear a coronet even if he broke his neck in the pursuit of it.

Lettice was looking healthy and well. To the astonishment of some, but perhaps not of others, she had recently married Sir Christopher Blount who was no older than her own son. The difference in age did not bother her in the least and she seemed extremely happy. As always, she brought Penelope up to date with the gossip of the town.

The most important news was that her son, Lord Essex, was favoured by Her Majesty even more than ever. 'My dear,' gushed Lettice, 'she is loath to be without him. He recently fought a duel with Mountjoy over her, and Robert was wounded in the thigh. The Queen banished them both from the court until they made it up and now, I believe, they are true comrades.'

'These royal goings-on still fail to interest me, Mother,' Penelope said wearily. She had a slight headache and there was a definite limit to the amount of gossip she could listen to.

Lettice was quite put out. Rising indignantly she gathered her skirt. 'I'll be on my way, then,' she said. 'It's about time you learned to control that bitchy tongue of yours.'

Penelope's drawing room once more became the meeting place for court personalities as she took her place among the top Elizabethan hostesses. A delighted Robert shamelessly lavished hospitality on anyone who could further his ends. One night with Essex to supper came Charles, Lord Mountjoy. As Lettice had said, they seemed to have settled their differences and were now constant companions. Charles was gracious and well-poised but extremely cautious. So many had fallen because of their amorous entanglements. Her Majesty liked to keep her young men on a short leash, but now, as he paid his courteous addresses to his beautiful hostess, both he and Penelope knew that their attachment was still mutual, and her heart leaped high in her bosom at the touch of his hand. At her supper table his dark eyes wooed her constantly, and at the gaming table they sat side by side, knowing full well that the hawkish eyes of Robert Cecil surveyed them. But that was as far as it went. Penelope had begun to realise that her impulsiveness had got her into many scrapes. This time Charles would have to make the first move.

Warily, she locked her door each night in case her husband came calling, but he did not bother her. As the season moved on he clung like a limpet to any who could aid his ambitions and his eagerness to beget sons seemed to have died down.

Essex was still unable to get the Queen to receive his mother and sisters at court. Nor did Elizabeth's love for Essex prevent her from slowly milking him of his estates, forcing him to relinquish them to pay the debts to the state that his father had accumulated in defending the realm in impoverished Ireland. Nowadays Essex often looked ill and fatigued, Penelope thought, and his crowd of friends seemed like weights about his neck, always asking and receiving favours from the generous, carefree person that he was.

In April of that year, Robert secretly married the demure Frances. Walsingham, widow of his great friend and comrade-in-arms, Philip Sidney. Once the family heard the news, they were most concerned for him. For a knight of the realm to marry without royal consent was considered treason and the Queen demanded fidelity from her favourites. It did not take long for his enemies at court to inform the queen of his misdeed. The Essex family and friends all waited anxiously for the Queen's anger to run riot. But she surprised them all by forgiving her young Adonis. The truth was that she could not bear to be without him. She needed the treasure of happy, laughing youth to brighten her life, and to ward off the dreaded approach of old age. His new wife, Frances, however, was another matter. The Queen refused to receive her, and forced the newly pregnant wife to live with her mother while she kept Essex at court.

Penelope was outraged by this news. 'Is it even a crime to marry now?' she cried indignantly.

In January 1591, Lord and Lady Rich attended the baptism of their new nephew, Robert Devereux, the future Earl of Essex. The ceremony was held at the grand church of St Olive's in the Strand and many noble families were listed among the guests – Russells, Dudleys, Hobys and Sidneys. As happy as any new father, when they came out of the church, Essex held his son high up in the air for the population to admire. The earl was popular with the man in the street and the waiting crowd let out an enthusiastic cheer, which did not please the jealous queen when she heard about it. Even her favourites could not seek the limelight.

That evening in Essex House, they held a grand family party. These children of mixed fortune were a close-knit family, circling around their beautiful, wayward mother, Lettice. The atmosphere that night was one of hectic gaiety as the generous Devereux welcomed the timid Frances into their bright social circle. All Lettice's children were present – the dark-eyed, moody Penelope, the fair, quick-tempered Dorothy, the studious, red-haired Walter and his new child bride, rosy-cheeked Beth Deakin from the north.

Their illustrious brother, Robert, had spared no expense in the celebration of the baptism of his heir, whom he would never see come of age. The food and drink was limitless, and the music exquisite. In the middle of the evening, the Lord Chamberlain's players presented a play, a hilarious comedy, and then there was feasting, dancing and gambling until dawn.

It was during the play that Penelope exchanged glances with Charles. Her face was flushed with wine and laughter, but he was looking soberly across the room at her. The admiration in his eyes set her heart racing, and she knew for certain that all was not over between them. He was neat and smart in a black silk suit and a scarlet waistcoat, so that he stood out among the social butterflies in their frills and furbelows. Beside him stood young Henry Wriothesly, Earl of Southampton, with his long golden curls, fabulously attired in white-and-gold brocade; the impression this young earl created was almost effeminate, for he was not yet pubescent. And as Wriothesly flicked his long lashes and placed an arm on Mountjoy's shoulder, Penelope was at once seized by a hot, jealous rage, even though she knew that the desire in Charles' eyes was directed only at her.

After the party, the family dispersed. Penelope and her husband returned to St Bartholomew's Square and almost immediately began to quarrel. Robert had been particularly obnoxious during the visit to Essex House and provoked continuous baiting from Lettice who rarely missed an opportunity to mock her foolish son-in-law. Robert Rich had always been terrified of all illnesses and was often trying out all sorts of concoctions and ointments to protect him from dying before his time. The latest concoction was an ointment made up of evil-smelling herbs, which he had smeared all over his body before he came to the party. No one could help noticing the pungent smell that emanated from Lord Rich all evening, least of all Lettice. Penelope was embarrassed for her husband and irritated that her mother had waved her fan violently each time he came near her.

'Oh, goodness me!' she had gasped. 'Whatever is that dreadful smell?' And she had turned to laugh scornfully with her friends.

Now in the small hours, the wounded Robert took out his anger on Penelope and made disparaging remarks about her mother and her new youthful husband. 'Why, Sir Christopher is your stepfather and younger than you!' Robert laughed.

Penelope reacted instantly. 'Why, you oaf! You perked-up little cockscomb. What right have you to criticise my family?'

'The right of your lawful husband,' he sneered in return.

'That's very debatable,' she retorted angrily.

'No fault of mine that I'm your husband,' he scoffed.

'For God's sake. Why don't you set me free?' Arrogantly and striding up and down like a caged animal she hurled abuse at him. 'Why, I hate you. I loathe the very sight of you and that evil smell you carry about with you. I've said it before and I'll say it again: You disgust me, sir.'

Robert Rich winced momentarily, but gathered up his courage. 'I realise that we are incompatible, madam,' he said, without looking at her. 'You can have your freedom because I have no longer any desire to share your bed. I have no need to; I have my three sons. You can do as you please.'

Penelope stopped her pacing suddenly and stared at him in disbelief. Then, as she began to understand, she said, 'Well, well! That is very interesting.' Her slow, sarcastic smile appeared, and then the full, red mouth dropped in a dangerous downward curve. 'We have found ourselves a mistress, have we? One who will put up with your filthy, sadistic habits, no doubt?'

He looked at her sheepishly, but made no denial.

'So now I have your lordship's permission to take a lover. Is it possible that you even have a particular one in mind?' she demanded coldly.

He squinted at her warily. She could see beads of perspiration on his brow.

'Some great lord no doubt,' she continued. 'Possibly someone who will benefit you at court . . .'

He backed away as the flicker in his eyes betrayed him. She knew that she was right.

'Ah,' she said glaring down at him from her greatest height. 'I've guessed it. A certain little fox with a rounded back?' The magnificent eyes held Lord Rich like a rabbit trapped in torchlight and a bejewelled hand lashed out and dealt him a vicious blow across the face. He stepped back, a red weal on his cheek.

'You dirty little pimp!' she screeched furiously. 'If I take a lover, he will be of my own choosing. And it will not be very difficult, I can assure you.' The very idea that she might become the mistress of Robert Cecil had outraged her. The knowledge that Robert Rich was hoping to arrange the alliance made her even angrier.

Lord Rich could obviously take no more. Blood was trickling from his wound. But he backed away now anxiously to escape from his wife's rage. 'I'll have no disgrace brought on my noble name,' he made one last effort to assert himself. But her flashing eyes made him turn and flee from the room.

'What noble name?' she yelled after him. 'Your family have never been anything except foul, money-grabbing traitors.' But he had gone. As the final insult left her lips, she sat down in a heap, exhausted and overwhelmed by her emotions.

Later that week, Penelope's troubles were added to

by the official publication of the sonnets that Philip Sidney had composed for her. Edited by Philip's sister, Mary, the sonnets became the talk of the court. That Lady Rich was the elusive Stella of his most famous sonnets, 'Astrophel and Stella', became universally known. Ladies whispered together behind their fans; men gave her provocative glances; young enterprising poets invaded her privacy; unknown ones sent her long epistles begging her to be their patroness.

Penelope was soon sick to death of all this notoriety and more so of the sneering comments of her husband. And all this talk of Philip revived forgotten memories. She had not read his sonnets before. Philip had only ever read them aloud to her. But now as she began to read them with a new understanding, she realised how passionately he must have loved her. She became depressed and conscious of having somehow failed him. And she began to loathe her husband more than ever before.

To her immense surprise, her only friend and ally concerning this affair was the neglected little wife of Sidney, the small, mousy Frances, now her own sister-in-law. 'Do not allow it to defeat you, my dear,' she said in her soft calm voice. 'Philip loved you with all his heart. Does he not prove it in his writing? It must hurt you to recall your moments together.'

Penelope smiled at Frances, grateful for her generosity. 'You were his lawful wife,' she said. 'I was only his mistress.'

'He died with your name on his lips,' Frances said

sadly. 'I never counted ours as more than a marriage of convenience.'

Filled with emotion, Penelope put her arms about the tiny Frances and embraced her affectionately. 'Forgive me, dear, if I unwittingly caused you unhappiness. You are so generous and life has not been kind to you. Now we are sisters we must take care of each other.'

And so the two women embraced warmly, beginning a friendship that was to last for the rest of their lives. Secretly, in the spring, Frances left town, supposedly for her mother's country house. Instead, accompanied by Penelope and some loyal servants, she took her two children – her daughter Elizabeth by Sidney, and Robert, son of Essex – and travelled to Wanstead, now the property of her husband, under the will of his stepfather, Lord Leicester.

They journeyed through the night so that it was in the red, rosy light of dawn that they passed under the tall elms that lined the drive. As the white Gothic portals of the great house rose to greet them, a feeling of well-being possessed Penelope. It was always the same at Wanstead; she did feel at home there.

'Why, how lovely it is!' exclaimed Frances as she espied the shining lake and the flowering lawns for the first time.

'Yes, it is lovely,' replied Penelope, 'and I envy you, Frances. I've always been so happy here. It's a good, peaceful house.'

'Share it with me, dear sister,' cried Frances, holding Penelope's hand. They smiled warmly at each other. Frances had meant what she said.

The early spring beauty of the landscape outside made them unprepared for the depressing gloom of the interior. The rooms were silent and empty with only a few old servants pottering about. Gone was the bright gaiety of her mother's time; the bare, high walls had been stripped of their sumptuous fittings; no paintings or tapestries hung on the walls, and no silver armour or gold plate gleamed in the sunlight. All the treasures that Leicester had acquired had been sold off to pay his debts to the Queen

'Oh dear,' sighed Penelope as she looked around the great hall. 'The Queen had the place picked clean, but do not despair,' she consoled Frances. 'I'll soon set things right.'

Penelope was always able to muster a huge amount of energy in any crisis and she did it now in her efforts to turn Wanstead back into a beautiful home. She issued orders to all the servants to fetch everything for their immediate needs. And a coachman was dispatched to London so that the store and larder could be restocked.

To her delight, on inspecting the state of the stables, Penelope found that her mother's old grey mare was still there, having been put out to pasture. In no time at all, she was riding out once more through the forest glades as she had done in her youth. Once more, memories of her lost Hawise haunted her. But the heavy guilt was fading and she wondered if Frances could ever fill the vacant spot in her heart. She suspected not. Frances was lovable, but very soft and weak. Penelope had already begun to lose a little patience with her at times.

Most of the servants who had served Wanstead for many years had all been dispersed to avoid undue expense. In no time at all Penelope had gone to the village and rooted them out – gardeners, cooks and serving maids. Within a week, the great house was running on oiled wheels once more and Penelope supervised the cooking, cleaning and washing until the house shone and smelt fresh and clean. And all the while, the real mistress of the house, Frances, sat with a demure expression on her face, her hands folded on her lap, watching and waiting for the promised visit of her lord when he could detch himself from the possessive queen.

Days and weeks went by and still Essex did not come. Frances would cry herself to sleep each night, while in the next-door chamber, Penelope would sit up writing letters to her mother, or to the governess at Leighs asking after her children, for she was terrified that they would forget her. She particularly missed the love of small, afflicted Charles. Without her children, and especially in the country, she did not feel complete.

Eventually, late one night, Essex did arrive, looking tired and travel-stained. He was accompanied by none other than Lord Mountjoy. As the men entered the hall, Penelope and Frances stood at the top of the marble stairs watching them. Letting out a delighted cry, Frances suddenly catapulted down the stairs into the arms of her husband while Penelope stayed where she was, as still as a statue. As Charles removed his wet cloak, his warm brown eyes roamed appreciatively about the great hall to rest on the figure of Penelope in a fine scarlet robe. She looked calm but a world of passion shone from her magnificent black eyes. Had she not returned to Wanstead because she had known he would come to her there?

That evening the four of them ate together. Frances was clearly very excited by the presence of her beloved lord and husband, and Penelope sat looking beautiful and serene. Only a slight trembling of the lips betrayed the desire that burned fiercely beneath her cool exterior.

Essex had contracted some mysterious fever some weeks earlier, and still looked very ill. He talked continuously of his intentions to get royal permission to take an army into France but Charles was silent and looked rather bored as if he had heard it all so often before. Penelope eyed him from a distance; she gazed on his handsome, dark-tanned skin, his heavily lidded eyes, and thought that she loved him even more.

When Charles entered her bedchamber later that night, a pale, silvery moon lit up the room. Penelope had been waiting for him. She stood breathlessly by the half-opened door, arms outstretched and her body throbbing with passion. Then the world outside ceased to exist. Hidden by the rich hangings on the four-poster bed, two souls became as one. This was her man. He loved her as much as she loved him. Never again would she feel lonely and unwanted.

After a few days, the restless Essex left Wanstead to ride to Chartley, his childhood home, to recruit more men for his forthcoming French campaign. He was quite unconcerned when his friend elected to stay at

Wanstead and await his return. 'You will be in good hands, I trust,' he said with a wink, and he rode off with a daredevil grin on his face, as his distraught wife retired to her chamber to weep her heart out.

Every day Penelope rode out on to the high weald with her lover, the gentle, courteous Charles, out into the open country where she had always found peace. One day they stood poised high on a hill, looking down into the valley. 'It's a beautiful spot,' Charles murmured thoughtfully, as he looked from the dark, mysterious forest in the east to the rich green, undulating meadows in the west.

Penelope laughed gaily and hung on to his arm. 'I knew you would like it here. It's my favourite place. Oh, how happy I am, Charles,' she exclaimed. 'You make me so happy.' Tears rose to her eyes.

Gently, he held on to her hands and looking straight at her, said very seriously, 'I wish that you may always find happiness, my love. The only regret I have is that I cannot be with you constantly to cherish and protect you for ever.'

'Such sentiment from you, my lord! It amazes me,' she scoffed lightly. She spoke with the habitual ironic humour, which she used to defend her pride.

'I love you, Penelope, as I never loved another,' he told her very soberly.

She stared at him, her heart beating swiftly with joy.

'I am not as other men at court,' he continued. 'I have no inclination to lie with the maids there. I value my healthy body and would not risk disease but you I cannot resist.'

The magic of the moment had been shattered by Charles' insensitive words. A sarcastic smile curved her lips. 'You are perfectly safe with me, sir,' she mocked. 'I do not even provide for my own husband.'

Remounting quickly, she gave her horse a good, hard whack and rode rapidly home. She was not really angry but rather sad that Charles was not a bit more romantic.

In the morning, Essex returned from Chartley to collect his friend. After saying goodbye to their women, the two soldierly figures rode off side by side. Spring had long gone and the flowers in the garden lay wilted and scorched by the hot summer sun. The weeks went by slowly and Penelope idled her time away at Wanstead without any more visits from her lover who was now with Essex in France. Frances was slightly more sociable now that she was pregnant once more, but she suffered from bad headaches and spent the long, hot days lying in a cool, shady room. Oblivious to the heat, Penelope spent her days riding through the forest or wandering through the lovely gardens of the magnificent house. All the signs told her that Charles with his loving had left her pregnant once more. But she did not care; having children was no problem as far as she was concerned.

One day she received one of her husband's long complaining letters. It accused her of neglecting him and her children, and informed her, with great self-importance, that he had been elected to go on an embassy to France. And it was essential, he wrote, that she return home immediately to manage the affairs of his many manors. Penelope was loath to leave Wanstead, but Robert now had her dowry tied up in his deals and she was sure that he would find some way of swindling her if she did not return. It all needed careful thought for it was a very complicated situation. He had no doubt found sexual satisfaction elsewhere, but still apparently had every intention of utilising her efficient energy for his own ends.

Then she thought of Charles and she became confused about what to do. Her lover really needed her, but he was so terrified of jeopardising his position at court and the ambitions he had worked so hard to achieve. Now here, within her was another small life, waiting until it was ready to be born into a world of uncertainty. One thing she was sure about: if this child was a male, she might even be able to persuade Charles to acknowledge him as his own. It was done even in the best of families. Had not her own late stepfather claimed responsibility for his illegitimate son and had not society accepted the fact? She was reminded again of a conversation she once had with Charles. She had been in one of those deep, pensive moods, when he had asked her: 'Tell me, Penelope, is Charles my son?'

She turned to him with a charming smile. 'Why, surely you must know that. He's the very image of you.'

Charles looked away as a sad expression crossed his face. 'It has always been my intention to beget a son to inherit my noble name. What a pity! I wish I could be sure that I fathered him.'

'Why, my dearest,' she said with light laugh. 'Do you not trust me?'

'I love you, Penelope, very sincerely,' he had replied. 'But I'd be a fool to trust you in matters which you cannot be sure of yourself.'

His words had hurt her deeply then and she had never forgotten them. This time she would make sure that she could prove the paternity of this little one by staying on at Wanstead until it arrived. Robert, in his chagrin, would deny this child, male or female, and then Charles would have no alternative but to step forth and protect her. Bravely she schemed, but turning over in her mind was the thought that if it was a girl her lover might not be willing to make that sacrifice. It could be the end of his career so far as the queen was concerned. Meanwhile, Penelope could do nothing but wait.

The next day she received a long letter from her mother who said that she had been staying in town, but was on her way back to Drayton Bassett now that the court had moved up to York because the dreaded plague had returned again to the city of London.

Penelope did not take much notice of her mother's letter, and that afternoon she rode into the village to collect some necessary supplies for the household. Travelling in a small waggonette driven by a groom, as they passed the village pump, she saw a small crowd had gathered. As usual, she surveyed them without interest. All news was exchanged round the village pump and today there did not seem to be undue agitation. But within a second, they had all dispersed, fleeing in every direction. Astonished by such a sight, Penelope called the driver to a halt. There she saw a grim procession coming down the road towards them, a long line of weeping mourners around a cart piled high with coffins.

'God in Heaven!' she gasped. Never had she thought to see such a procession here.

'Get back home quickly!' she commanded her driver. 'The plague has come to Wanstead.'

Later that day, she breathlessly helped the weeping Frances to pack up her belongings and children.

'Go immediately to your mother's house,' Penelope said. 'Do not go near any town. Take your mother and then all of you go to Chartley. My brother would never forgive me if I allowed his son to run the risk of infection.'

'But Penelope, where will you go?' wailed Frances.

'To my children, of course. Someone must protect them.'

Once she had seen off her sister-in-law, Penelope packed up her own belongings and, with her servants, rode off through the night to Leighs.

9

Come Live With Me And Be My Love

For three more long years the plague raged fiercely up and down England, and again Penelope remained at Leighs virtually imprisoned within the sheltering walls. Again the gates were bolted and barred and armed men patrolled the grounds to prevent the entrance of intruders.

The enterprising young Essex had squandered another army out in France and returned to the bosom of his queen. Up in York, in the safety of the court, he enjoyed in secret the lovely maids-in-waiting, with whom it was always his inclination to dally. Robert Rich had returned from France, but had remained up north with the Shrewsburys, not daring to come any closer to the blighted city of London. During those years of pestilence the grass grew in the streets there, the whole social whirl had disappeared because entertainment was forbidden, and whole families were wiped out.

For Penelope and her family, life flowed peacefully and placidly by. Her two elder sons were becoming very grown-up. A tutor was preparing them for public school, where they would go when it was safe to leave the confines of Leighs. Her daughters were lovely.

There was tall, willowy Lettice with her dazzling red hair; small, blonde Isabella who was thoroughly spoiled and demanding but also charming; and the tiny new baby, born a few months after Penelope had returned to Leighs.

But it was her youngest son, Charles, who still gave her the most pleasure. At four years old he was still thin and weedy, and his velvet-brown eyes did not see very well. He was backward in his speech and stumbled nervously against the furniture. Penelope thought of him affectionately as her little lame duck, and she took him right into her heart, loving and fussing him, and endeavouring to teach him to speak more clearly, and guiding his faltering steps around the room. She enjoyed countless hours playing with little Charles and her relationship with him made the long stay at Leighs worthwhile. Even when she gave birth to her last child, Charles was still her baby, clinging to her skirts. There had been an air of quiet mystery about the new little one, and Penelope had named her Essex, after her illustrious brother.

Thus, when the plague finally abated and it was safe to travel again, Robert Rich returned home to find that the cuckoo had invaded his nest once more. No amount of probing, sneering or threatening would make his wife reveal the name of the child's father. Unperturbed by his abuse, Penelope made her contempt for him obvious. Her dark eyes held his trapped as she coldly announced, 'It's a wise child that knows its own father.'

Slowly the towns came back to life as everyone

– rich and poor – began to rebuild their lives after
three years of disaster. Complete families had gone,
they had either left the country or been wiped out by
the sickness. Among the aristocracy, there were plenty
to take their place, and it was not long before the fighting and bickering between the factions at the royal
court had begun again in earnest. And at the centre of
this new society was the young Earl of Essex, who,
after several brilliant victories in battle, was now a
mature and very famous man. His home, Essex House,
was the centre of the new society, and he entertained
lavishly, heaping favours on his followers and support-
ers with liberal generosity.

His sister was not there to join in with the festivities.
At Leighs, the Essex marshalands were in flood. The
weather was cold and the general atmosphere very
depressing. Every day Lady Rich gazed out over the
waterlogged grounds and longed for the bright lights
of London. Now almost thirty, she had visibly aged
during her long stay at Leighs. Her hips were wider,
and her face was fuller, but she still possessed the same
flamboyant beauty that had brought her fame – the
alabaster skin, the dark, brooding eyes, and the full red
mouth that turned down discontentedly at the corners
as she looked out on the desolate scene. It was soul-
destroying for her to live in a Puritan community,
coping with her cold, sneering husband and his peculiar habits, quarrelling incessantly with Miss Thorpe
over the children. Lazy fun-loving Penelope could not
bear it for much longer. Word would reach her of the
great happenings in town – parties, plays and many

grand events. Were not her brother and Charles at the centre of them all and thoroughly covering themselves in glory? Whereas here she was, drab and untidy, with a child always hanging to her skirts. Desparingly she dreamed of flags flying, trumpets blaring, mounts rearing, shining armour and handsome men.

Until her pompous little husband returned, she had not been unhappy at home with her children, but now his presence turned Leighs into a place of misery for her. Quite apart from his own irritating behaviour, he had packed her two elder sons off to a school and encouraged the girls to prefer the company of Miss Thorpe to hers. And much to Penelope's distress, the governess had made pious little prigs of them both. A coarse jest or a foul oath from Penelope in a moment of provocation would make them register their disapproval of her. They told her repeatedly that it was wicked to play cards or even to sew on the Sabbath. God would surely punish her if she continued to sin, they warned.

Penelope loved them but this Puritan upbringing was more than she could tolerate. At least there was always her little Charles by her side clutching a beloved wooden soldier, his deep-set eyes so beseeching. She looked down at him now and patted his head as she pondered for a while. This child really needed her, but how much longer could she bear the life at Leighs? She began to think with sensuous pleasure of the tough muscles and creamy skin of her lover Mountjoy. To the devil with Lord Rich, she thought. She would return to town and take small Charles with her. He would fret if she left him behind and besides, was he not the link that bound her to Lord Mountjoy?

On an impulse, she began to prepare for her journey. Robert could not stop her going; he was in Chelmsford, in his capacity as justice of the peace, judging a long-drawn-out witch trial. This time she would travel in style, taking the family coach with its six fine bay horses, the oldest and most esteemed of the coachmen, two serving maids, her complete wardrobe and all her jewels.

The inquisitiveness of Miss Thorpe was aroused at the extent of her preparations. She hovered around, her sharp face pinched with curiosity. 'Are you taking a long trip, madam?' she asked.

Penelope stopped her packing and glared at the governess. How she detested this long-nosed Puritan! And she was quite sure that Miss Thorpe was a household spy for her husband. 'It's none of your business,' she snapped. 'Kindly confine yourself to affairs of the nursery.'

Miss Thorpe bristled indignantly at the snub, but she went on her way, her mouth in a grim line. It looked as if her ladyship was going for good, she thought. Lord Rich would be informed.

Having gathered together all her belongings, Penelope collected small Charles and left for London. She sat in the bouncing coach, rosy-cheeked and breathless with excitement, feeling like a young bride eloping to her lover. Wondering where she should go, she knew that it would not be possible to go to St Bartholomew's Square, for her husband had let it. With his shrewd business sense he overlooked no opportunity of making money. So she decided to go to Essex House. Frances would welcome her, she was positive of that.

London had a strange desolate air about it as the coach ploughed through seas of mud. A grey mist hung over the neglected houses and many of the streets were quiet. But as they came into the vicinity of Essex House, the noise emanating from it and the bright, swinging lanterns outside distinguished it from all others. The other noble residences lay quiet and empty, but here, in the centre of the Strand, Lord Earl Marshall, Robert of Essex, held a court that competed with the Queen's in its sumptuousness.

At the sight of Penelope, Frances extended a very warm welcome to both her and young Charles who was soon installed in the nursery with his cousins. Later, in a small cosy parlour the two women talked, catching up on all that had happened over the last three years. Penelope was struck by how much Frances had changed physically. She was thinner and seemed even tinier than before. Her thin brown hair was flecked with grey and the pain lines in that sweet face told their own story. Penelope was quite shocked and saddened to hear that Frances had had several miscarriages lately and had lost one son in the plague. Penelope also knew that, according to court gossip, all was not well between Essex and his wife; a certain court beauty, known as fair Bee, was back on the scene. But as always, the placid Frances did not complain or bewail her fate. She just sat quietly listening to Penelope's long tale of the misdeeds of Lord Rich.

'Stay here as long as you want, dear,' her sister-in-law said. 'I'm sure you'll find much to amuse you,' she added with some bitterness.

Penelope's stay in Essex House proved to be very invigorating. Fresh air blew in from the Thames at the back gate over the busy landing-stage and the motley throng of boats and elaborate barges. There was much coming and going, for many visitors from St James's and Richmond Palace came down the river to call on his lordship. The house was a hive of activity and Essex had fitted out various apartments to house his numerous friends. The two Bacon brothers almost lived there and Fulke Greville, his layabout cousin, seldom went to his own home. Endless foreign ambassadors paid fleeting visits. The whole pattern of life was varied and exciting and cost a small fortune.

Penelope plunged eagerly into this whirl of social activity, so hungry was she after those dull years at Leighs. Every day there was a grand array of shows and parties with visits to the surrounding noble houses and entertaining in return. She was a good asset to her ambitious brother. Her warm, vivacious personality made her a charming hostess in comparison to the faded, unhappy Frances.

After a while, their mother came to visit. Lettice was ageing but she still had her lively, bitter humour. She was highly painted, her hair was dyed bright red and laden with jewels. Accompanying her was Dorothy, who was more mature but sad having lost her beloved husband, Tom, in a riding accident. She was now unhappily married to the moody, drunken Thomas

Percy, Earl of Northumberland. And so, except for the gentle, studious Walter, who sadly had gone to his death in France, the Devereux were all together again. Although Robert of Essex was the highest in the land, his own family always came first with him. At twenty-seven he was tall, thin and frail; his shoulders were slightly hunched and he always wore a harassed expression as if the yoke of favourite were too heavy for him to bear.

All through the winter, into the spring, the merry-go-round kept turning. Penelope was often made to feel quite dizzy with the balls, cards and late nights. And there were the attentions of the young gallants who surrounded Essex. Each one hoped to be knighted by him, for Essex, in a haphazard fashion, had knighted many of his friends, much to the dismay of the Queen and the chagrin of his enemies. He, however, quite impervious to the storm clouds gathering, made merry while he could.

Penelope was now content and secure in her love affair with the serious-minded, chivalrous Mountjoy, who was very much the right-hand man of her brother. Charles, in turn, was completely absorbed in his beautiful mistress. Night after night he sent a heavily hung barge to bring her secretly along the Thames to his house in Savoy Hill. She bloomed like a full-blown rose in the sunshine of this illicit love. But, as always, her happiness was to be short-lived.

Lord Rich suddenly moved back into town, re-opened his grand house in St Bartholomew's Square and began to snoop about with a cruel smile on his ugly face, hoping to catch Penelope in the arms of her lover. If he could do this he could denounce her publicly as an adultress. The common people put their erring young maidens in the stocks and aimed filth at them; high society had other methods, but they were just as devastating.

On hearing of Lord Rich's arrival in London, the wary Mountjoy moved swiftly out of town, on the excuse that by royal command he had been made governor of Portsmouth Castle and that such a royal favour would be most detrimental to refuse.

Penelope was desolate without him, but consoled herself with her brother's new guest, a lively Spanish gentleman, called Señor Perez, who had been a spy for both sides in the fighting. He had escaped from a Spanish prison and was now receiving great hospitality from Essex for information received. Both Essex and his sister enjoyed his vivacious company but they soon discovered that he was a homosexual.

'He prefers the bed of the Bacon brothers to mine, thank God,' Penelope gaily informed the rather shocked Frances. But the Spaniard was useful to her brother, so she felt it was her duty to cultivate and amuse him and this she did very well.

After a while, Lord Rich began to change his tactics. Once he realised that among all her admirers, only Mountjoy was his wife's lover he became wary of offending the great Earl of Essex, for was not Mountjoy his much-respected comrade in arms? Instead of the continuous spying, therefore, he sent officials to remove her son Charles from her care.

Penelope, in her high-handed manner, sent them all packing.

The next visit to his wife was a personal one. This time his approach was one of entreaty but with him were gentlemen whom Penelope recognised as lawyers to witness the conversation. As confidently as ever, she informed him that she had no intention of parting with Charles.

'I warn you, madam, I wish to educate my own son,' Lord Rich's shrill voice cried. 'And I shall take legal proceedings to make sure that I do.'

'You cannot be sure if he is your son,' she jeered.

His unpleasant face paled. 'Now, madam,' he said nervously, 'you and I know he is my son.'

'Prove it!' she retorted.

Robert had begun to perspire, and she knew that she was wounding him deeply.

Now his voice rose in temper. 'Have I not taken one bastard of yours under my roof without reproach? This child I claim as my own. He must be returned to Leighs and brought up in the company of his blood brothers. I command it!' he screeched.

Penelope looked away as a slow smile, designed to infuriate him, curved her lips. 'I won't let him go,' she said simply.

'By God!' he gibbered. 'I'll fight you. Neither you nor your illustrious brother can afford a scandal. I'll take you to the highest court in the land,' he threatened.

Penelope held her own temper in check and continued to mock him as he stormed on, but inwardly she was worried. There was no legal protection for a woman in a case of this sort. If he went to court she would be condemned as a whore. And then Essex would not support her.

Her fears were confirmed later that day when she sought advice from her brother. 'Look here, Penelope,' Essex said loftily. 'I don't condemn you. I am a father of an illegitimate child myself. If Mountjoy wants to load you up with children, he had better come forward and acknowledge them, but I'm afraid you will have to let this child go. It's the law of the land. You do not stand a chance of defeating Lord Rich.'

After a week or two, Penelope's mind began to waver. Her best-loved child was still tugging at her heart-strings, but Lord Rich persisted. He soon visited her again, this time waving a court order. 'But, of course, if you wish to return home to your rightful position and bring my son with you,' his squeaky voice continued, 'I will drop all proceedings.'

'Get out of my sight!' she shouted irritably. 'I'll bring Charles back in the morning.'

'My sincerest thanks, madam.' He bowed low, an unpleasant smirk of triumph on his mean features.

She had a sudden desire to rush at him and tear his hair out, but she stood still, looking calm and proud until he had left. And when the fury of her temper dissolved into tears, Frances came to comfort her, while little Charles came and held tightly on to her arms. 'I don't like Papa,' he said expressively.

She cuddled him close. 'Oh, dear,' she sighed. 'We do have to go back home, my darling.'

Like a bird which had been freed from its cage, she

was about to return to captivity. Unable to bear the thought, she vowed that she would find another way to escape, down to Portsmouth, perhaps, and providing that Charles still wanted her. She felt depressed, sick and headachy, and nothing could comfort her.

That evening, she went to a new play, accompanied by Señor Perez, her Spanish escort. From the theatre she went on with him to a gaming house and came home at dawn. But her thoughts were of Charles and the enforced separation from him and upon the misery of returning to her husband.

Next afternoon, she returned home to St Bartholomew's Square. There was no red carpet of welcome as she trailed desolately up the ornate staircase holding Charles by the hand. Robert Rich kept his distance, but produced a tutor for the boy, who was whisked away to a back room. For much of the afternoon, she could hear his little voice in the distance, raised in protest as he demanded to see his mother.

Unhappily, she lay back on her bed with her weary head on the pillow, and placed an arm across her aching eyes. Then, suddenly, she noticed a red blotch on her white skin. She rose, went to the mirror and to her horror saw that her face was covered with a maze of scarlet blotches. 'Oh my God!' she cried. 'I've got smallpox. Get the physician!' she cried to the maid, almost fainting with fright.

The physician came quickly and immediately confirmed that she had smallpox. He told her that she must go into quarantine, and Charles was to be removed from the house. In the midst of a raging delirium, she heard the protesting wails of her son as they marched him off away on the long journey to Leighs. Then for seven weeks she was imprisoned in her own quarters with only two women to take care of her. On Lord Rich's instructions, his home-brewed remedies were used on her. The one that was particularly irksome to her was the draping of the windows in red flannel. This, according to his lordship, would prevent the skin from getting permanently marked. She often demanded for it to be taken down, but the hard-faced women had received their instructions and ignored her complaining. 'Piffle!' screeched Penelope. 'Take the damned things down. I'm stifled for fresh air.' But they took no notice.

It is possible that the cranky Lord Rich knew more than Penelope had given him credit for, for at the end of her stay in bed, she had recovered without a blemish on her lovely face.

Throughout that time he was also kind to her, sending in fruit and items of news from the court. But he did not come near; he was too afraid of the infection himself.

The summer had disappeared and given way to rainy autumn by the time she came down the stairs once more. She was pale and slightly thinner, but she had not lost one bit of her proud, haughty demeanour. She lay on her convalescent couch in the small parlour and began to receive visitors once more.

Lettice dropped by, breathless and blustering after a session of gossip-gathering and visits to her numerous relatives around the Strand. 'Oh, how fortunate you were, my dear,' she said to Penelope as she arrived. 'Not a spot, not a blemish.' She peered inquisitively into her daughter's sober face. 'My goodness, when I think of poor Mary Sidney, I realise how lucky you are. She wore a mask for the rest of her days. I was so anxious that I indeed dreaded visiting you,' she admitted.

Her daughter was hardly listening to her mother's chatter for she was thinking of her lover Charles. She had heard that he was back at court and she was aching for a sight of him.

'Your brother is planning another campaign,' gossiped her mother. 'And it's possible that Lord Mountjoy will accompany him. As will your loving husband, or so I hear,' she added spitefully.

'Lord Rich to sail with Essex!' Immediately Penelope cheered up and began to take an interest. 'It's very interesting,' she said thoughtfully. 'That little toad would never risk his neck at sea unless there was something very worthwhile in it for him.'

'With a bit of ingenuity and a lot of luck, he might disappear overboard,' Lettice jested.

'Where are they bound for?' enquired her daughter.

'On to some remote Spanish island,' replied Lettice. 'And all the young gallants are falling over themselves to sail with Essex. They're actually paying good money to join this venture; every fool expecting to be knighted.'

Penelope suddenly felt concern for her foolhardy brother. How long would it be before their avaricious ruler brought him low? It sounded as if he were becoming rather too high and mighty.

With a small hand mirror she carefully examined her face and smoothed her unwrinkled skin. Yes, she supposed she had been very lucky. She had mocked Lord Rich with his fads and pills, but she supposed she ought to be really grateful to him. If she had been terribly pock-marked, she would have never faced her lover again.

Her mother's shrill voice broke in on her thoughts. 'For the Lord's sake, cheer up, Penelope. You're about to get rid of your husband for several years and you still have your lovely looks to charm another.'

Her mother's cheerful banter was slowly getting on her nerves. 'I thought you said you had an urgent appointment, Mother,' she said gloomily.

Lettice rose majestically, wounded by Penelope's remarks. 'All right,' she said. 'I can take a hint. You always were a little vixen, even in the best of health.' With that parting shot her elegant mother drifted out.

Penelope lay still, dreamily longing for the ardent embrace of her lost lover. What would she not give at that moment for the comfort of Charles' arms? Her pride would not allow her to send a message to him. Had he not deserted her in her hour of need? She lay sick and faint with apprehensive longing when, as if by telepathy, a discreet manservant entered with a crested note on a silver salver. She snatched at it with trembling hands, and broke the ancient seal of the crest of the Mountjoys. Her lips moved as she read it: *I must speak with you alone. I am waiting in my coach outside.*

Within moments, Penelope had run down the marble stairs and was locked in Charles' close embrace.

'It is hopeless,' he whispered urgently between their kisses. 'I simply cannot survive without you, Penelope.' His tears ran onto her hands as she tenderly caressed his worried face.

'Oh, my lover,' she returned. 'How happy I am to be in your arms again.'

Charles pulled the window hanging closer. 'Let's go to my house,' he murmured. 'It will be safer there.'

Willingly she went with him, cuddling up close, until they reached his house at the top of Savoy Hill. Instantly, he carried her to bed and they made love as never before, with passion, lust and gentle tenderness.

'It broke my heart to think of your beauty being destroyed,' Charles said afterwards, all but in tears. 'I kneel in homage,' he cried, going down on his knees beside her.

Penelope was lying full-length and naked upon the bed. Placing her hands behind her thick hair, she looked down at her toes. Some devil within her tempted her and the coal-black mirrors of her soul looked steadily at him. 'I belong to you, sir,' she said slowly and deliberately. 'To none other. So why can't you gather enough courage to face up to Lord Rich?'

Charles avoided her gaze and looked distinctly uncomfortable.

'Declare to the world that I am your mistress and I shall be content,' she said.

With her challenge thrown down before him Charles became more evasive. 'My love,' he cried taking her hand in his. 'I am due to sail away to sea, possibly for a long voyage. How can I make such a hasty decision?'

Penelope pulled her head away. 'You are a moral coward, sir,' she accused him.

He bowed his head sheepishly. 'Yes. You may be right, Penelope. As you say, I am a coward in such matters, but I would not go away and leave you to face the consequences of such an act. I am going on active service; there is always a possibility that I might never return.'

Penelope sniffed and stared at him scornfully. 'Have I not already faced such a condemnation from society every time I have your child within me?' she cried.

He hung his head, his brown eyes extremely sad. 'Don't add to my anxieties, Penelope, I beg of you,' he pleaded.

The magic had gone, and she knew it was useless to try to persuade him. Slowly, she began to dress while he sat head in hands and with furrowed brow.

'Then this must be our last farewell, my love,' she said, 'because I can no longer stand this life of secrecy. Each day I grow older. Soon the bloom will have gone from the apple and you will look elsewhere.'

'Oh, don't speak like that, Penelope. Don't belittle our love,' he begged.

'The answer is in your hands,' she told him, coldly.

'I swear to you, darling,' he cried, 'that if by some chance I can avoid taking this long voyage we will go away together, down to my own country home in Devon. I'll give up court life and become a farmer. We will leave the world behind. Will you come with me and be my love?' He held her hand to his lips, his eyes searching hers as he awaited her reply.

'You know full well that I will,' she said, 'but I also know that fate will never grant me such a favour. I'll still be here, a bright social butterfly with other fools queuing for my attentions.'

'Penelope!' He sounded quite shocked. 'Don't be so bitter.'

'I'm sorry,' she said sharply, 'but that is just how I feel.'

Taking her cloak, she swung it violently about her shoulders and stalked off, leaving her gloomy lover behind and all alone.

Her husband was standing in the hall when she got back home. With hands behind his back, he greeted her with a leer. 'I trust you are now fully recovered, madam,' he sneered.

But Penelope was too distraught to rise to the bait. She pushed past him without a word and retired to the sanctity of her own chambers where she remained for the next two weeks. She refused to see her husband at all but after a while, she accepted visitors. There was a long, weeping visit from Frances who was now eaten up with jealousy of the maids at court. Then her sister came to see her after having quarrelled with her drunken husband. Finally, her cousin Elizabeth Vernon appeared – another dark Devereux beauty, but a shocking simpleton. She told Penelope and Dorothy of how she was enamoured of the perverse young Earl of Southampton, Henry Wriothesly. Declaring that she was dying of love, she wept a sea of tears at their feet because the ageing Queen had fiercely objected to this union and had driven them both from the court.

'Everything is so gloomy,' remarked Dorothy once their cousin had left. 'Nothing seems as bright as it used to be.'

'It's probably because we have all grown up at last and found that the world is not quite how we saw it as children,' Penelope said philosophically.

Once more the war-mongering Essex sailed off with Her Gracious Majesty's blessings to put an end to the Spanish dogs. Once more he took with him many young men of noble families, each one determined to obtain laurels under the banner of the valiant Lord of Essex. With him went his friend Mountjoy. And also with him this time went his unpopular brother-in-law, Robert Rich. This perverse little man was fully convinced he could sail into the sunshine with his famous relations; the Spanish treasure ships were an added inducement. His great kinsman, the Earl of Essex, as impoverished as always, had been very grateful for the financial aid provided by the wealthy Lord Rich, so that to Penelope's great satisfaction, her husband sailed off to the islands on the long voyage that might take two years.

A couple of weeks after the fleet had been due to sail, Penelope was still at St Bartholomew's Square. Now feeling the freedom given her by her husband's absence, she could not make up her mind whether to travel to Leighs or stay in town, and she had a feeling of inner happiness as if there were special days ahead.

She dressed in a loose gown of a brilliant shade of

pink, delighting in the feeling of freedom the flowing robes gave her limbs. 'It cheers me up,' she informed her maid as she wrapped it about her ample bosom. She wore the gown – and little else – all day. Her burnished mane hung down below her waist. With her sloe-black eyes and full red mouth, she still had the voluptuous beauty that had dazzled so many in her youth.

Outside the house, the storm that had been raging for two weeks continued. The rain poured down in torrents and a wild wind tore across the country and surrounding seas. That day the Thames rushed flood-tide through the City and news reached St Bartholomew's Square that a rough coastal gale had driven Essex's grand fleet off its course.

But despite the weather and the bad news, Penelope's spirits remained high. The rain had died down a little, and so she stood on the balcony of her town house and looked down the hill towards the end of the Strand and St Paul's. In the depths of her mind, the certainty that this was a special day persisted.

A heavy gust of wind carried a host of raindrops dancing along the street. Apart from a few beggars huddled in doorways, the street was deserted, although an occasional carriage would drive in or out of the ostentatious gateways further down the street.

Dreamily, Penelope surveyed the dreary scene, wondering vaguely why her heart felt so light. Then her eye suddenly caught sight of a figure walking laboriously up the hill, fighting against the wind and hanging on to his wide-brimmed hat with both hands.

Instantly her heart leapt; the figure looked just like Charles. But that was impossible, she told herself. He was miles away at sea. Yet how like him this man was, with the same tall, heavily built shape. She shook her head, blinked and looked again. It had to be some figment of her imagination. Now she could see a familiar dark suit and scarlet waistcoat. He had to be some royal messenger on an urgent errand. Vainly, she tried to dismiss her excitement. As he came nearer the man removed his hat and placed it under his arm. A tuft of black beard on his chin blew about in the wind and his dark hair was swept back from his brow. Penelope gasped. It was him! But why was he walking? Mountjoy never set foot on the ground if he could ride. Something was amiss.

Now he had reached the front steps of the house and was running quickly up them.

Frantically, she ran down into the hall to meet him. Something terrible must have happened, she thought, if he, always so wary, should now be approaching Lord Rich's house in so bold a manner. Then, under the gaze of the shocked servants, Lord Mountjoy went down on one knee before her on the marble floor in the front hall.

'Come, live with me, my darling,' he said, his arms stretched out towards her.

She drew him into a small ante-chamber and held him close. 'What has happened, my love?' she cried in terror.

Mountjoy laughed and ran his strong fingers through her lustrous hair. 'Nothing has happened,' he assured her. 'In fact, this is the finest moment of my life. I have made my decision. You are now Lord Mountjoy's lady and the whole world shall know it.'

'Then my husband is dead?' she cried.

Mountjoy shook his head and smiled. 'No. Last time we met he was but half-alive, but certainly not dead,' he grinned.

'Don't jest!' she cried. 'I can't bear it. Tell me what is going on!'

'Come with me, Penelope,' he said, suddenly seriously. 'Come now, I cannot wait. And remember, it is forever . . .'

'But, my lord,' she protested, 'you are to sail with Essex.'

'Not now I have been recalled.' He smiled again.

As his words sank in, Penelope also began to smile slowly. 'You, my lord, are to stay ashore while my husband sails with Essex? Why, it's too incredible!' She laughed with relief.

'Her Majesty recalled both Southampton and me because we are not married and as yet have no heirs to carry on our noble names. We are not to be allowed to risk our lives. Your brother's fleet is back in port to be refitted after a bad storm, but then it will go ahead.'

'Oh, God bless good Queen Bess!' Penelope cried jubilantly.

Mountjoy held her close. 'But that's not all, my love. I have leased Wanstead from your brother in return for the money I invested in his venture.'

Penelope clasped her hands together in joy. 'Beautiful Wanstead! I can't believe that this is all happening,' she exclaimed, 'yet I knew that today was special. I felt it in my bones.'

'Break all the ties that bind you, my darling,' he begged. 'Come, be the mother of my heir.'

'My lover,' she declared impulsively, 'I'll come with you at once just as I am.' And together they went down the stairs to his awaiting coach that had just arrived.

'It's rather wicked but delightful that you are clad only in this loose gown,' he said, as his hands caressed her in the privacy of the coach.

'I come to you, my lord, with empty purse and almost naked because I care for nothing but our love,' she declared passionately.

Black night had descended by the time they reached Wanstead. A silver moon lit up the long line of elms and cast haunting shadows over the lake.

'How lovely it looks,' she exclaimed. 'I have always known that this would one day be my home. I've always felt it in my heart. How wonderful that you, my lover, have made it possible.'

So, like two young love-birds, they settled down at Wanstead, leaving the cares of the world outside completely behind. The hidden depths of Charles' character balanced perfectly Penelope's own impulsive nature. And at last she was living with a man upon whom she could pour out her affection, so long pent-up during her marriage. So began, in beautiful Wanstead, the happiest part of Penelope's life.

10

The Plot

Days of delight fled by. On warm summer days, the lovers would sit beside the silver stream that ran bubbling and dancing through the estate and into the green woodlands. Dreamily, Penelope would sit beside her beloved Mountjoy while he fished, both silent, preoccupied. When it rained, she would join him in the huge library while he sorted and dusted the precious books that he had collected during his student days. For years they had been stored away but now they found a home in the deep bookshelves that Lord Leicester had never filled.

Charles also had a large collection of lead soldiers, which, in moments of leisure he would sometimes arrange and organise in mock battles. He was a self-sufficient man and in his quiet, calm way he was never bored. Gradually he built up their home, always returning from London with some treasure or another; perhaps a piece of ancient silver or rare glass, or a painting by one of the Italian Masters, whose work he loved. He loved a bargain and always planned his money carefully so as to afford these luxuries.

With her belly heavily swollen with a new life once more, Penelope was content with this quiet existence. She gathered roses from the garden and filled the house with huge jars of them so that their sweet scent pervaded the air. Then when the flowers faded she began to make pot-pourri with the dried petals from a French recipe her mother had sent her. She had seldom known such contentment as that which she experienced while awaiting the birth of Mountjoy's heir.

Snow glistened in the parklands and a robin hopped on the sill when the first cry of their son announced his birth.

Charles held the baby very close. 'I thank you, darling, with all my heart,' he told his exhausted love. 'This child is mine, I know that he is really mine!' he cried.

Penelope smiled weakly but tears crept into her eyes as she thought of his first frail little son now sent away to a grim school in the north. 'Nevertheless, this child is still a bastard,' she murmured.

But Charles hardly seemed to hear her. 'I'll call him Mountjoy Blount. Two noble names will stand him in good stead.'

This child would be well-loved and wanted, but Penelope still worried that he was not legitimate. When Lord Mountjoy announced to the world that he was the father of a natural son and heir to succeed to his ancient estates, the news did not cause much gossip, nor did the fact that Lady Rich was now openly acknowledged as Mountjoy's woman – after all, this had been known for quite some time. Both Charles and Penelope had, however, expected some sort of comment from the palace, but Her Majesty preserved a stony and somewhat alarming silence.

Elizabeth was busily engaged in squabbling with Essex over the loss of the ships of his fleet in the bad storm of the autumn. He had been driven back to port, forced to lie at Plymouth for a refit, while the noble young men, having become disenchanted with the voyage, began to desert him and to return to town. The first inkling Penelope had of the return of Lord Rich was a letter to Charles from Essex. In a postscript Essex wrote: 'I have been forced to put my brother-in-law ashore, his health was so poorly. I did not want to feel responsible for his death.'

When she read this, Penelope laughed heartily but she checked herself when she saw the look of dismay on Charles' handsome face. 'I'm sorry I laughed,' she said, holding back another giggle, 'but the idea of that absurd little man roughing it aboard a battleship is just too funny for words.'

But Charles was now frowning as he read the date. 'The letter was forwarded in September, yet there is no sign of Lord Rich in town,' he said soberly.

'No, my dear. He will stay holed-up in some warm inn with his pills and potions. He won't be travelling anywhere until the spring comes,' she informed him with a note of contempt in her voice.

Charles nodded but as he continued to peruse the letter, his brow creased with more anxiety.

'Charles, my love, don't look so distressed,' Penelope pleaded, placing her arms about him. 'I'll never leave you, whatever he threatens.'

'It's the scandal that worries me,' he muttered.

'Nonsense!' she exclaimed. 'What can they do to us?'

'Those dogs at court are growling and chewing all the time now that Essex's back is turned. I am worried that the blow, when it comes, will fall in our direction.'

'Don't be so morbid,' she cried impatiently. 'If trouble comes, I'll face it. I'll not sit on my arse and wait for it.'

Charles was shocked at the coarseness of her words. 'Behave yourself, madam,' he ordered quietly with a frown.

But Penelope began to laugh her high, clear, infectious laugh that no one could resist. Soon Charles was laughing with her as he relaxed again, happy in the knowledge that his love for Penelope Rich was worth any scandal it might bring upon him now.

Later that month Penelope received a long letter from her mother informing her that she had forcibly detached the girls from the dreadful Miss Thorpe and had them to stay with her at Drayton Bassett for Christmas. The boys had spent their school vacation with her and she had no intention of returning her granddaughters to Leighs just yet; they were all, she wrote, having such a good time.

'Just like Mother,' sighed Penelope, but she was glad that her children were safe with their grandmother at her estate with the horses and dogs and all the country affairs she indulged in. They would all be enjoying themselves there. Lettice also mentioned in her letter that Catherine Hastings was travelling north to take young Charles under her wing. Ever since her beloved Walter Devereux had died in battle, Catherine's kind heart had been looking for someone else to mother.

'Well, at least my mother's taken the worry of the children from my mind,' Penelope remarked to Charles, 'but, my God, what an explosion there is going to be when Lord Rich eventually returns to Leighs!'

Placidly, she settled down with her new baby and her lover. Now that she knew her children were being looked after, the world outside mattered less than ever. But as she had predicted, in the warmth of spring, Lord Rich arrived at Leighs, to be met with tales of woe from Miss Thorpe about the departure of his girls. Immediately, he dispatched servants to Drayton Bassett to force Lettice to return them. Then he dashed off to London to complain to Essex at the behaviour of his sister. He could rouse little interest there – Essex had plenty of his own troubles and did not want to hear. So Robert Rich petitioned his old crony, Robert Cecil, who was now the Queen's secretary. But even then he was treated with cold disdain. Outraged, he tried to appeal to the queen, but on discovering that all such doors were firmly closed to him, he resorted to the civil law.

The long legal epistles arrived for Penelope at Wanstead when Charles was away from home, having just been made Commander-in-Chief of the new army Essex was gathering.

Infuriated by the legal documents presented to her by Lord Rich's emissaries, Penelope flung them on the floor and stamped on them, shouting loudly that her wretched husband had to divorce her. She had no intention of going home.

After much fuss and a lot of arguments, some sort of compromise was reached when the girls were returned to Leighs and Essex diplomatically persuaded Lord Shrewsbury to take that infernal nuisance, his brother-in-law, away to France on an embassy with him. Robert Rich, feeling the importance of his assignment, went in the autumn leaving Penelope in peace to have her second child by Mountjoy. Becoming pregnant every other year was her life-long habit. She was happy to be so prolific and grew even more beautiful in the clean, fresh air of Wanstead and the sunshine of her love.

Essex, after his successful venture to the islands, was even more popular than ever and once more the right hand of the ageing queen, but he was still restless and uneasy, dallying with the maids at court under the nose of his jealous patron. So it was that when Ireland rebelled against oppression, he rode off once more with banners flying and trumpets blaring, to conquer that unhappy country.

From the balcony of Essex House, Penelope watched her brother's new army ride away, magnificent in golden armour. She waved as her gallant brother rode away, followed by his close friends Sir Christopher Blount and Lord Southampton. Even from her position high up on the balcony, she could see that Essex's face was thin and pale as if he were under heavy stress.

Charles was there, too, but as head of his command, he was to stay in England and escort the army onto the ships in Wales. He looked fine and handsome, and Penelope was very proud of him as he rode by. But her worried thoughts returned to her brother. Was it not that God-forsaken land that had defeated their brave father? Mist and bog-land, a furious, untamed population. Could they be the downfall of a second Earl of Essex, too?

The next day, she returned to Wanstead with her sister-in-law, Frances, and her silly cousin, Elizabeth Vernon, who had now secretly married Lord Southampton but was afraid to stay in town in case the Queen discovered that she was pregnant. Elizabeth had been married on Essex's insistence, for Southampton had been a most unwilling bridegroom. The dark Devereux cousin had mooned over him for so long, that theirs had become a marriage of obligation.

Penelope was not particularly fond of Elizabeth. Her meekness and subservience to men irritated her, as did her little lisp and mild, doe-like expressions. She made her feelings known to the sweet Frances. 'I'm fed up with Elizabeth and her dear Henry. She's so weak!'

'Oh, Penelope, don't be unkind,' begged Frances. 'Elizabeth is young, and so much in love.'

'God knows how he ever managed to get her pregnant,' Penelope declared bitchily. 'I always thought his inclinations were in the opposite direction.'

Frances's lips twitched primly as Penelope referred to the widely known homosexual activities of young Southampton, but she passed no comment.

Elizabeth came hurriedly towards them one morning, her cheeks flushed. Her curls had escaped from her snood and dangled haphazardly about her face. 'I'm very worried,' she cried. 'My mother has written to say that there is bad news from Ireland. Our men are starved and harassed. I do hope my Henry is safe.'

'Knowing your Henry, he will not court danger,' mocked Penelope harshly.

'It's a God-forsaken island and the folk are very wild,' commented Frances.

'Did not my own dear father give his life and his wealth to help conquer that damned bog?' returned Penelope.

The three women looked sadly at each other, each concerned for her kith and kin. While their children played happily in Wanstead's great garden, they sat in a group sewing, two of them awaiting childbirth.

Penelope was the first to be delivered in June of another bonny son. Lord Mountjoy rode up from London to congratulate her.

'I've run out of names,' she jested. 'Now you must find one.'

'St John,' he said, proudly, holding his son aloft, 'the patron saint of the noble Blounts who rode with them to the crusades and protected them at Floddenfield.' Thus as military-minded as ever, Mountjoy named his second son.

'How fares my brother Essex?' she enquired once the excitement had died down.

Charles' expression of joy turned to one of gravity. 'Not so good,' he said simply, and then was silent as though not wishing to think of bad matters in this moment of happiness.

But Penelope pressed him. 'Charles, seriously. I am concerned for him. He is facing much trouble, not only in battle, but also from the court. I'd prefer you to stay in town. He has many enemies and is very much in need of a loyal friend.'

'Yes, Christopher Blount has been recalled and Southampton demoted,' agreed Mountjoy. 'I fear all is not well out there. I shall return to court and protect your brother as best I can.'

So once more the loyal, patriotic Mountjoy returned to help keep back the jackals who were out to destroy Essex, and to make sure that the Queen was not detached from her support of his venture in that unhappy country.

When he had gone, Penelope was seized with boredom. Suddenly she could not bear the constant sitting and sewing; or the tedious chattering of Frances and Elizabeth. For a while she thought of visiting her mother at Drayton Bassett, but when she realised that Lettice's husband, Charles's younger brother, had returned from the war, she knew that she would only quarrel with her mother. No, there would be no peace at Drayton Bassett. So she changed her mind, and then suddenly decided to visit her daughters at Leighs.

'Is it wise?' asked Frances. 'I think it would be better to stay away.'

'Lord Rich is either in France or Shrewsbury,' replied Penelope. 'He's definitely not at Leighs. And it would be nice to see my girls; I might even bring them back to Wanstead,' she added thoughtfully.

'I will take good care of the babies, Penelope,' offered Frances, 'if you still think it's a good idea.' She knew it was useless to argue with her sister-in-law once she had made up her mind about something.

Two days later, Penelope travelled in a comfortable carriage to Leighs, taking with her her own servants and plenty of presents for her daughters in the hope of winning their goodwill. But the atmosphere at the family home had not improved. It was still gloomy, frigid and religious. Numerous long-frocked parsons seemed to haunt the stone corridors – many of them, according to the icy Miss Thorpe, refugees from religious persecution on the continent who were just passing through.

Penelope's girls had grown considerably since she had last seen them. Lettice was tall, willowy and rather disdainful; Isabella was a true flaxen-haired beauty; and podgy, little Essex giggled incessantly and did not know her mother.

Undaunted, Penelope was determined to stay and get to know her family once more. And she returned to her duties as the lady of the manor. She visited the farmer tenants; went to church in the village; and to the school at Felsted where her sons were being educated. Everywhere she went she was received graciously, and she felt very glad to be recognised as the mistress of the immense estate once more. At Wanstead she had found peaceful isolation. This was an entirely different world, and most of the inhabitants preferred the mistress to the master. Lady Rich, they thought, was fair-minded and trustworthy, while Lord Rich was avaricious and very treacherous.

Finding that she was enjoying herself, Penelope prolonged her stay at Leighs in the hope of coaxing some love for her into the hearts of her cold, religious young daughters.

News from London took a long while to reach the rural population at Leighs. Gossip, scandals and anxiety were not so important to country folk. So when the storm broke and swept over her beloved brother, she was unaware that he had lost his nerve contending with Irish fighting tactics, or that he had left Ireland without consent, and had ridden home in pursuit of Lord Grey, determined to get to the Queen first and had made all haste to Nonsuch Palace where the court was.

As Lord Grey was still ahead of him with his story of the Irish Armistice, Essex, when he arrived, burst straight in upon the Queen, catching her in déshabillé in her bedroom. Penelope knew nothing of all this or of the fact that Mountjoy was now to take her brother's place in Ireland. Ironically, she heard the news from none other than Lord Rich.

He rode in one night – it was raining hard and he was soaked to the skin – looking very alarmed and even more so at the sight of his estranged wife sitting at her own fireside.

'I did not expect to find you here, madam,' he wheezed. He seemed to have a very bad cold.

She moved aside as he came close to the fire,

coughing and shivering. She rang for a servant to bring hot drinks.

'I came alone,' he gasped. 'I could not trust anyone. I have with me all the private papers of Lord Essex. He sent a message to me personally to take charge of them.'

'Why? What is wrong with my brother?' she asked in bewilderment.

When Robert Rich told her what had happened, she still did not seem to understand.

'Are you a fool, woman?' his cracked voice announced impatiently. 'Don't you see the seriousness of what he has done? He is committed for trial on a treasonable charge. Things look black for him. He encouraged his men to question the strategy of invading Ulster and instead of attacking the Earl of Tyrone, as he had been ordered to, he made a truce with him. Then, against express orders forbidding him to return, he left Ireland and came home. The man's a fool.'

'I cannot believe it,' she murmured, still shocked by the tragic news and barely able to take it in.

Robert coughed and sputtered noisily. 'I must take to bed. I have caught a severe chill,' he complained.

Thinking confusedly about her brother, it then occurred to her that Charles might also be implicated and in trouble. 'I must go,' she said suddenly.

Robert Rich read her thoughts. 'Don't hurry,' he sneered. 'Your lover is to be sent to Ireland. In all probability, he is on his way already.'

She ignored his scornful words, knowing that she had to leave at once. Ordering her carriage, she bundled her servants out of bed and rode through the stormy night to London.

Tired and tousled, she arrived in the early morning at Charles' house in Savoy Hill just as her lover was breafasting in bed.

He looked astonished as she burst in on him. 'My dear Penelope,' he exclaimed. 'Whatever possessed you to ride through the night? And what were you doing at Leighs? I was sure you were safe at Wanstead.'

'Oh, my dear,' Penelope gasped, panting breathlessly. 'I was so afraid I would miss you. Lord Rich informed me that you are to replace Essex in Ireland.'

'Not immediately, you goose,' he said, quite unperturbed, 'but I shall be going. Essex must be tried first.'

'Do you think he will be cleared of the charge?' she asked anxiously.

'He will if he gets a chance to explain. Her Majesty will forgive your brother anything,' said Mountjoy with confidence.

'Oh! I hope so fervently. Meanwhile, I can retire with an easier mind.' She smiled coyly. 'Will I see you later, my lord?'

'Try to prevent me,' he growled with a laugh.

Suddenly Penelope looked sad as she thought about the meaning of the Queen's order. 'My love, however will I get on without you?' she asked wistfully.

Mountjoy shrugged. 'I presume that you will return to Leighs . . .'

'I certainly shall not,' she replied angrily, annoyed that he could suggest such a thing. 'You know I only went there to see my daughters.'

He raised his hands in peaceful protest. 'I apologise, madam,' he said humorously. 'Don't lose your temper. Now, go and get some rest – I'll come up later.'

For the rest of the month of August, Essex was imprisoned in York House. The Devereux family members gathered to commiserate with each other. His mother tried hard to gain admittance to the Queen to plead for her son, but was refused, and although his wife, Frances, was allowed to bend her knee to beg pity for her husband, it did no good at all. The young Earl had overstepped the mark this time and had brought royal disfavour upon himself in no uncertain terms.

It had often been his custom in the past to feign illness to ward off the royal wrath. Therefore, when rumours began to circulate that he was ill, no one believed them. In fact, this time he was not crying wolf. He really was ill. Nevertheless, his family was forbidden to visit him.

When Essex had first been imprisoned, Penelope and his other sister, Dorothy, had gone each day to the house of Philip Sidney's younger brother, Robert, and from his roof had looked down into the courtyard of York House to watch Essex when he was brought out for exercise. They would wave to each other and smile, and even that limited and brief contact gave the women comfort. But now he never came outside, and they began to get very anxious as the illness that had laid him low became progressively worse. Persistently, his womenfolk pestered the court for his release, but to no avail. They all knew that Essex had to humble himself, grovel at the Queen's feet, before there was a chance that she would give in.

With Mountjoy on his way to Ireland, Penelope drew upon all her immense energy, and pulled every possible string in an effort to free her brother. Each failure increased her hatred of the Queen. She wrote a secret letter to King James in Scotland, begging him to help Essex. Fervently she pleaded with young Robert Sidney, who had such high standing at court and she asked him for the family's sake to petition the Queen. He had become a good friend of hers over the years – indeed, she had recently become godmother to his first son – but in the end it was all to no avail.

Essex had committed an unforgiveable crime. Not only had he defied her orders in Ireland, but he had burst in on the queen at Nonsuch Palace, catching Her Highness without her wig or her mask of make-up. Not only her prestige, but her vanity, had been hurt.

While in Ireland, Essex had contracted the dreaded flux – the disease his father had died of. The iller he became the weaker he grew until there was no fight left in him. So sick was he that he had to be lifted from his bed in sheets. The Queen was not entirely unconcerned; she sent her doctor to him, but he was still not reprieved. Again his family gathered in Essex House to pray for their beloved Essex and comfort each other.

But not many of them could do much except weep. Lettice was too distraught to be of any help. Frances had recently been delivered of a small girl and had not yet recovered from the birth. She looked ghastly, walking the house and weeping most of the day. Their cousin Elizabeth Vernon and her new husband had also taken up residence at Essex House, blatantly defying the royal wrath by doing so. They were too concerned with their own problems to know what to do about Essex. So it was left to the resourceful Penelope to act.

Again she wrote to King James begging him to intercede for Essex, and she sent a note to Mountjoy in Ireland urging him to use his forces to aid her imprisoned brother. Finally, as a last resort, she wrote to the Queen herself. But her dislike for Her Majesty must have been evident in the tone of the letter, for in spite of the passionate pleas for the life of Essex, Elizabeth read threats into it and was furious.

At Christmas the bells tolled mournfully across the land announcing the death of the Earl of Essex and the nation wept for its young hero. But he had not died, and by the New Year, he had begun to recover. By this time it was his defiant sister who was in trouble. The Queen was now fully aware of Penelope's contempt for her and was determined to do something about this unruly young relation.

On hearing of the Queen's rage, Penelope's family insisted she flee, that she leave town and lie low at Wanstead, and so, with Elizabeth Vernon in tow, Penelope did precisely that, planning to stay quiet until the Queen's anger had cooled. But within weeks she was arrested, brought back to the house of Robert Sidney and forbidden to move until the Star Chamber had been assembled to consider the case.

There was an uneasy atmosphere after Penelope's arrest among the young earls who had supported Essex, for there had been many underhand negotiations. Would this woman betray them? But strong, alert and as astute as always, Penelope coolly surveyed those bearded old men of the Star Council – acquaintances of her youth, friends of her father, and the long, thin face of Robert Cecil, who was now Chancellor, having stepped so easily into his old father's shoes. 'I wrote what I thought and what I think,' she told them in an unwavering voice. 'I write defiantly and ungrammatically without one qualm of contrition . . .'

The results of Penelope's mock trial were pleasing. After a few days of haggling she was set free and the only request from Her Majesty was that Penelope return to Leighs to nurse her sick husband. Everyone was immensely relieved but perhaps not so much surprised, for was not Penelope the Queen's kin? The memory of her own sad mother, Anne Boleyn, was reflected in Penelope's dark eyes, those mirrors of the soul, which were a Boleyn heritage.

It was a very nervous, harassed Uncle Knollys, as the Queen's emissary, who gave his niece a good talking to. 'Her Majesty insists that you return to Leighs. Your husband is very ill; it is doubtful that he will survive.'

Her lips curled disdainfully. 'He hated me in life, so he won't need me in death,' she said curtly.

'Now do be sensible, my dear,' begged Uncle Knollys. 'You have escaped with your life. You are lucky. What you did was audacious. In fact, it was considered treason by some who thought you should suffer the fate of traitors.'

'Well, I would have disappointed them,' replied Penelope loftily. 'They could not have hanged me because I am in my usual state of pregnancy.' She looked up at him with a saucy grin.

Her uncle was not amused. 'Madam, I pray, let this be a lesson to you to control your rash impulses in future.'

Penelope scowled and let her mouth drop sullenly. What an old bore he was, she thought. Why did he have to interfere? She stared at him gloomily, as he stuck out his podgy belly and dusted his brow with a fancy handkerchief. 'Upon Lord Rich's demise, the estate will belong to your sons. Will you bring disgrace on them at the beginning of their young lives?' he asked.

'I have another family at Wanstead which you all seem to have forgotten about,' she retorted rudely.

'Those children will be taken care of adequately. Kindly do as you are bid, Penelope and appreciate what others have done to save your life.' He spoke angrily now as he began to lose his temper. The veins stood out in his temples and his eyebrows shook.

'All right. I'll go, but only under protest,' she said eventually, realising that it would do no good to resist. And so reluctantly she returned to Leighs and her ailing husband.

She was severely shocked at the sight of Lord Rich. He lay on his bed in a dimly lit room, his body swollen, and his eyes sunken as he gasped painfully for breath with gaping blue lips. Several doctors hovered over the bed complete with their instruments of torture. For weeks, Robert Rich had been constantly bled and sweated, probed and stuffed full of evil substances. With his morbid fear of illness and dread of pain, the man was practically out of his mind.

Filled with horror, Penelope stared at him; but then pity took over. Perhaps it was because she understood Robert so well, or perhaps she remembered how he had saved her beauty from the smallpox, or perhaps it was just an instinctive gesture of kindness, but she knew that, whatever her feelings for him, she had to help him now. 'Get out of here!' she commanded the doctors. 'I'm his wife. I shall take care of him.'

Shaking their grey heads and protesting loudly, the medical men departed.

Slowly and skilfully, Penelope gently nursed her husband back to health. Absorbed as always in matters of the moment, she devoted all her incredible energy to nursing her hated spouse; intense pity was the only emotion she felt. And so, with the aid of Robert's loyal manservant, she set her mind to pulling him through, without the expense of the eminent physicians she had so abruptly dispensed with.

'It is my opinion,' she said, 'that Lord Rich is suffering from a severe chest complaint.'

The manservant looked admiringly at this courageous, unsentimental woman and was quite happy to help her in her task.

'He has ample pills and potions,' she said. 'And I'm sure that you are well versed in the art of dispensing them.'

'Certainly, my lady,' replied the servant. 'My master has often been subject to severe bronchial colds and we have always conquered them before.'

'Good,' she said. 'Bring the pills and potions here and we can get on with it. Those bastards were torturing him with their probing and bleeding.'

So mistress and servant bathed and soothed Lord Rich's chest, and poulticed his lungs. Together they sat up all night as he came through the crisis, shouting and raving in a feverish sweat. By the end of the week the patient was out of danger and, although he was still dreadfully weak, he was slowly improving. Penelope however, was exhausted, but her gallant effort had even been recognised by Miss Thorpe, who brought her nourishing food and began to insist on taking over while she rested. Miss Thorpe's respect was one thing, but among the servants at Leighs there had always been many who preferred the mistress to the master, and their admiration for Lady Rich was now complete.

As the better weather came, Robert was able to sit out on the balcony overlooking the garden. He was pale and wan, but as bad-tempered and perpetually unpleasant as ever. 'Well, madam, I suppose I should consider myself very grateful to you,' he said to Penelope one day with a distinct sneer in his tone.

'You'll be pleased to hear that you don't need to,' she replied shortly. 'I'd do the same for any stranger in my care.'

'I note, then, that there is little change in your attitude, madam,' he whined.

'If you think I will ever become subservient to you

again, sir,' she said icily, 'you are a bigger fool than I take you to be.'

After that exchange, they could only continue in the same vein. As the summer ticked by, they sat in the garden when it was possible, bickering relentlessly. And, as the days went by, Penelope's belly began to extend. There had been no news of Mountjoy. He seemed to have disappeared into the misty bogs of Ireland. She sorely missed his soothing companionship – and gradually felt the melancholy atmosphere at Leighs beginning to overwhelm her. Her daughters kept themselves busy with their music, their dancing and their studies, and were still cool and aloof towards her, showing little affection. As always, her mother kept her informed of recent events in town. One letter brought the welcome news that Essex had finally been released from York House and returned to his own residence. But, Lettice wrote, he was kept under constant surveillance. His family and friends had been turned out of the house; and many servants were being dismissed as Her Majesty, still unforgiving, began to call in all his debts to her. She had taken away the privileges he had enjoyed while in her favour and seemed determined to ruin him financially.

With inner fury Penelope read of her brother's sorry plight. His health and fortune were reduced to shreds, just as her father's had been in royal service. On the other hand, Mountjoy was covering himself with glory, having overcome the rebellious earls in ill-fated Ireland. Mountjoy's success did not surprise her, but no news from him hurt her very much.

In August, the weather was good and her sons came home from their school holidays. They were now quite grown up, well-mannered and gracious. And Robert Rich was on his best behaviour in the presence of his two much-loved sons, Robert and Henry. Lazily, Penelope lived each day, relaxed as she always was when she was pregnant, until the boys returned to school. Her husband, now fully recovered from his illness, began to prowl about the house, interfering with everything and everybody and his odd eyes watched her beadily as she steadily put on more weight.

Late one afternoon, Penelope was in the garden collecting the large blooms that she loved to arrange about the house. Holding a sharp pair of shears, she bent over breathlessly, snipping at the long rows of sweet peas. As she inhaled their scent her head began to swim pleasantly. Robert Rich came up and stood beside her, his small, mean eyes surveyed her mockingly. 'You should be careful, madam,' he said. 'Too much exertion in your condition could be dangerous.' A smirk hovered around his irregular features.

Penelope put her hand to her back and stood up, looking at him in concern. This was the first time he had referred to her already well-advanced pregnancy.

'I presume that I am to have another of your bastards foisted upon me,' he sneered.

She froze. 'No, sir!' she cried. 'I intend to return to my own home as soon as it is convenient.'

The expression on her husband's ill-favoured face became ugly with anger. The small, uneven teeth showed in a bestial grin. 'What home, may I ask? Not

Wanstead, I'm afraid. Lord Mountjoy will not require your presence when he brings back his Irish bride.'

Penelope's mouth dropped open in dismay. Robert obviously knew something that she did not, and that was why he had come over to her. 'I'll leave tomorrow,' she declared, defiantly, 'and I swear by all that's holy, you can die a thousand times. I'll return no more.'

'Do not try to hoodwink me, madam,' he snarled back at her. 'I know you were forced to come back to Leighs; otherwise you would have shared the same fate as your brother. I was your protection, your husband by law.'

Penelope's throat seized up with rage as her fingers convulsively clutched the sharp garden shears. How she wanted to dash at him and stick them into his sneering face! For a second she hesitated as the impulse almost overwhelmed her, but then she quickly dropped the shears to the ground. 'I do not believe your malicious lies,' she cried. 'I hate you, you sadistic beast. I'll go from this house at once.' She gasped for breath, choked with exertion and temper.

'Please yourself,' Robert said casually, 'but I warn you, if you do, I'll denounce you as a whore and an adulterous wife. Once you leave my protection, you can never return.'

Penelope tossed back her head in anger. 'Coward! Fool!' she screamed. 'I don't need you. Divorce me, and let me live my own life.'

'Lord Mountjoy is contracted to marry the Earl of Ormonde's sister, so don't burn your boats, my lady,' Robert warned.

'Cease!' she screamed at him. 'I don't want to hear. My God, I should have killed you, not nursed you. Devil! Son of Satan!' Quite beside herself now, she hurled more insults at him. 'I'll go. Get me a mount!' she cried to a servant. And, kicking over the basket of sweet peas she had cut, she ran to the house. 'Get me a cloak, you dolts,' she shouted at the astonished servants.

A warm cloak was handed to her and she ran to the stables.

'Let her go,' commanded Lord Rich as his manservant made to follow her. 'She will ride off her evil temper.'

'But in her condition,' muttered the man, 'it could be dangerous.'

'To Hell with her!' declared Lord Rich. 'Now that her brother is so out of favour with Her Majesty, I have little need for my wife any longer.' With a cynical grin on his face, he turned and went back to the house.

On a grey stallion – a son of her mother's grey mare – Penelope rode like a mad thing with her cloak floating out behind her. Despite her condition, she sat in the saddle with ease. Her mind was almost blank with hate and fury as she rode through the muddy Essex lanes all alone in the direction of Wanstead. But underneath her anger, one concern nagged at her constantly: she had to find out the truth about Charles' betrothal. In her heart of hearts, she knew there must be something in the story, that she might lose her beloved Charles.

The hours passed slowly as the horse strode on.

Penelope was becoming thoroughly exhausted. Her back felt as if it were almost breaking and the child within her jumped about protestingly. At dusk she was clinging, half-fainting, to the reins, but her brave stallion, who had been reared at Wanstead, knew the way back home. With little guidance from his rider, he left the road, and jumped hedges and ditches. As the cool mist of the evening came down, she fell forward and clutched him lovingly about his long, white mane and dozed off as he galloped valiantly on. And now a rosy dawn cast ruddy hues upon the lake at Wanstead. On the last lap of the long journey he galloped down the long drive and halted, sweating, outside the house.

Penelope slipped off into the arms of the servants who carried her, screaming with birth pangs, up the steps. In her semi-conscious state, she recalled only the tall elms in the shadowy half-light but she knew she was home.

Before morning, a tiny child was born, as dark and tiny as Charles had been. It was not a difficult labour but, added to her earlier exhaustion, it took longer than usual to recover from. But when she did finally emerge, blooming with the glow of motherhood, she discovered to her surprise, that the house was full of guests. Lettice, Frances and Elizabeth Vernon were all staying at Wanstead.

'Her Royal Highness had us all turfed out of Essex House,' explained Lettice, 'so we decided to come here.'

Penelope was delighted to have such company and was content to be back in her old bedchamber. 'It's so good to be home,' she exclaimed, lying back against the pillows. 'Wanstead has always been so good to me.'

Elizabeth Vernon rapturously held the tiny new baby in her arms. Recently delivered of a boy herself, she was full of maternal bleatings. 'Dear cousin,' she said to Penelope, 'do let's call her Elizabeth,' she lisped looking eagerly towards the bed.

Penelope's good humour quickly turned into irritation at her feeble cousin. 'No, no,' she snapped. 'That's a name I abhor.'

Elizabeth looked aghast and tears crept into her eyes. 'How can you say such a thing, Penelope? It's my own name,' she said miserably.

'Please yourself,' replied Penelope with a shrug. 'I'm sick of child-bearing and I've run out of names,' she complained.

Lettice decided to step in before Elizabeth dissolved in a pool of tears. 'Well, you have had your share of babes now, Penelope, so perhaps it's just as well,' she said humorously, trying to brighten up the atmosphere. 'We've just heard that Robert may be able to come here from Essex House before long. Her Majesty has deigned to allow him to leave. It will be nice if we can all be together for Christmas. It has been a sad year.'

Penelope was pleased for her brother but she had something else on her mind. 'Mother,' she said quietly, 'tell me the truth about Charles.'

Lettice averted her dark eyes from those of her daughter. 'Until Essex comes, we have little news from court,' she replied evasively.

Penelope bit her lip to hold back a wail. 'So, it is true,' she whispered. 'Charles is to marry an Irish earl's sister.' Her dark, tragic eyes looked reproachfully at her mother.

'A rumour dear. Quite unfounded,' murmured Lettice, shaking her head reassuringly. 'You know what it is like at court. There's always gossip.'

'I just can't believe that Charles would desert me,' Penelope murmured in confusion.

Lettice gently took her daughter's hand. 'My dear,' she said softly, 'should it happen, it will be only for ambition. It will not affect you or his love for you.'

As Lettice tried to console her, Penelope turned her face to the pillow. Seldom had her mother seen her so desolate. 'Not affect me, Mother?' she spoke into the pillow. 'What are you saying? What about my sons and my new daughter?' The pillow was damp from her tears.

Lettice patted her hand. 'He is a man of honour. He will provide for them,' she said complacently.

Now tears were pouring down Penelope's face. 'Oh, Charles, my lover,' she wept. 'What will I do without you?' And no amount of comforting by anyone could console her.

Essex's proposed visit to Wanstead did not take place for several weeks. Urgent business matters held him in town as he fought to save what was left of his vast estates and watched his former friends desert his sinking ship. If he was out of favour with the Queen, Essex's patronage lost its attraction.

Eventually, he arrived at Wanstead in early

December. Penelope was terribly shocked at the sight of his harassed face and emaciated body. He had grown a beard in prison which made him look older than his years. This discreet visit to his well-loved family had to be kept a dark secret from the jealous, vindictive queen, for he was still kept under restraint most of the time. His women folk fussed and spoiled him lovingly. Once more they were all together, so they made merry and tried to throw all their troubles aside.

It was during that secret visit to Wanstead that the first idea of rebellion was born. In the library, surrounded by Mountjoy's books and lead soldiers, Penelope and her brother would sit and discuss his predicament.

'I wish I were like you, Penelope,' Essex told her. 'You have such a strong spirit. What can I do? Her Majesty is determined to ruin me. I'd give my soul for her. How can I approach her to beg forgiveness?'

'God in Heaven!' exclaimed his sister. 'What does she expect of you? You have served her well and she treats you like this. But remember that she is old and surly, and will not live for ever.'

'It's possible that she will outlive me,' he said gloomily.

'For God's sake, Robert,' she snapped impatiently, 'Get up and fight. What does she want of you? How much more can you stand?'

He stared soberly at her. 'I don't know,' he said simply. 'All I know is that I have many enemies and the few friends I had are now deserting me.'

'But the people will support you. The man in the street – are you not his hero?'

'Memories are short, sister,' he said despondently.

'There is the Queen's nephew in Scotland and, as yet, she has named no successor.'

Robert looked at her gravely. 'You are very astute, Penelope, but it would be dangerous to play one against the other.'

Penelope grasped him by both hands and looked urgently at him, confident that she had come up with the answer to their problem. 'I'll help you, dear brother,' she said, 'but do not allow her to cast you underfoot and trample you. Are we not a noble family with royal blood on both sides?' Penelope was hard and bitter at the desperate plight of her brother and in her disappointment with Mountjoy, who did not confirm or deny his involvement with the Irish earl's sister.

They spent many more hours in the library, while he dictated letters in a secret code to King James of Scotland and to Mountjoy in Ireland, begging for their support. Thus the seeds of that fatal rising to come were sown during the visit to Wanstead.

As Essex plotted with his family and a few loyal friends, the rival Cecil faction at court was also busy preparing for the day when the great queen died. Envoys were secretly dispatched to Spain to establish links between the royal house there and the Cecils. For the Spanish infant was in the direct line for succession to the English throne.

Just before Christmas the Devereux family gathered back at Essex House for the festive season. When they were not having furtive meetings, they held parties, got merry and celebrated with the few friends that remained. Heedless of the future, they went to plays, gave splendid balls, visited relatives and ignored the great Gloriana sitting like a faded spider in the royal web. Essex and his friends, including Sir Christopher Blount and Lord Southampton, went about the town hitting the high spots and neglecting their wives, spending the remainder of their great inheritances on gambling and women.

Throughout this time, Penelope was depressed and mournful. Every day she asked herself why Mountjoy had not contacted her.

Her mother's mood was not much better; and Lettice was very apprehensive and did not like the way the wind was blowing. She was terribly afraid that her son's rebellion would fail, and was therefore opposed to it. Although she dared not say anything to Essex himself, she warned her drunken young husband, Christopher, not to get involved. 'Don't join Robert,' she urged. 'Don't be a fool. The silence from Elizabeth can only mean one thing. She is getting ready to pounce, and I can assure you she will do so soon, and without warning.'

'Tut, tut, my dear,' Christopher mocked. 'Her Majesty is getting old. She has to fall sometime, anyway.'

Lettice flushed. Any reference to age annoyed her. This fresh, blond young man whom she still loved so much had almost ruined her with his extravagant ways. Now it seemed, he could not be dissuaded from joining her son in what might be a fatal endeavour. 'Well, get on with it, then,' she said sharply. 'But don't say I didn't warn you. I may be getting on a bit, but I have had a lifetime's experience of the wiles of Elizabeth Regina.' So, wisely, she pushed this concern from her mind and devoted herself to her household, her hunting parties and her many grand-children.

Meanwhile, Penelope in her forthright fashion, and despite her own unhappiness, had dived deep into the plans for her brother's rebellion against the old queen. Egged on by Essex, who was so grateful to have her support, she rode out to various country families who were still loyal to the Devereux, endeavouring to gain their support.

As the New Year approached, the whole family was still at Essex House for the annual celebrations. Essex had become very moody – one moment being ecstatically happy, the next being plunged into the deepest gloom Sometimes he became so melancholy that he shut himself away in a darkened room for days on end. When this happened, his devoted sister watched him anxiously, and sometimes even wondered if he was fully aware of what he was doing. But most of her thoughts when she was alone were centred on Charles and the sad fact that he still had not been in touch with her. All she could do was live in hope that he loved her as ever before, and she dreaded the day when news might come which would finally deprive her even of that.

The Essex Rebellion

One day in early January, the sun shone down upon the Strand and the river, unusually quiet, flowed placidly by. But the calm was tense, a herald of the other storm to come. Most of the big mansions were shuttered and empty. News of the planned rebellion had spread and those not wishing to be involved had left town.

In contrast, the courtyard of Essex House was a hive of noise and activity. Soldiers drilled in the square. All sorts of layabouts and vagabonds lounged about the gate. There were heretical parsons bitter to the heart, priests from Catholic families who had been hounded from place to place. They had gathered either to seek asylum or to find a leader in the defiant young Earl of Essex. Young men from his estates in Wales and from Chartley camped in the grounds, fencing, larking about and playing dice. No secret had been made of this insurrection, but the older and wiser nobility stayed away, for they believed no good would come of it.

Inside the house, Essex and his friends breakfasted after a hectic night. They had all crossed the Thames on that previous evening to watch a performance of *Richard II*. The Queen had previously banned the play because it presented the life of Bolingbroke, a usurper of the

English throne. Essex had paid the players well to defy the ban. Did he, in his confusion of mind, have visions of himself as Bolingbroke taking over the throne of England? It is hard to say as he still insisted on his loyalty to the Queen. What he did was to lead, three-parts drunk, his followers through the streets, intent on taking over the City of London and making it his stronghold. But he had overestimated his popularity. The City remained steadfast to the Queen. Men and women who had previously always cheered their hero would under no circumstances take up arms against their monarch. Thus, on that sunny morning marching to disaster with his motley band of followers behind him, Robert, Earl of Essex, condemned himself to death.

When the news came of Essex's disastrous attempt to overthrow the queen and his subsequent arrest, Penelope immediately organised the escape of herself and Frances and Elizabeth with their children. Her mother had managed to get away from London, to flee to her sister, Lady North, who had remained loyal to the Queen. She would travel on to Wanstead from there, she said. Penelope, as fearless as ever, rowed a small boat down the swift-flowing Thames to the Blackwall Ferry, where she arranged for a carriage to transport them all to Wanstead. At nightfall, the children were being cared for and the women waited anxiously for the news of their men.

News of Essex came which made it clear that this time his downfall was complete. That he had broken down under the strain of interrogation and implicated all his friends and his devoted sister, Penelope, came as a shock, but in the estimation of his loyal family, Essex could still do no wrong. Of Penelope he had said: 'She has a proud spirit. You would do well to look to her.' To the proud, wilful Penelope, this was almost a compliment.

From January to February he fought for his life in the Star Chamber but he knew that he could expect no mercy from the Queen, or, indeed, anyone, this time. On Shrove Tuesday, as his women were kneeling in the old chapel at Wanstead to pray for him, Queen Elizabeth signed Essex's death warrant. The next day, that handsome head was severed from his body and four heartbroken women dressed in black, knelt together and wept for their beloved Robert.

Penelope knelt on the cold stone floor beside her weeping mother, trying so hard to find some contact with God. But her heart was hard and bitter and her thoughts kept drifting back to haunting tragedies in her past. Soon she was thinking of poor little Patrick Russell who had died because of Penelope's impetuosity. Could it be that she was also responsible for her brother's death? Had she not urged him to defy the Queen? Had she not urged him to become a traitor? Mercilessly, she flayed her conscience.

All afternoon she prayed but no help seemed to come from Him. Oh, why was she so headstrong and wilful? Why did she destroy so many people with her rash behaviour? When no answers came to any of these questions that tormented her, she finally railed against the being whom others called God, the wonderful God of love and beauty, who on this bright Lenten Day had not one scrap of comfort for her.

The next day, Lettice prepared to flee to Drayton Bassett, terrified about what was to happen to her fine young husband who had been arrested along with Essex. Christopher had no title. He was a traitor. They would hang him and disembowel his lovely body and stick his fine head on a spike on Tower Bridge. 'Come with me, Penelope,' Lettice cried. 'The Queen's fury will descend on you too. Escape! Go to Ireland, to Mountjoy. I'll care for the children.'

Penelope's mouth twisted in a bitter smile. 'No, Mother. I will not run. Let them come if they want me. I am not afraid. Just assure me that my family will be cared for. That is all I ask.'

Unable to cope with Penelope's attitude, Lettice shook her head in despair before whirling around to leave, her black cape swinging behind her.

Elizabeth and Frances also left discreetly with their children, each one to her own family, who had been loyal to the Queen. Soon Penelope was alone at Wanstead with only Mountjoy's children and a few old servants. In the park the daffodils waved their glorious golden heads, each one seemed to her to be a terrible reminder of her brother's head, while the eerie silence of the little river seemed to beg for Charles to return and sit fishing placidly and contentedly from the bank. Every day, Penelope walked through the forest along the soft, shady paths. Even the tall trees deepened her loneliness; her heart was swollen with grief that she could not release.

As summer came, she wandered more in the gardens, gathering blooms and seldom speaking, except when she played with her children on the green lawns. Her dark eyes were always alert, watching and waiting for the Queen's guards to come to arrest her or for Mountjoy to return to love her and rescue her from her loneliness.

As the days became shorter and the evening cooler, Penelope would sit with her family about the log fire in the hall, the boys at her knee and the tiny girl, Elizabeth, on her lap, still waiting for some news or for the axe of the law to descend. She dreaded leaving her lovely children but otherwise she did not care what happened to her.

Then one day a messenger came from Robert Sidney with the news that she had waited all the summer to hear. By some miracle Charles had escaped any imputation of being concerned in the plot with Essex, though everyone knew he had been up to his neck in it. After all, had he not promised Essex the support of his Irish troops? But instead, he was to return home to glory having defeated long-suffering Ireland once more and made peace with the rebel earls. At least he would not lose his life, she thought, but why had he never got in touch with her?

'Your father has deserted us, darlings,' she told her wide-eyed youngsters when she had finished reading the message. But her two fine boys and her little daughter did not seem to mind or even care that their mother's heart was breaking at Mountjoy's neglect.

The long winter closed in and she spent many hours reading or telling the children fairy stories. There was still no news from Charles or any command from the

Star Chamber, but there was gossip among the servants who said that the Queen had gone into a decline and had scarcely spoken a word since the death of Essex. They said that all the jollity had gone from the court. The younger folk stayed away and only the old faithful remained.

The good news and rest from anxiety soon brought Penelope back to normal health again. In the spring, she rode through the green woods or the park, accompanied by her sons on their ponies. Gradually, news began to drift back from Charles, whose loyal manservant came to Wanstead bringing home equipment and a verbal message that Lord Mountjoy would return soon now that peace had been restored in Ireland. Penelope was hurt that he had not sent her a written letter, but she reminded herself of how wary he was, and how he trusted no one. It was probably his caution that had saved him after the Essex Rebellion. In fact, he was the only survivor of that affair. Sir Christopher Blount had been beheaded with the rest of them. She knew that she had to be brave and trust Charles; she had to be sure of his love. Now he was only awaiting a summons from the Queen and then he would return to England. Just one letter going astray could condemn him. No, she had to be patient. And deep in her heart she knew that no onther woman had taken her place. Restored in her faith once more, she took heart to go on living and look forward to the future.

Now that Penelope's illustrious brother was dead, Lord Rich had no more use for her. During Essex's trial, when she had been under suspicion herself, he washed his hands of her and publicly declared her to be an adulteress. He had retired to Leighs where he kept himself considerably quieter, and when he published a legal document declaring himself to be no longer responsible for her debts, Penelope could only smile. The pompous little ass! She was well able to support herself, without any charity from him.

The days passed slowly and, by the next spring, it was evident that the old queen was dying. Undaunted by the danger she had been in, Penelope renewed her correspondence with King James in Scotland knowing that he would be the new monarch.

Then an extraordinary letter came at last from Mountjoy who was prepared to put pen to paper to tell her the good news that he was on his way home and bringing a guest – that grand old rebel, the Earl of Tyrone – who was prepared to swear an oath of allegiance to the dying queen. But Mountjoy was just too late; as he landed on British soil, the Queen died. All the tears and bloodshed that had washed over his proud country would trouble her no more.

It was a bright spring day when Mountjoy finally came home. Penelope stood in the great hall, a child each side of her while little Elizabeth skipped gaily forward to greet the papa she had never seen. The two warriors entered from sunshine into shadow, Charles' familiar stocky shape beside that grand old man, Tyrone, whose red hair was now silver and his beard snow-white. But his Irish blue eyes still shone clear and bright. The tiny Elizabeth, irresistible with her tight black curls and her red dress, curtseyed gracefully as she had been taught, but piped up in a squeaky voice: 'Which one of you is my papa?'

With a deep, throaty laugh, Charles bent down and scooped the child up in his arms to hug her. This little one was to be his love and joy for the rest of his life.

Penelope was delighted to welcome the grand old Earl. She remembered him from her childhood when he had been a guest of her father's at Chartley. Mountjoy was cool and calm and somewhat self-important but Penelope was happy that he had come home to her at last – and, to her relief, there was no mention of the Earl of Ormonde's sister to whom, it was once alleged, he was engaged.

Once more Wanstead became alive and was full of guests, with Mountjoy's staff and the Earl's household and young Irish Lords eager to enjoy their stay.

When the old queen lay peaceful in death and the new king was on his way from Scotland, everyone in England had wondered what the new reign would bring. In fact, to Wanstead at least, it brought prosperity. One of King James' first acts was to make Lord Mountjoy Earl of Devonshire and to Penelope he restored the title that had used to belong to her family – the ancient name of De Bourchier, a noble Norman baron. She also received the complimentary title of Countess of Essex, which gave her precedence over all the other ladies at court, an ironic fact since she had always disliked court life so much in the past.

And so, Penelope Devereux rose proudly from the ashes, harder, more bitter and ambitious than ever before.

In May, she rode to the border with a group of ladies from the court to greet the new Queen Anne of Denmark, whose entrance to England had been delayed by illness. The blonde, naive Anne, who spoke little English, was given a warm welcome, and all the ladies of the court were anxious to do service for her. A group of duchesses had ridden to the border with their pretty daughters, each falling over the other to greet the new queen, but much to the chagrin of the others, Anne immediately took to the attractive, forthright Penelope. It was that wide smile and happy manner that had singled her out and swept Anne off her feet. Penelope rode at the Queen's side all the way back to York, where the court was again in residence for fear of the return of the plague in high summer.

Later that year, fabulously attired, she rode ahead of all the other grand ladies in the coronation procession; then when Anne set up Grand Court in Greenwich, it was the Countess of Essex who was Lady of the Drawing Chamber. Conscious of the power she now had, Penelope wanted vengeance upon former enemies: 'I'll make them pay for every slight that has been cast on my family and each and every one of them will suffer for what they did to Essex,' she declared one day.

The calm, placid Mountjoy looked very alarmed. 'I've had my share of battles, madam. I am tired and need only peace to reside in my own home.'

This was not the only issue which was to divide the new duke and duchess in their few remaining years together.

The End of an Era

It was the spring of 1604, one year after the death of Queen Elizabeth. After the initial excitement about the new king had died down, it soon became clear to everyone that King James I was proving to be a very alarming change from the late queen, and there were many who already regretted the demise of that great Gloriana. In spite of her bad-tempered tyranny, at least the Queen had always been loyal and fair-minded to her subjects. In contrast, James was canny, mean and crafty. He liked to play one man against the other and, having brought his own Scots followers with him, he then gave them first place in court as the old and loyal courtiers were gradually pushed out. Many old families retired gracefully, but some clung to the shreds of the old glory while James milked them of their estates. In addition, his fondness for blood sports and his obsession for fondling young boys were frowned upon by the old courtiers.

Fortunately, Penelope and Charles were above all this. The new era brought them prosperity. Together, as Earl and Countess, they had attended the grand coronation and were warmly welcomed by James, despite the fact that they were not legally wed. His young queen, simple-minded and very fond of pleasure, was always at loggerheads with her husband, and preferred her own court at Greenwich to his. She became very fond of Penelope, admiring her bright, forthright character and the way she contemptuously swept aside the spiteful venom of those other grand duchesses seeking favours from the Queen.

Even though he was well-favoured, Charles was not so happy about these changes. He was appalled by the drunken ribaldry of the court and had been terribly shocked to see Penelope, partly clad in a voluminous gown that had shown off most of her plump body, lounging back in a ridiculous manner in a curious seashell-shaped carriage. Several other much younger ladies dressed as mermaids in fish tails and not much else appeared with her in one of those elaborate masques that the Queen loved. This one was a carnival procession, lavishly produced by Ben Jonson at great cost but which amounted, in the end, to no more than a drunken orgy.

'God in Heaven!' Charles had protested after this particular occasion. 'Enough is enough. I was really ashamed of you. What is our society coming to?'

Penelope frowned impatiently. 'Oh, don't be such a prude!' she retorted. 'Let us enjoy life. It passes quickly enough as it is.'

'Such licentiousness is not my idea of enjoyment,' Charles answered primly.

'You do as you please. I will not go as a snail into my shell to please your puritanical ideas.'

Soon afterwards, Charles left London and went home to Wanstead and the company of his beloved daughter, Elizabeth. Penelope was really enjoying court life as never before, and she was determined not to back down. So she stayed and continued to make merry and to hold down her high place in Queen Anne's court. She hunted and walked in the park with Anne and her string of little dogs.

There was a string of admirers following her, too, for she was still at the heyday of her beauty. One was Herbert, the young son of Mary Sidney, and so much like his Uncle Philip that Penelope's heart missed a beat when he first paid his addressed to her. He was a very persistent youth who clung to Penelope with passionate devotion. And when he declared his love for her in his poetry, his whole family became quite alarmed. But Penelope was quite unperturbed. Like a glossy bright butterfly, she warmed herself in the sunshine of this young, courtly love and flitted from court to court in the wake of the fun-loving Queen Anne, neglecting her home and family in the process. It was as if she had to compensate for the lonely years when she was starved of gaiety.

Charles, meanwhile, attended meticulously to his duties as a peer of the realm, but had retired from military affairs. He wisely stayed clear of the treachery of the King's court and was regarded by His Majesty with amused tolerance.

Lord Rich divorced his wife eventually and immediately remarried a wealthy widow. The laws concerning divorce and remarriage had not been fully clarified since the Reformation. But most people took the view that a divorced woman could not remarry. This did not worry Penelope at the time. She was content to be free at last from a husband she loathed. But as time went by, the fact that she was known as the Countess of Essex did not compensate her for the fact that to most ladies at court she was still only Mountjoy's mistress and her children were bastards.

Her eyes would light suspiciously on any group of noble ladies whispering behind their fans. And during her infrequent meetings with Charles, heated arguments would break out. She demanded loudly that he should petition the King to give them royal permission to marry. But Mountjoy neither liked nor trusted James. He hated the rat-race at court, with the ever-increasing number of low-bred Scotsmen leap-frogging their way into power. He was sickened by the King's liking for small boys and his barely concealed homosexual tendencies. Charles felt that it was still necessary to be very wary. King James had disposed of many of Elizabeth's ministers, and plots were being hatched all over the country. Charles wanted no part of the new court. So the rift between himself and Penelope began to widen.

Matters came to a head when Penelope again became pregnant and it was clear that her fertility was undiminished. Once more she attacked Charles. 'I swear to you I'll not give birth to another bastard,' she cried dramatically.

Charles's brow furrowed in distress at her imperious manner. He did not think it was possible that he could have fathered another child, for his virility seemed to have left him since his sojourn in Ireland. But Penelope was adamant. There was no mistake, she told him, and there had been no other man. Had Charles ceased to love and trust her? She wailed at him miserably.

'No, my darling,' Charles calmed her. 'You are my true love, but what do you want me to do?'

'I want us to be wed,' she cried. 'Let us marry secretly, just as my mother did, at Wanstead.'

Charles looked worried. 'We are dealing with a moody, unreliable king. It is very risky,' he warned.

'Don't be such a coward!' she sniffed. 'What can he do? We live as man and wife. He has embraced us as loyal subjects.'

Mountjoy sighed, knowing that it was useless to argue with her now. 'As you wish then, darling,' he said simply.

For a second, Penelope stared at him in astonishment, scarcely able to believe what he had just said, but then she flung herself at him joyously and almost knocked him over. 'My love, I thank you with all my heart!' she cried. 'No more will my lovely children be slighted,' she added triumphantly.

Arrangements for the marriage were made quickly and the services acquired of Mountjoy's private chaplain, a young priest called William Laud, who later became the famous, ill-fated, Archbishop Laud.

In the grand, silent chapel at Wanstead, in the same spot where the Lord Leicester had sworn his love and loyalty to her mother, Penelope married her man, Charles Blount, Lord Mountjoy.

She was exhilaratingly happy, but Charles was worried and very subdued, still anxious about what the King's attitude would be if the news leaked out. Penelope did not care. Delighted to be lawfully wed to the man she loved, she spent much of the Christmas celebrating and eating and drinking too much. One night she danced much too hectically and in the New Year she miscarried. By the time she was confined to bed everyone knew that Penelope and Charles had secretly married.

While she was still recuperating at Wanstead, Charles paid his courtesy visit to the court at Whitehall and received a terrifying shock. Always before, the King had greeted him with a coarse jest and a friendly welcome. This time he was met with a raging incoherent tornado of abuse. He was dismissed with loud oaths, told never to enter the King's presence again or bring that saucy bitch, his mistress, with him. Completely overwhelmed, Charles put up no defence of himself or his wife. He left hurriedly for his town house on Savoy Hill to nurse his wounds, which he feared were fatal.

That God-fearing king, who not only wrote religious tracts, but continually spouted parts from the Bible, had been deeply offended by the secret marriage. News of it had been almost immediately reported to him with glee by Penelope's so-called friends. James was outraged that they, whom he had taken under his royal wing, had flouted him, defied the law of the church as he saw it and committed sacrilege. No divorced woman had ever been allowed to remarry. Wholeheartedly, King James defended the church. His own dubious practices were another matter.

Immersed in gloom, Charles returned a few days later to Wanstead, where his wife was resting. Despite her miscarriage, she seemed relaxed and happy to have eventually got what she wanted. Busily she planned her new wardrobe for her return to Queen Anne's court the next month, stuffing herself with sweetmeats and lazing around half-dressed. How would he tell her? Charles nervously anticipated the burst of violent temper that would surely descend upon him. He found it almost impossible to accept that fortune, always so good to him, was with him no longer. He walked into the house with a sad expression on his face and his small daughter Elizabeth came forward with her charming smile to greet him. As the child put her small hand in his, Penelope waved a languid greeting to him from her couch. The gentle domestic scene pained him. Passionately he put his hands to his face. 'Oh, Penelope, my darling,' he wept. 'We are ruined. What have we done to our children?'

Astonished by his outburst, Penelope leaped to her feet and went towards him with great consternation. 'Whatever's the matter, my lord?'

Ashamed of his display of emotion, Charles kept his face covered. 'I have been dismissed from the court, abused and insulted,' he sobbed into his hands.

Penelope placed a slim hand on his arm. 'Now, my dear, control yourself. Explain what you mean,' she cajoled.

'We did wrong, Penelope. It would have been wiser to leave well alone. The news of our marriage has leaked out and deeply offended the King.'

'Nonsense!' she said defensively. 'Why should it? He knew of our affair.'

'It's because he believes that we committed a sin against the church,' replied Charles.

'Damn the church!' she shouted angrily. 'Am I supposed to condemn my own children because of the laws of a church?'

'The King is the head of the church, my dear, and you have flouted him,' he told her. 'You were not allowed to remarry.'

'Damn that frowzy old Scotch toper!' she yelled. 'How dare he interfere? I shall petition the Queen.'

Charles just shook his head and retired to his room where he sat in a depressed state compiling a long, rambling epistle explaining, begging and defending his love and his honour to the King. His wife, meanwhile, in full battle regalia, left for the Queen's palace at Greenwich.

Queen Anne was cool and apologetic but clearly had no intention of involving herself in strife with her husband in this matter. She was very fond of fresh faces and in Penelope's absence, had already acquired a younger livelier concerned. Penelope was distressed by the Queen's unsympathetic response but her pride would not allow her to beg, so she returned to Wanstead very bitter, though still proud and haughty.

The following year, however, was a long, dreary, unhappy one for husband and wife at Wanstead, with each one blaming the other for their downfall. Charles kept to his study, writing endless, wordy appeals to King James which were completely ignored. He began to publish his thoughts and his defences in various pamphlets that were circulated.

Meanwhile, the gloom of her surroundings crept over Penelope like a cold, clammy mist. She became inactive, pale and languid, got fatter and more shapeless, spending her time eating and drinking, or just lying down and dreaming of past glories. She succeeded, most of the time, in ignoring a dull ache in her belly and bleeding which had not ceased since her last miscarriage.

Few visitors ever came to Wanstead now because neither Charles nor Penelope had any inclination to entertain. The garden lay neglected, the rooms unused. The boys had gone away to school and one day Lettice arrived to collect Elizabeth for the summer. She had arrived as bright and vivacious as ever. Despite her husband's execution and all her troubles, she had survived. Her hair, now a fine silver, was piled high in the latest fashion. She wore country clothes and talked continuously of dogs and horses, hunting and country life. Her house at Drayton Bassett now seemed to be a fashionable rendezvous for all the young society folk from the town – sons and daughters of her old friends who came to ride to the hunt and make merry in the company of that undefatigable grandmother.

'God in Heaven, Penelope!' she cried, when she first caught sight of her daughter. 'What a confounded mess you are in. Pull yourself together, girl! It's not the end of the world yet.'

'Mind your own business, Mother,' returned her daughter, tartly.

Lettice arched her fine eyebrows. 'You still have the same bitchy tongue, I notice,' she said quietly.

'Perhaps I have,' replied Penelope, 'but that's entirely my own business.'

'Please yourself,' shrugged Lettice, 'but now that you've finished child-bearing, you had better watch out – you could quite easily go into a decline.'

That shaft went home. Penelope's own astute mother had sensed that her daughter was ill and hiding the fact. But Penelope said nothing in response and bade small Elizabeth farewell.

'Go with Grandmother and be good. I'll come and see you soon,' she said gently.

'I want to stay with Papa,' sobbed Elizabeth, clinging to Penelope's gown.

'He is very busy with his book. You will only distract him. Go with Grandmother and have a good time.'

Penelope's illness grew worse so that she could not face the journey to Drayton Bassett. But still she refused to admit to anyone that she ailed, nor would she seek expert advice. She just continued to laze about the house hoping that she would recover.

Charles avoided her and she him, for both their hearts were breaking with loneliness without even their children in the house.

Silver threads appeared in Penelope's lovely hair, dark rings encircled her wonderous eyes. She wore loose, flowing, untidy attire – a sight the meticulous Charles could not stand – but still the peaceful beauties of nature comforted her. She loved more than anything to wander in the woods or relax in the garden.

When winter laid its cold, white carpet on the ground, she sat alone by the fire thinking of past glories and telling herself that when spring came she would feel much better.

Only one old friend went to see her in those dark, gloomy days – loving, loyal Frances, her diminutive sister-in-law. She arrived full of sympathy and love, and alive with a vigour which a new husband and a revitalised religious fervour had brought her. Frances, surprisingly, had married again a young, good-looking highlander, so much like Essex in appearance that it was a painful sight for her sister-in-law to see them so happy together.

For her part, Frances was shocked at the sight of the beautiful Penelope and how much she had aged. 'Come home with me to Scotland, darling,' she pleaded. 'The air will revive you.'

'Perhaps in the spring,' Penelope replied, but her tone was listless.

Frances looked puzzled. 'Why not come now?' she asked.

'I am not sure,' Penelope replied vaguely.

Frances was taken aback by the change in the usually forthright and confident Penelope, but with a new husband, who truly loved and admired her in a way she had not experienced before, she could not stay with her friend. Her son by Essex was now a page at court, being brought up as companion to the King's son, Henry. And her husband had vast estates in Scotland. Frances had become a Roman Catholic when she married – a secret which had to be kept from

King James who had no time for the Papists. Now she was returning to the Scottish highlands to live in the remote isles and Penelope was sad to see her go.

In March, Charles suddenly dressed himself in his best suit and announced that he was going to London. 'I have decided to stay in town for a while,' he told Penelope. 'I am determined not to neglect my seat in parliament. It is my right as a peer of the realm and I must consider the future of my sons.'

From the gloom of her chamber, Penelope stared suspiciously at him; there was a tiny tug at her heart as she beheld him dressed in his best attire but with a pathetic expression on his ravaged face. 'Then it's hardly possible that you will need me around,' she said sarcastically.

'I have considered the possibility of you returning to live in town with me,' he said. 'It's not good to shut ourselves away. It is better to face up to the world. Also, the upkeep of this house is expensive. It might be more sensible to live at Savoy Hill.'

Penelope pulled her robes around her shoulders and thrust out her chin. 'I've no intention of leaving Wanstead,' she cried stubbornly.

'I only leased this house from your brother,' replied Charles with patience. 'The lease will shortly need to be renewed.'

'So we are now paupers as well as outcasts,' she jeered, turning away in disgust.

'Do be reasonable, Penelope,' he begged. 'I only want what is best for us both.'

After a moment's hesitation, she turned back and

looked at him slightly shame-faced. But then she said impatiently, 'Go! There is no need to make a fuss. As for me, I'm not ready to face those treacherous swine at Whitehall yet. Have I not suffered enough in their hands?'

He took a step towards her but then, wary of the hard expression on her face, stopped. 'Farewell, my love,' he said tenderly. 'I trust you will join me when you are well.'

They embraced politely and Penelope watched Charles' portly figure mount his horse and, with just a few loyal serving men, ride away to town. Now she was really alone and for some strange reason she did not mind.

As the fierce March wind bent the tall elms and rustled the dead leaves along the paths, she walked slowly in the immense grounds of Wanstead, so glad to be alone, with time to think. She often sat in the deserted rose arbour. The trellis was bare, the wood cold and damp, but there were warm memories, vivid ones, of the elegant Philip Sidney declaring his love for her there. Her gaze swept the wind-blown lake; wild birds flew over its surface, their shadows moving swiftly against the cloudy wind-swept sky. It was cold, blowy and desolate, but to her, infinitely beautiful. Wanstead wrapped her round like a comfortable blanket. She felt safe and secure here and was troubled only by the knowledge that she should be deciding to leave it for London, a prospect she found impossible to face.

Over the months, she had gradually accepted that her vibrant good health had deserted her. Each day that passed she became more conscious of the ache inside her, and she would tell herself that she should consult a physician. Now forty, she was at an age when women developed strange ailments. Her mind would jump from her health, to her husband. Yes, she must be more tolerant with Charles, she told herself. Perhaps she would join him in town, and get back to their old companionable relationship. Each day she reflected on these things, but each day she did nothing about them. March winds gave way to April showers; the primroses bloomed and the buds formed on the rose trees. She walked in the rain admiring them with slow and stately steps, her hair wet and her loose garments blowing; and still she could not make the final decision to go to London. Meanwhile, Charles did not return, nor had she any news of him.

One wet night, a carriage drove a breakneck speed up the drive, and from it stumbled her husband's loyal aide. He had been with Charles in the army. Hat in hand he knelt on one knee in the entrance. 'My lady,' he cried breathlessly. 'I beg you to come immediately. His lordship needs you. He is so ill that I am sure he is near to death.'

Penelope was shocked by this extraordinary news and could hardly believe what she had heard. 'Where is he?' she cried. 'What's wrong with him?'

'He's at his home in Savoy Hill,' replied the servant. 'In the beginning it was just a severe chill but over the last two days he has taken a turn for the worse. He has difficulty breathing and he continually calls out for you, my lady.'

'Why wasn't I informed about this before now?' she demanded, her shock giving way to anger and concern.

'It was all so sudden, my lady. His lordship was very upset over the trouble with Lord Rich and did not leave the house for a week.'

'What do you mean?' she asked. 'What trouble?' She had begun to gather her belongings to travel to town.

'In the house, my lady. Lord Rich is now Earl of Warwick, having purchased a peerage from His Majesty, and he had words with his lordship.'

Those dark almond-shaped eyes suddenly flashed with temper. 'Good God! Do they sell peerages now like barrels of apples?' She muttered scornfully. Then she lowered her voice. 'Don't tell me that Lord Rich insulted my husband?' she said.

'I am afraid that he did, my lady, and his lordship did not retaliate; he just walked away.'

'Oh, God in Heaven!' she cried. 'Is there no end to the impudence of that little toad?'

All the way to London sitting in the bouncing carriage, she fumed. How foolish she had been to let poor Charles face those fiends all alone; she should have faced them too. Well, she was not yet dead. She would let them see that they had not defeated her. Vowing vengeance on Lord Rich, King James and all her deadly enemies, Penelope's old spirit revived.

When they arrived at Savoy Hill, she hurried up the steps to reassure and protect her man. But Charles lay on his bed, silent except for his rasping breath which came slowly and with difficulty. To her horror, she saw that his face was almost blue. Pushing past the priests and doctors who surrounded him, she knelt by the bed. 'It's Penelope,' she whispered tenderly. 'I am here to take care of you.'

At the sound of her soft voice, Charles turned his head with difficulty to take one final look at the woman he loved so dearly. 'Farewell, my darling,' he whispered with his dying breath. Then his gallant spirit left the world that had rejected him.

Penelope gripped the bedclothes in anguish. 'Charles, don't leave me!' she cried. She began to beat the bed with her fists. 'It's not true! It can't be.' She wept uncontrollably, clutched at her husband's body, tore her clothes and finally had to be taken by force from the death chamber. She quietened a little but continued to weep as if her heart would break.

Later, the servants carried her, exhausted, to bed. The doctor pulled down her heavy, closed lids and examined her high stomach. 'Madam,' he said, 'you must get some medical attention. Your own health is not as it should be.'

Among the remaining Elizabethans there was great sorrow at the death of Lord Mountjoy in the prime of life. And the rumour that his distraught widow was very sick quickly spread about her large family. No one could really believe it; it hardly seemed possible that the fiery, vibrant Penelope had been laid low, that she had a malignant growth in her womb, that the body that had been so prolific was now diseased. She had little chance of recovery, for there was no knowledge in those days of how to operate upon this condition.

Friends and relatives came in a steady stream to visit Penelope at Savoy Hill. That the truth should be withheld from her was universally agreed; so they came, concerned and anxious but feeling inadequate. Her aunt, Lady North, sent many comforts and offered her home to Penelope. Her sister, Dorothy, sad and harassed, travelled down from the grim castle in the north where her rebellious husband was deep in a plot to unseat the King. She now had two children, but was not happy with the moody, drunken Henry Percy, Earl of Northumberland. Her cousin, Elizabeth Vernon, was now a fine lady. Her husband had been released from prison where he had been sent for his involvement in the Essex Rebellion, and was now in high favour at court; but Elizabeth wept when she saw her sick cousin.

Penelope was irritated by such scenes and generally scornful of the sudden concern of her family. Only to sweet Frances did she speak frankly.

'Don't try to fool me, Frances. I know I have a large growth within me,' she informed her sister-in-law. 'I have felt it there ever since I lost that child.'

Tearful, Frances looked at her beloved sister, her strong, reliable Penelope, who had always been there when she had needed her. 'Oh, darling!' she cried. 'I pray that dear God will be kind to you, but do not lose hope, it might be curable. You may recover.'

Penelope shook her head adamantly. 'No, Frances. I am convinced it is fatal and that the end will come slowly but surely.'

'Hush, darling, don't talk like that,' sobbed Frances.

Tears rushed down her cheeks at the thought of losing her friend. 'Pray!' she urged. 'Trust in God!'

Penelope nodded, unmoved by Frances' religious fervour. 'I know that you became a Roman Catholic to please your new husband,' she said quietly. 'I just hope it will not lead you into trouble.'

Frances clutched impulsively at her hands. 'I shall never regret having done that, Penelope,' she said. 'I have had such great peace of mind.'

'I envy you, sweet sister,' Penelope mocked with a weak smile. 'Peace of mind is something I have not had for a long time.'

Frances squeezed her hands tight. 'We have been through hell together, you and I,' she whispered. 'Let me help you find peace and happiness now.'

'I can't believe it possible,' Penelope replied soberly. 'Why, I cannot even pray any longer.'

'Come with me to the highlands,' Frances begged. 'There is someone there you must meet.'

Penelope shook her head. 'No,' she said. 'When my lord is laid to rest I shall return to Wanstead. That was where we spent our happiest days. I'll stay there until my end is nigh. If all you say is true, it's possible that he and I will meet again.'

'All right,' agreed Frances. 'Then I will return to Wanstead with you and send for Anthony to come south. He is my husband's true confidant and friend.'

Penelope's pale face brightened with a slow, roguish smile. 'Good gracious, Frances,' she said with a light laugh. 'What makes you think that I am in any condition for masculine company?'

Frances wiped away her tears and managed a smile herself. 'You have not changed, Penelope,' she said. 'I shall send for him and when you meet him you'll know what I mean,' she added mysteriously. 'Take care, darling,' she said as she left. 'I'll be back soon.'

But Penelope's troubles were still mounting. With his usual perverseness, King James had decided that Mountjoy had to have a grand military funeral, so arrangements were made to bury with full honours the deserted hero, conqueror of Ireland and once companion-in-arms to the gallant Essex. All the newly knighted young men, anxious to show off their finery, assembled together, bearing their recently acquired banners and heraldic coats-of-arms. King James freely sold those English titles to the highest bidders.

There were all in place, ready for that long, slow march to Westminster Abbey where Mountjoy was to be laid to rest. The few remaining old Elizabethan courtiers were not so keen to march with this bevy of Scots. They were sad for Mountjoy, who had been a gallant gentleman, but made excuses not to attend. They insisted, however, that his natural sons should walk beside his coffin. So Penelope's young sons, Mountjoy Blount and St John Blount, walked amid the other nobles, with Prince Henry and his cousin, Robert of Essex, and young Rich, now heir to the Earldom of Warwick. The blue-and-gold arms of the Bourchiers were not allowed to be displayed, nor were the banners of the Devereux. This was considered by Penelope's family to be a direct insult, and as a result, the Knollys, Careys, Norths and Devereux all boycotted the funeral. Penelope also decided not to attend the funeral. Instead, she lay in bed weeping her heart out.

And again dark thoughts descended upon her. Charles was being honoured now, but the last years of his life had been wretched. She had made them so, demanding their secret marriage. Nor had she sought to cheer them by coming to him in London. How was she to die in peace when she carried so much guilt? Little Patrick, Hawise and her love, her dear brother and now beloved Charles – all had died or suffered through her own fault.

In the evening, Frances arrived with a comfortable coach to take her sister-in-law home to Wanstead. She was accompanied by a young man. He had a lined face and scraggy body, so his correct age was hard to guess, and he spoke in a low, husky whisper as if there were some impediment in his speech. But he had an attractive manner and his clear blue-green eyes were quite compelling.

'This is Anthony.' Frances introduced him as they were seated facing each other in the coach.

Penelope took the cool, gentle hand he offered and knew immediately who, or what he was, and that the correct introduction should have been Father Anthony. He was a Jesuit priest, a fact that shone from those gentle, long-suffering eyes. The moment he touched her, Penelope felt calm and comforted. Father Anthony seemed to spread an aura of peace about him.

Frances was taking a risk by bringing this priest to meet Penelope like this. These were still dangerous times. No one was sure of James's reaction to the Catholic faith even though his own mother had held to it. Father Anthony, however, had spent many years in prison and had been racked and tortured for his faith. But Penelope was surprised to find herself glad to have a Catholic by her side.

Once back home at Wanstead, she seemed to recover. Every day, she strolled in the deserted gardens with Father Anthony. Every day they sat by the lake, to watch the afternoon sun playing hide-and-seek with the clouds and casting bright, dancing shadows over the water. A family of swans lived on the lake, and they often floated majestically by – father, mother and a long string of brown cygnets in a precise line.

'At last I'm beginning to feel at peace,' she remarked one day. 'I've always had the strange feeling that this would be my last resting place. It looks as though this will come to pass.'

'Death is not the end, only the beginning,' Father Anthony said gently.

'Oh, I do wish I could believe it,' she cried. 'Father, I have no faith. What is to become of me?'

Father Anthony folded his white hands in his lap. 'There is always time for repentance,' he told her.

Penelope looked at him sideways. 'Not for me,' she said softly. 'I've been too wicked.'

The priest gazed at her with his steady eyes. 'Jesus welcomes the sinner,' he murmured.

She stared soberly back at him. Her black eyes still shone from her fading face. 'Will you instruct me, Father? I feel the need to find the peace and beauty of your religion.' Now she knew that Frances had been right.

Father Anthony drew a deep breath and took her hand. 'It is my greatest desire to lead you into the arms of Mother Church,' he whispered huskily.

They walked back to the house, holding hands. 'I have never meant to be bad,' she told him. 'In fact, sometimes I think I was just thoughtless.'

'I do understand,' he replied. 'There will be time. I will stay with you until my own life, which has not long to go, comes to an end.'

Penelope stopped and turned to him questioningly. 'What is it you are telling me?' she asked.

'You cannot have failed to notice the huskiness in my voice,' he said. 'I too have a growth. In my throat. There is a lease on my life, but it is God's will that I shall be able to fulfil this last task for him.'

'Is that why you were released from prison?' she enquired.

'Yes. To the custody of my friend and patron, Lord Clan Kirriad.'

She held compassionately onto his thin arm as a strange feeling came over her. Cheerfully she said, 'Then the way will not be lonely. Maybe we will travel it together.'

'God willing,' said Father Anthony.

All through that long summer she feasted upon the beauties of Wanstead – the glowing jewel in the dark, green forest that she loved so well. She no longer rode; she strolled languidly along the leafy paths and each day knelt with Father Anthony in the old chapel where she had married Mountjoy. Each day she took a little religious instruction; she was content and happy. As her beautiful body faded, her mind became calmer but also very much alive.

Every day she walked through the grounds with the priest, telling him about the stormy life she had lived; of her unhappy marriage; her love affair with Philip Sidney; her secret marriage to Mountjoy. Often she spoke of the death of young Patrick Russell at Bisham Abbey and of her beloved Hawise.

'Do you think I was responsible for their deaths?' she asked, happy that she could now even bring up the subject. His answer gave her much peace of mind.

'No, my child, you were just an instrument of the devil. You were all alone in a wilderness,' he said.

'If I had not goaded my brother Essex and called him a coward, he might be alive today,' she said soberly.

'It was the will of God, my dear,' Father Anthony persuaded her gently. 'You have paid in full measure for any wrongs you have done in this world. Rest upon God's mercy and pray for me.'

Then he told her of his life, of his imprisonment, his travles on foreign soil and his happiness that he had been allowed to help her to find peace, to meet his own death close to her.

No one else came to Wanstead during this time. The world had forgotten Lady Penelope, and her family could not face up to anything so final as her imminent death. But Penelope did not mind; Father Anthony's company was all she wanted. At Drayton Bassett, Lettice had gathered Penelope's children about her. She gave them fine parties and made merry each day in an effort to take from their minds what was happening to their lovely mother. And Penelope was glad for that.

The winter was long, but peace still reigned in the large house. When the primroses began to bloom in the spring, Penelope was wandering weakly in the garden and, as she stooped to gather a posy of primroses and wood violets, she fell. Her servant saw her collapse and went to her aid. Soon she was laid gently in her bed from which she was never to rise again.

Her last words were to Father Anthony. She said quite clearly, 'I want to be buried here in a secret place, according to the Catholic rite. I want no one but you to know of my grave.'

'It shall be as you wish,' he whispered, as with tears in his eyes, he began to administer extreme unction. And as he prayed for the repose of her soul, Penelope's beautiful dark eyes closed for the last time.

Father Anthony lived only two weeks after Penelope's death and the parish priest buried him in the village churchyard. All traces of the grand house at Wanstead have now disappeared and there remains only the large lake and some of the tall elms. When the breeze rustles them at night, voices from the past are wafted among them; at full moon a tall figure in flowing robes walks gracefully around the lake and through the trees in an aura of calm and contentment. Lady Penelope Devereux died in peace and the spirit of that beautiful courageous lady still lingers on.